MAKE ME WILDER

WILDER ADVENTURES BOOK ONE

SERENA BELL

JELSBA
MEDIA
GROUP

Jelsba Media Group

ISBN 978-1-953498-09-0

Icons made by Good Ware from www.flaticon.com

1

LUCY

I almost choke on my coffee. Liam is here—with flowers.

I can see him through the conference room window. He strides toward me, a big bouquet in his hands, every bit as hot as that night, six weeks ago, when I hooked up with him after the comedy show.

I never thought I'd see him again. We'd agreed it was just a one-night thing, and at the time, I was totally okay with that.

But in the weeks since then, I've been regretting not getting his number, or giving him mine. He was fun to talk to and good in bed, traits that are rare by themselves and a unicorn together. I've thought about trying to look him up, track him down. How many Liam Johnsons could there be in Manhattan?

Um, yeah. Quite a few. So I didn't even go there. We'd agreed. And I didn't want to be a stalker.

But now that he's here, I'm remembering how hot he is: slightly ginger-y blond hair, dazzling blue-green eyes, and a killer hard-won gym bod. All packaged today in a gray suit, black button-down, and silver-and-blue tie.

And he brought me flowers.

He opens the conference room door, and I rise out of my seat, ready to run to him. In my whole life, no guy has ever shown up at my work with flowers. This is a grand gesture. He found me, he came to my workplace with flowers, and now he's walked into the middle of a brainstorming session with my boss, Gennie, and two of my other female coworkers.

I think I just fell in love with Liam at second sight.

If this were a movie, I'd run into his arms and kiss him, but I hold back, because this isn't the movies, and my boss is here.

"Oh my God, Liam," I say. "How did you find me?"

Gennie turns to look at me.

Both of my coworkers turn to look at me.

Liam turns to look at me.

Wait a second.

Why wasn't Liam looking at me?

I realize that Gennie has stood up. And taken two steps toward Liam. Confusion is written all over her face.

My coworkers don't look confused. They look horrified.

I am very slowly—like slow-motion car wreck slowly—piecing this together.

Liam is not here with flowers for me.

He is here with flowers for my boss.

And I said that thing aloud. The thing about *how did you find me*? We all heard it. Liam. Gennie. Jasmine and Pilar.

"It's not what it looks like," Liam says. To Gennie. "Gennie, whatever you think, it's not that."

"If you'll excuse me," Gennie says. She doesn't say what

she will do. She just picks up her laptop and her iPad and her notebook, stacks them neatly. Gennie is always calm, always deliberate. She is calm and deliberate now as she takes her things and walks out of the conference room, Liam hurrying after her with the flowers, turning to give me a look that is both apologetic and chiding.

"Um," Jasmine says. "I should—"

She and Pilar get up. Both move toward the door.

"Wait!" I call.

They reluctantly turn back.

"Help?"

They exchange a look. In their faces I see all the questions that any sane woman would have in this situation. Should their loyalty to Gennie trump everything? If they stay, will they be betraying her?

And if they go, won't they miss out on the chance to find out what the hell is going on?

"I have to get back to work," Jasmine says. Not a surprising decision. Jasmine is Gennie's best work friend. She slips out of the conference room without a backward glance.

But Pilar hangs back. She gives me a sympathetic look.

"What did you do?" she whispers.

"I didn't know he was her boyfriend," I whisper back. Oh, *God*. I'm dead. I'm fired. I'm dead and fired and jobless and did I mention dead?

Also, I'm a terrible person who sleeps with other women's boyfriends. But I'm not that person. I swear I'm not. I would never knowingly be that person.

Could I accidentally be that person? Apparently.

"I didn't know." My voice is a tiny, wispy thread.

"She can't fire you if you didn't know," Pilar says.

I never said *fired* out loud, but apparently that is where both our minds have gone, which isn't reassuring at all.

This is a terrible time to be flooded with passionate love for my job, but that's what's happening. I love, love, love my job. I love marketing and I love working for a really good marketing company and I love figuring out how to market goods and services to women, which is what our team specializes in. Gennie is a generous boss, fair and creative. Jasmine and Pilar are excellent colleagues. Besides, to survive in New York City, I need an income.

"How long have they been a couple?" I madly hope she will say less than six weeks.

"Two years."

I shrink like a poked slug.

"But they broke up three months ago and only just got back together." Pilar holds up hopeful crossed fingers.

Salvation.

"It was six weeks ago."

Pilar nods. "That was when they were broken up." Her eyebrows draw together. "But how did you not recognize him?"

"I've never met him."

"Didn't you meet him at the Christmas party?"

"I wasn't at the Christmas party." My voice is small again.

"You weren't at the Christmas party?"

The Grand Plan Christmas party is not to be missed. But I did. I shake my head. "I had—other plans."

I told myself that this year, at this job, I would finally do things differently. I wouldn't hang back like a shy preschooler sussing out the playground vibe. I wouldn't say *no* when I should say yes, then make lame excuses. I'd go to the effing Christmas party.

After the e-vite went out with the details, I kept meaning to buck up, put on my big girl pants, and show the hell up... but while I was waiting for the injection of courage that never came, I missed the RSVP deadline.

So I stayed home, ate Ben & Jerry's and watched *Die Hard* and *Love Actually.*

But I don't tell her any of that.

"Well, what about Friday night happy hour? I know he's stopped by a few times—" I can almost hear the "tick, tick, tick" of Pilar's brain working through this puzzle and arriving at a conclusion. "But you've never come out to happy hour, have you?"

"No," I say.

"And you don't follow any of us on social media."

Now she sounds like she's adding up my crimes. Calculating out my sentence.

I shake my head.

"Why not?"

"I only use social media for work," I say.

"But happy hour?" The way she says 'happy hour' makes me feel so nerdy.

"I—" I gulp air. "I should go pack my desk."

I sneak one last glance at Pilar, who looks at me with so much pity that I have to quickly turn away.

I've JUST FINISHED PACKING my desk when Gennie calls me to her office. Seated behind her big, bossy desk, she has never looked so cold and intimidating, not even on the day I interviewed with her, a year and a half ago. And that was one of the scariest interviews I've ever done, though later I realized that Gennie reserves that side of her personality for interviewees. And as I discover today, for employees who sleep with her boyfriend.

"I am so, so, so sorry, Gennie. You have to believe me, I had no idea who he was."

"I do believe you," she says, her voice as terrifying as her demeanor.

"I would never. Never in a million years. Girl code..."

I apparently can no longer complete sentences. My eyes fill with tears, but I *won't cry*. I won't.

There's something in people that senses weakness, my mother said, after we left Atwell, the small town that soured me on small towns. *They sense it and they go in for the kill.*

Gennie looks like she would like to kill me.

"Do you even understand why I'm so angry?" she says.

"You have every right to be mad! I slept with your boyfriend! Not that I knew he was your boyfriend. And not when he was your boyfriend. But the fact remains, I did. If I were in your shoes, I'd be furious with me."

I suddenly realize it doesn't matter whether or not she is going to fire me. I have to do the right thing. I've made things impossible. Uncomfortable. And whether I did it on purpose or not, it's my fault. There's only one way out. I'll have to quit.

"I want to make this as easy for you as possible," I say quietly. "I'll give you my letter with two weeks notice as soon as we're done in here."

Gennie's perfect eyebrows nearly touch her hair. "Lucy." I brace myself. "I'm not mad because you accidentally slept with my boyfriend when he wasn't actually my boyfriend. I mean I am. Of course I am. I want to strangle you with my bare hands and bury the body where it can never be found. Mmmm. Actually, I want to strangle him with my bare hands and bury the body where it can never be found. Or?" She tilts her head. "Strangle both of you?"

I wince.

"Sorry. Too much honesty? It's just, he wasn't supposed to rebound. He was supposed to pine and realize how much he'd taken me for granted." She sighs. "Which he did, eventually, but he may have slept with half of Manhattan on his way to doing it."

Gennie comes out from behind the desk, pacing. She kicks off her heels and strides back and forth in her stockinged feet. Then she stops, turns, and points at me. "But whatever, I get it, you didn't know, and he didn't know who you were. He was just, you know, doing what guys do when they're hurt." She crosses her arms. "But I'm mad at you because if you had even *once* come out to happy hour with us, or gone to a Christmas party or a rooftop barbecue or a housewarming party for anyone at work, or followed even one of us on Facebook or Instagram or... you would have known who Liam was." Her voice has gained strength and her finger is jabbing the air. I take a step back.

"I'm mad at you because I've been working with you for more than a year and you literally have no idea what's going on in my life, none! And I literally have no idea what's going on in yours. I didn't know you like comedy clubs or sometimes hook up with strangers—"

I wince, but there's no judgment in Gennie's voice. Just... sadness.

"And if you'd just let any of us be friends with you like we've been *trying* to do, this wouldn't have happened."

I feel awful and try to find the right words to tell her so, but they stick in my throat.

"But no," she says. "You had to be an ice queen and go your own way and now I have to work with you knowing you know what my boyfriend's O face looks like."

"I—I know."

The ice queen thing—it's not like I've never heard it before, but it still hurts.

She's not saying anything I don't know.

I'm *that* coworker.

The one who isn't really a very good "team player."

The one who isn't really a "people person."

Or, to put it the way Darren did when he broke off our three-year relationship last year, I'm *unknowable. A black box,* he said. *I kept waiting for you to open up to me, but now I know it's never going to happen.*

I've realized he was right, and since then, I've vowed to be better. Any armchair psychologist could tell you I'm closed off because my dad proved himself so untrustworthy in every possible way, but that easy assessment doesn't mean it's simple to fix.

"I meant what I said about giving notice," I say. "You don't have to work with me, I'll move on."

She throws her arms in the air. "Have you heard *anything* I just said? You are *not* giving notice. No notice!" She buries her face in her hands. "Oh, Lucy, *what* am I going to do with you?"

"Fire me?" I suggest. Again.

"I'm not firing you," she says.

"But I—"

I can't, I think.

I can't come to work knowing that within a day or so, everyone at work will know the story of what happened. How I stood up, all soft and eager and vulnerable, with my feelings showing all over my face, and said, "How did you find me?" like the heroine of a romantic comedy, except I wasn't the heroine.

I was the comic relief.

Gennie's expression softens.

And now it looks an awful lot like pity, too.

I would so, so, so much rather she hated me.

"Listen. I totally get it if you need a little time. Maybe a leave of absence. Say, three weeks. Take some time off. Let both of us reset."

"Please just let me quit," I beg.

She shakes her head. "If you sucked at your job, I would. But you're the best I've got, and I'm not letting you go that easily."

"Thank you." My voice is small again, but at least steady.

"I won't let this get in the way of what's best for the team or the business," Gennie says. "And I know you won't, either."

I thank her for the three weeks leave of absence. For her generosity in not firing me. I apologize again, while she waves it off.

When I go, though, I take the box with me. The one with the contents of my desk.

I think, *I'm never coming back here.*

A woman dressed in a pale gray pantsuit and spike heels crouches over the rain grate on Main St.

I'd be less shocked to see a Sasquatch.

No one in Rush Creek dresses like that. And no one in Rush Creek looks like that. Long cornsilk blond hair, narrow waist, flared hips. The way she's squatting emphasizes all her curves, and there are plenty of them. I know this because I'm staring at her.

I need to stop: A fish out of water like this woman can only mean trouble for me.

But wait!—my foolish dick begs—*if she's just passing through, she'll be the fun kind of trouble.*

This is how mistakes get made.

I am outside the feed store with a forty-pound bag of dog food slung over my shoulder, stopped in my tracks as the first few drops of rain begin to fall. My shoulder starts to ache, Buck is back home, waiting to get fed, and I'm staring at gray pants stretched tight over the world's most perfect ass.

What the hell is that woman doing here, *dressed like* that?

I think about the last beautiful stranger I met who was dressed all wrong. Who was all wrong in every way.

What the hell is she doing?

Then a whole bunch of things happen at once.

I hear the sound of a distressed duck.

I'm a hunter, so I know bird calls, but even if I weren't, I would spot the mama duck immediately. She's agitated, hopping around on the sidewalk above the grate. It's the corner of Main and South, on the side with the bookstore.

I hear another sound, high pitched and persistent.

Ducklings, cheeping, panicked.

Okay. I know what's going on.

This storm grate is a magnet for duck disasters. Every spring, at least one brood has to be rescued.

I reach for my phone to call my friend Josiah at Oregon Department of Fish & Wildlife. He'll have those little dudes out of the drain in seconds flat.

And then she turns her head and I see her face for the first time. Perfect oval, clear pale skin, big blue eyes, cute nose, wide mouth. Her eyes meet mine, and I guess something about me suggests that I'm the kind of guy who's good in a crisis, because when her gaze locks with mine, I see her relief.

"Hey—" she calls. "There are ducklings down there! Can you help me?"

All thoughts of calling Josiah slip out of my head. Josiah's a good-looking guy. Women go nuts over him. And for whatever reason, I don't want this woman to go nuts over Josiah.

I want to be her hero.

Which is pure, total, complete, and utter bullshit. One: I have enough going on in my life. I don't need to be anyone else's anything. And two: nothing—I repeat, *nothing*—about this woman suggests that she's anything but temporary.

Right about then, my gaze drops from her beautiful face to her silky cream-colored blouse. The rain is falling harder now. I wonder if the rain will ruin her top—or make it see-through. Even from the other side of the street, I can see the contours of her breasts and the shadow of an edge of lace. I drag my eyes back to hers, just as a car swings around the corner, too close and too fast. She gasps as it splashes muddy water onto her pants. But her eyes stay on mine, the question between us.

She's clearly not going anywhere until the ducklings are okay.

Next thing I know, I'm at her side.

It's getting late, and dusk is starting to fall. The shops are closing down. There are a few cars passing on the street, headlights on. One slows to a crawl. "Hey, Gabe!"

"Hey, Joe!" I call back. One of the shop owners in town, heading home for the evening.

"You all good?"

"We're good!" I call back.

"Who's your friend?" he asks, angling his thumb in the direction of the newcomer.

I roll my eyes at him, and he laughs, speeds up, and heads on.

"Hey," I say to her. "What's going on?"

She bites her soft, pink lower lip. "We have to get them out."

I crouch down, and sure enough, there are several duck-lings, drab yellow balls of fluff, swimming in circles, crying for mama.

"Let me just put this away"—I shrug to indicate the dog food—"and get some stuff from my Jeep, and I'll be back."

Her makeup's starting to run. The dark streaks make her look like she's been crying, even though I can tell she hasn't. Maybe that's what pushed my rescue buttons. I don't know. But whatever it was, when she smiles at me like I've just saved her day, I feel like a big hero. And I haven't even done anything yet.

I tell myself it's no big deal. Everyone wants to be a hero for a beautiful woman with a pretty smile.

I cross to my Jeep, wave to Tom Morrow who's shutting down the feed store, sling the dog food into the back, and rummage around. I hope like hell I can repurpose something to help her. If I had the Wilder Adventures van with me, I'd definitely have more options.

Luckily, the last time my brother Brody borrowed the Jeep he left a bunch of fishing gear in it, including a net. And I can use the tire iron as a crowbar, so I'm pretty sure I'm set.

I jog back across the street, passing by two of my sister's mom-friends who greet me warmly. They're wearing jeans, rain boots, and rain jackets with the hoods up, and as I rejoin the duckling woman, I'm struck again by how out of place she is in her city girl costume. I bet she owns a little folding umbrella that would be blown to bare spines and ragged nylon in two minutes in a Pacific Northwest windstorm.

As I crouch down by the grate, she crouches next to me. "Hey. Thanks. I didn't know what to do. I was going to try to call someone, but I didn't know where to start. I googled 'ducklings in grate' on my phone, and then you showed up—"

"Best thing to do in this situation is call Oregon Fish & Wildlife."

She gives me a sidelong look under long, damp eyelashes. "I could still do that—"

"Nah. I've got this."

"Thank you," she breathes.

I wiggle the tire iron under the edge of the grate as she watches. I can feel her next to me—the warmth of her body, her slightly sped-up breathing. My own breathing hooks itself into hers, my pulse kicking up. I tell myself it's just the adrenaline of a rainy duck rescue, but I know I'm full of shit. This isn't adrenaline, it's lust.

I'm going to pin it all on the spike heels. I'm apparently a sucker for them, even though it makes zero sense. I should be all about women in hiking boots, the kind who know how to pitch their own tents and manage a rifle. Instead, I'm thinking about this woman—who I've never seen before and whose name I don't even know—wearing those heels in bed.

Her eyes settle on me. I can't stop being aware of her gaze as I use the tire iron to pry up the grate. The city girl makes a little sound of relief and appreciation as the grate pops loose.

That sound has nothing whatsoever to do with sex. Nothing.

Tell that to my suddenly perked up cock.

"I didn't know the grate came up like that," she said. "I just figured it was screwed down."

"Nah."

"Have you done this before?"

"Seen it done."

She looks at me like I set the earth in orbit. Her makeup situation has gone from bad to worse. Her hair is wet and limp, with strands stuck to her face. And all I want to do is fix it. Run a thumb under each of her eyes to clear away the smudges. Brush the sodden strands off her cheeks. Get her somewhere dry, wrap her in a blanket.

And ask her fucking *name*.

God, Gabe, you giant dickweed.

"I'm Gabe." Better late than never.

"Lucy."

Her gaze flicks away from mine—breaking eye contact that's too intense for comfort—and then, unexpectedly, she laughs.

"What?" My eyes track hers to the Rush to Read Books window. In spite of the fading light, we can see the display— picture books about ducklings.

"It's like they came to this corner for a reason," Lucy says, a bounce of delight in her voice. "Do you think the owner would like it if we took photos for her? She can add them to her display."

"Uh..." The suggestion has caught me off guard, but it's perfect. "Yeah. I think Jem would love that. We can do that after we get them out."

Lucy pushes a strand of damp hair back. I realize she has the net in her hand, and I reach to take it from her, but she bends and dips it into the drain. She tips forward onto one knee, probably destroying her expensive pants, but she doesn't seem to care. The fluffy babies are still yelling their little heads off below us. She scoops the first one up so I grab the hoop as it surfaces, then gently tip the soft, warm ball of fluff onto the sidewalk. "There you go, little dude," I tell him, as she leans down for the next one. I try to keep my eyes off her ass, and I'm mostly successful.

Mostly.

As each duckling reaches safety, it scurries to join the

mother who has been supervising warily. When the last is freed, they hurry off together, mama and babies in a tight parade, as I snap photos for Jem, and Lucy watches them waddle off.

"Ohhh, look at them," she says, her hand covering her mouth. Then she turns her gaze on me. Her eyes shine with tears. "We saved their lives. Thank you. I'm so glad you turned up when you did."

I cough. I hate having a big deal made over stuff. "Yeah. Well. Glad I was here."

I bend down to reset the grate. When I stand up, I catch her gaze on my ass. Our eyes meet. And she doesn't look away.

Well, well, well.

Now I'm *really* glad I was here.

"You, um, want to get a drink?"

As soon as the words leave my mouth, I realize exactly how ridiculous they must sound. She's dripping wet, hair plastered to her face, makeup running, cream-colored silk so saturated now that I can see the faint outlines of peaked nipples, even under the shadow of her blazer. My cock hardens even more.

Of course she doesn't want a drink. She wants to go wherever she is supposed to go, take a hot shower, and put on warm clothes. That's what I should want, too, because I am equally wet, although my green t-shirt, Carhartt pants, and leather hiking boots are more up to the task than her businessy clothes and fuck-me shoes. Plus, I have to get home and feed Buck, whose forty-pound sack of dinner is sitting in the back of my Jeep.

Still, my better judgment doesn't come online. Instead, I say, "Forty-five minutes. Meet me at Oscar's."

I gesture toward Oscar's Saloon and Grill, Rush Creek's local gathering place. She turns to look, and I try to see it as she would. Pretty sure she's east coast, and I wonder if Oscar's Western-style false facade looks kitschy through her eyes.

Then I wonder why I give a shit.

I don't know what the hell I'm doing. I don't even know why she's here. She could be just passing through, in which case she's totally fair game. But she could also be new to town, and that would mean she's off limits.

I tell myself I'll find out first. Before I let things get out of hand. While I can still set boundaries.

Her pretty blue eyes are moving over my face, trying to figure me out. She bites her lip. I'm ninety percent sure she's about to say no.

Then she bites her lip again and shrugs.

"Okay," she says, and her mouth turns up at one corner, almost a smile. There's something wary in it, but also—eager.

And fear pulses through me, because it's possible I already missed it. The time before I let things get out of hand. The moment when I could still set boundaries.

It's possible it never existed with her.

3

LUCY

I'm dripping wet. I hurry up the main street toward my hotel, trying to soak in as much of the town as I can while I literally absorb water into the hems of my pants.

Even sopping wet, and even through my bone-deep dislike of small towns, I have to admit Rush Creek, Oregon, is charming. I pass by a coffee shop that's still giving off the rich dark smell of coffee and some kind of fragrant ginger tea. A slim woman is closing it up for the day and has stopped to exchange a few words with the bike shop owner next door, who has his helmet slung over one arm and a pannier under the other. Their warm conversation reminds me of how that guy in the car called out to Gabe, how Gabe knew the bookstore owner's name. This is definitely the kind of town where everyone knows everyone else.

The kind of town my mom and I have stayed away from since I was twelve.

I can see that, despite the local sense of camaraderie, Rush Creek is a town in flux, like my mom said. It's got a strong Western vibe. There are feed stores and tack shops and outdoor equippers tucked in among the gift and ice cream and bookshops. But I also note a bunch of shops catering to the town's recently surfaced hot springs and its new wedding venues—gifts, beauty products, and, yes, wedding dresses.

Most of the buildings have that low, boxy Western style and the pale brown long-plank siding to go with it. A few of them are cottages, with brightly colored doors and shutters. There's a log cabin or two and an old-style Western train depot, painted red. Flower barrels, rain barrels, and benches squat at intervals along the sidewalk, and the lampposts are tall wooden Ts hung with Craftsman-gaslamp-style lights.

It's got a totally different flavor from the Vermont town where I grew up, but it's just as cute and quaint in its Western-flavored way.

It would be fun to explore some of the shops, if I have the time and the sun comes out. Taking into account that it's all Small Town and therefore Not My Thing.

I climb two wide concrete steps, enter the lobby of the Depot Hotel, and cross to the reception desk.

"Oh, hon," says the woman behind the desk. She's wearing a cowboy hat. "You look like you could use a hot drink." I guess her to be sixty-something. She has ash-blond-and-silver hair and leather-tanned skin.

"Oh, God, that sounds good," I breathe.

"Why don't you help yourself to tea or coffee on the sideboard there and then come back and we'll get you checked in."

"Thank you," I say, dismayed to feel teary again. Ever since I blew up my job, small things get under my skin. Now fluffy ducklings and an offer of hot tea can wreck me. Go figure.

I fix myself tea. Just holding the steaming paper cup between my palms makes me feel better. I hadn't realized how cold I was.

The lobby of the Depot Hotel is dark and cozy, bare log-style with a roaring fire in the heavy stone hearth, chunky geometric prints, and an antler chandelier. There's a big leather couch in front of the fire, and it's calling my name. Loudly. But if I sit down now, I won't get up again.

God, that sounds good.

I force myself to head back to the desk.

"That's better," the clerk says, smiling at my drink and then at me. "Name?"

"Lucy Spiro."

She taps on the keyboard. "Single occupancy, double bed, three nights, right?"

Uh-oh. "Three—weeks."

"I've got three nights here." My stomach drops at her apologetic expression. "I'm so sorry, Ms. Spiro. Our system says three nights. And I wish I could say we have something for you, but the Spring Festival starts this weekend, and we're booked straight through the weekend and next week."

"Can you recommend another hotel?" I ask.

She winces. "Oh, hon. Everyone's booked up. Six towns in the festival, so hotels as far as Bend are full."

"Let me just—" I scroll on my phone, looking for the email with confirmation, hoping against hope that the mistake is the hotel's—which would at least put them in a position of having to find a place for me—but as soon as I see it on my screen, I realize I'm out of luck. It says three nights. I put my palm to my forehead. How did I not catch that?

Maybe because you were busy trying to get out of town as fast as possible? So you wouldn't run into anyone you knew from work?

Right. That.

I realize my forehead is still in my palm and look up to find the woman behind the desk eyeing me with a combination of sympathy and alarm.

"I'll be okay," I reassure her. "Worst case scenario, I'll stay with my mom and her new boyfriend in his Airstream."

Her eyebrows go up. "That sounds... crowded."

"Yes," I agree. The Airstream where they're living until they close on the new house would be tiny, even if Gregg didn't have two cats (that I'm allergic to) and a ginormous, drooly dog. Also, my mom and Gregg are still very much in the honeymoon bonk-intensive period of dating, and the last thing I want to think about is my mom having sex. I'm happy to believe I was the product of immaculate conception. "It's pretty bad. But I'd have a place to sleep."

"There's that," she says brightly. "I'll keep an ear to the ground for places with rooms."

But she doesn't sound optimistic.

I guess it's not surprising that the run of bad luck that bounced me out of New York isn't over yet. These things tend to hunt in packs.

She hands me the keycards and tells me my room number. "Good luck finding a place to stay."

I ride the elevator up and swipe myself into the room. The lone queen bed has a bedspread that looks like a cribbed

Native American pattern, and the walls are decorated with posters from the now-defunct Rush Creek Rodeo, but otherwise, it's your basic generic hotel room, probably about a decade from its last update, but clean and serviceable. The events of the last hour have totally caught up to me, and I collapse on the bed and stare stupidly into space. I don't know what I was thinking, saying yes to Gabe's drink invitation.

I wasn't thinking. I was feeling. Feeling the intensity of his dark brown eyes, the force of what he wanted from me. He was looking at me like I was the last slice of chocolate cake on the platter or a glass of ice water on a hot day.

Forty-five minutes. Meet me at Oscar's.

He'd practically grunted it. It should have been a huge turnoff. But it was the exact opposite. It was a light switch, flipped to the *on* position.

I'm the light switch in this scenario.

When I first spotted him, coming out of the feed store with the huge bag of dog food slung over his shoulder like it was a sack of feathers, I can't begin to explain what happened. I'd been standing there, wanting to cry along with the poor ducklings and their freaked-out mama... and then there he was. Maybe it was just that he was a local and I figured he'd know who to call for help with the ducklings, but I swear it was more than that. He looked like the kind of guy who doesn't wait around for other people to make stuff happen. He looked *take charge*.

And he did. No questions asked. He took stock of the situation. Jogged across the street, still hoisting his ain't-no-thang dog food bag, rustled around in his manly Jeep, and returned with tools. Which he wielded.

I guess I'm saying it's one thing to have a bunch of tools in your Jeep, and yet another to know how to use them.

Plus—and I really don't think you can discount this—he's insanely hot. At least six-two, ruggedly built like a guy who works with his body for a living. Tanned skin, dark hair a little too long and shaggy, in the best possible way. Several days of scruff clinging to a hard jaw, a strong nose, but a yummy mouth and dark, broody eyes.

And he smells so good. Woodsy, masculine, and magnetic.

I was already a goner before he started talking to the ducks. "There you go, little dude," he said, after we freed the first one. And then, "That's it, go keep your brother company." And "Hey, man, she's this way," when the third one started off in the wrong direction.

How can any one human being be so adorable and so hot at the same time?

I wanted him to take charge of me the way he took charge of the duckling situation.

I wanted him to murmur to me the way he murmured to them. Only more rumbly and grunt-y, close by my ear as he braced himself over me.

But that was before I discovered I needed a new place to stay. Before I looked at myself in the mirror.

I won't be able to make myself presentable in twenty minutes. It would take a hot shower and a blow dryer and my whole makeup kit. Forty minutes minimum. I sink down on the toilet at the thought, wrecked from a day of travel and the drama of babies separated from their mom and being wet and cold for so long.

Yeah, no. As much as I want to be Gabe's slice of chocolate

cake tonight, I want more to crawl into a warm bed and sleep this day off.

I call Oscar's and ask for Gabe, and I haven't even started to describe him when the woman at the other end of the phone says, "Yeah, hang on a sec, hon, he's right here."

Right. Small town, the kind of place where everyone knows everyone and there are no secrets. Of course they know who Gabe is. And if I'd showed up and left with him, everyone would have known that, too.

That said, I know better than anyone that even in a big city, things are sometimes way too close for comfort.

Gabe comes to the phone. His voice is deep, deeper than I remember it being in person. "Hey," he says.

"Hi, um, this is Lucy?"

Did I really ask that like a question? "This is Lucy," I say, with more certainty.

He chuckles, a low, rough, totally delightful sound. "You're not here."

"I'm so sorry," I say. Meaning, *Sorry, not sorry.*

"You're going to stand me up."

My body likes the way he made the words a statement and not a question, low, rough, and absolutely certain. My nipples prickle with delight. Or because I'm chilled to the bone.

"I'm cold and tired," I admit. "And I have a meeting first thing in the morning. I should never have said yes. Also, it turns out I screwed up and only booked myself for three days in this hotel and I'm staying three weeks, so I have to find another place to stay."

"Tell you what," he says. "I can help with that. I know everyone."

Right. Small town.

"Are you at the Depot Hotel? I'll come there. There's a bar downstairs, and we can get spiked hot drinks. I'll sort you out."

He says it syrup-slow, almost a drawl but not quite. He's not asking. He's telling me. *I'll sort you out.* And I love it, even though I pride myself on being a woman who controls her own destiny... and does a pretty damn fine job at it.

Tonight, though? Tonight, I want to be sorted.

It's been that kind of month.

"Okay."

The word slips out before I can stop it.

"I'll be there in ten minutes."

I end the call, race into the bathroom, and churn myself into a frenzy redoing my makeup and fast-blow-drying my hair. Then I throw on clothes at a breakneck pace and head downstairs to meet my destiny.

Okay, let's not kid ourselves.

I head downstairs to meet Mr. Tonight.

4

GABE

I wait for her a long time in the lobby. Long enough that if she were anyone else and this were any other date, I'd have left. I hate getting dicked around and made to wait. But she sounded pretty miserable on the phone, and apparently I can't resist the urge to jump in when this woman needs help.

I'm not a big fan of the over-the-top "Western" decor in the Depot Hotel. Cowboy hats and boots hang from thick log columns, and the paintings rehash a bunch of not-okay cowboys-and-Indians themes. But the fire is warm and the leather of the couch is well-worn, and I had a long day at work, so I'm happy to sit and relax.

"Hey," says a soft voice, and I turn to find her standing behind the couch.

"Hey. Oh. You look... great."

"Thank you."

She's whipped herself back together. Her sunny blond hair is clean and straight—none of the damp wisps that clung to her face in the rain. There's no sign of the makeup that streaked her face earlier. She's wearing eyeshadow and some glossy pink lipstick that makes her lips look slick and kissable. And she's changed into what I'm sure are her "casual clothes"—a soft silky-looking top that clings to her fucking amazing tits and a pair of dark jeans that hug her ass, thighs, and calves. She teeters on another pair of shoes whose spiky heels make me want to beg her to keep them on in bed.

I'm not surprised she's all polished again. I'd guessed from her clothes and shoes that she probably wasn't a woman who liked to be out of control.

But I want to see her the way she was before. Rumpled, messy, passionate. Too caught up in the moment to worry about whether her hair is done, her makeup is neat, or her clothes are just-so.

I get a vivid mental picture of doing that to her. Kissing her into not giving a shit about anything except wanting more.

"Bar's this way," I say, instead, and lead her toward the back of the bar, to the small quiet corner.

We sit, and I order us two Irish coffees. She raises her eyebrows at me but doesn't protest.

"Where ya from, City Girl?" I ask.

She blows out a laugh. "New York."

"That was going to be my first guess."

"Does it show?"

"Hell, yeah. Clothes, hair, makeup. I can tell East Coast from a mile away. You can see it in the way people move. Fast. Leaning forward, almost, like they're always going some-where in a hurry, even when they're not going anywhere at all. They're the tourists who'll almost run you over on the sidewalk."

"We're not all like that."

I shake my head. "No. Some of you *think* you're not like that, but that's because you've lived there so long you've lost track of how normal people walk."

She squints at me. "And what, the West is the standard for normal? You're all in slow motion. I go to the grocery store and I trip over you. Everyone stops at all the four-way stops and is like, 'You go.' 'No, you go.' 'No, you go.' And meanwhile if we were in New York or Boston, twenty people could have gone. Also, the way you talk?" She draws out the last few words into a bad imitation of a southern drawl that sounds nothing like Western Oregon's relaxed, slightly flat speech.

"I talk like everyone else talks. You're the one who sounds like the Chipmunks holiday special." I deliberately speed my last few words up to demonstrate.

That makes her laugh again.

"So what's a New York girl doing in a town like this?"

She hesitates. Bites her lip. I get the distinct feeling she doesn't want to answer, and I make a mental note. Right, no personal stuff. But then she says, "Well—my mom's here. She moved here about a year ago to live with her boyfriend."

"You're Adele's daughter!" The words pop out before I can think better of it. If she doesn't want to tell me about her life, she definitely doesn't want me to already *know* about it.

She makes a sour face. "I should have guessed you'd know who she is."

"Told you I know everyone. My mother plays Bunco with her."

"Of *course* she does," she mutters. "Small towns."

"*Small towns?* Wait a second. Are you knocking small towns?"

"Everyone knows everyone else. Everyone knows everyone else's business. And everyone feels entitled to everyone else's business."

"Everyone looks out for everyone else."

She rolls her eyes. "Not my experience."

"You've lived in one before."

"Yeah. When I was a kid."

She doesn't elaborate. Instead, she says, "When things... went south for me back in New York, I asked my mom if I could come stay. I think she felt guilty she couldn't put me up, so she booked a hotel room for me instead, and got me some work."

"Like a job?"

I have to admit, my heart drops to the floor when she says work, because if she's staying long-term in Rush Creek, then this isn't going to happen tonight. I'm not interested in anything except one night of fun.

She shakes her head. "Just a short-term client. I'm in marketing. I specialize in marketing to women."

It makes total sense to me that Lucy's in marketing. Marketing people are always polished and in control. I bet she has an expensive leather portfolio that she carries her work around in.

She starts telling me about how women make most of the buying decisions in households, even if men are the ones who end up being the primary users of whatever gets bought. And about how women need to trust a brand before they'll buy it, and feel safe with it, which are different needs than male buyers have.

"So I work with people, help them capture the female buyers or audience, help them build that trust. And the gig I'm doing here, the one my mom hooked me up with, is helping a business reach more of that market."

"The *New Rush Creek*," I mutter. There's a banner flying over Main Street that says that in gold script. Every time I see it, I cringe. Way too close to home.

"Not a fan?"

"That's an understatement."

"I did my research on Rush Creek and the New Rush Creek, but I wouldn't mind hearing how you see it," she says. "It always looks different from inside the story."

That's for sure. I've never thought of myself as a guy who resists change, but I hate what Rush Creek has become.

"It used to be mostly a rodeo town, but then about five years ago, the rodeo shut down and this hot spring that had been underground popped to the surface. It was like some totally fucked up—" I eye her to gauge if my language is going to offend, but she waves it off. "—cause and effect. Goodbye rodeo, hello hot spring. One day we were all cowboy hats, tack, and tents, and the next, weddings, women's spa vacations, and romantic getaways. Now if you want to succeed, everything has to smell like lavender."

She makes a soft sound of understanding and sympathy.

"The shift gave all of us whiplash," I say. What I don't say, because it's such a sore sport for me, is that it screwed Wilder Adventures right to hell. Wilder's the outdoor adventuring outfit I own with my family. We've had to work twice as hard the last few years to get half as many clients—while equipment costs have skyrocketed.

I wish like anything it were otherwise, but business is in the toilet. Which reminds me of something she said earlier.

"You said something about things going south in New York?"

She shakes her head. "Let's not go there."

"Fair enough. I hate New York. Happy not to go there."

She grimaces, then nods, then admits, "It's a love/hate city. But I love it. I love that you can have anything you want, any time you want it. You can have anything you can dream of delivered to you in a couple of hours. Any kind of takeout. Food from a country you've never heard of before. You can see any movie, any play, any concert. You can have your laundry picked up, cleaned, and returned to you and never have to leave your apartment. And I love the anonymity. I love going for days without running into anyone I know. I love that no one knows who I am most of the time."

"The exact opposite of a small town."

"Exactly."

I try to imagine it, and a part of me can see the appeal—no gossip, no expectations, no history. Sex would definitely be easier. I limit my encounters to one-nighters with out-of-towners and a few friends with benefits. Out-of-towners dry up in the off season. Friends with benefits gets stale. Neither of those choices is the perfect solution, but they're better than getting involved. Believe me.

"But you—love Rush Creek?" she asks.

"Lived here my whole life. Can't imagine living anywhere else."

"And your family's here?"

"My mom, my brothers, my sister, my niece and nephew."

The bartender brings our Irish coffees. Lucy lifts hers to toast, and I clink glass mugs with her. She takes a sip and ends up with whipped cream on her nose. Very cute. I reach out to gently swipe it off. And her lips part. I drag my gaze up to her eyes, and her breath catches.

Life's short and Lucy's right here. I reach out a hand, cup the back of her head, and lean in. When our mouths touch, hers soft and warm, she lets out a gasp that sends blood roaring through my veins. It takes all the self control I have to draw back and enjoy how beautiful she looks, just kissed: blown pupils, pink cheeks, and slack lower lip.

"Wow," she says softly.

"Yeah. More where that came from."

Don't get me wrong. I could have kissed her into next week. I can still feel the imprint of her mouth, and I'm shot through with the need to lick into her and explore. But I like the look on her face right now. Wanting. I'm okay with drawing this out, letting her feel the tug between us.

I like that feeling too. That sense of possibility. Not too long from now, I'm going to make Lucy come apart, make her cry my name. I'm going to make it so good for her. No need to rush, though. The anticipation is part of it.

"So what's the business?" I ask, as if I'm not mentally undressing her. "The one you're consulting for?"

"Uh—" She looks completely undone, which is a total turn-on. I love that I was able to make her mind go blank like that. This is what Lucy looks like when she's so caught up she can't be all polished and controlled and organized.

"What *is* this?" she asks, gesturing between us. I know what she means. You don't get this kind of chemistry with everyone. It feels rare, and good, and dangerous, in the best way.

I've got my mouth open to say something along those lines, when she says, "Wilder Adventures."

My mind is on the question of whether I want to strip off Lucy's clothes or watch her take them off slowly, so at first, I barely register her words.

Then something in the pit of my brain—the part that leaps back from a snake on the trail before I'm even aware I saw it—gets it, and my stomach twists into a knot. She's answering my question. As in, "What business are you consulting to?" Answer: "Wilder Adventures."

Apparently, I'm shaking my head, because Lucy starts to look alarmed. "What?" she asks, and then, before I can answer, because she's a smart cookie, "Oh, *shit*."

We stare at each other.

"You're going to have to explain this to me." It comes out a growl. "How are you in town to consult for my business, and I don't know anything about it?"

Lucy doesn't flinch. Apparently, I'm not the first pissed-off business-owner she's had to face. "Gabe," she says slowly, her eyes searching my face for clues. "Gabriel *Wilder*. You, um— had a lot more hair. And a beard. In the photos on the web and the business page."

"It was time for a change." It's a dumb thing to say, but I'm in a daze, trying to understand why my mom appears to have hired a consultant without telling me.

Lucy watches me like I'm a bomb that might go off. Which, let's be honest, I am.

She chooses her words carefully. "Your mom hired me to make Wilder Adventures more female-friendly. A little, um, lavender along with the hiking boots and hunting rifles and fishing charters."

"Yeah. Got that." I'm going to kill my mom. In slow painful stages. "Wilder Adventures doesn't need to be more female-friendly. And it *definitely* doesn't need any lavender."

"That's not what your mom thinks," she counters.

"What exactly did she tell you?"

"That she owns Wilder Adventures and runs it with the help of her five sons. That I would meet all of you tomorrow morning. I take it she didn't tell you that part."

My hands tighten into fists, an attempt not to slam one of them down on the bar in frustration.

The thing is, Wilder Adventures is not actually mine. My mother still owns sixty percent of it. It's true that I run it, but there's no official org chart anywhere that says that. There has never had to be. Everyone who matters knows it, and my mother has never stuck her nose where it didn't belong.

But if my mom wants to hire someone to stuff those little mesh bags filled with lavender and tied with itty-bitty silk bows into everyone's sleeping bags...

I can't actually legally stop her.

My body tenses with helpless rage. I can't believe she did this to me.

Lucy is watching quietly.

I take a deep breath and cool off. I don't have any legal authority over my mother, but that doesn't mean I have to roll over. I can fight back. I can put my foot down.

"Yeah. Well. Not gonna happen."

This time it's closer to a roar than a growl, but Lucy still doesn't flinch.

"It sounds like maybe you and she need to have a little chat?" she suggests, in a voice she might use with a tantruming two-year-old. Which I suspect in this situation, she would say I am.

Guess no one's getting laid tonight.

Gabe's pissed. Like, *really* pissed.

Our goodbyes are... awkward. The kind of awkward that can only come from a situation where two people are about to have sex and then discover that they're, well, enemies.

I'm pretty sure Gabe's pissed at his mom, not me, but...

The sexy mood is as dead as the Dollar Store on Christmas Day.

If I were the kind of woman who believed in signs, I'd think the universe was trying to tell me to quit it with the one-night stands. Too risky. You could end up sleeping with your boss's on-again off-again boyfriend... or the guy whose business you're about to turn on its head.

But I'm not that woman. I don't believe in signs, and I don't think there's anything wrong with wanting uncomplicated sex. I'll just have to get better at double checking for complications *before* I lock lips.

"I'll see you tomorrow morning," I tell him. "At the meeting."

The look he gives me screams "over my cold dead body," but he manages not to say it. "See you tomorrow morning," he grinds out. He throws a twenty down on the bar, slips off his stool, and stalks toward the door before I can say anything else, like, "Let me pay for my drink."

Which is probably a good thing. He needs to have it out with his mom before anything else happens. Definitely before I take a shot at explaining to him why Wilder Adventures *does* need to diversify if it's going to capture the new market.

I don't panic. This happens occasionally with consulting, when someone at the client company gets blindsided. One of my jobs as a consultant is to make sure all the key players buy into my work... although, it's best if the person who hires me does that before bringing me in.

Obviously, Barb Wilder didn't. There were no hints that she wasn't truly in charge of the business. And damn it, I asked her if there was anyone else I should talk to before I showed up at a company meeting, and she said no.

Either Barb and Gabe are locked in an epic power struggle or she lied to me.

I'm going to have a heart-to-heart with her about the trust relationship I need to do my job well.

Suddenly all the exhaustion from earlier rushes over me, and all I want is to go back to New York. In the years I've been working in marketing there, I've never out-of-the-blue discovered that someone's mom was using me to manipulate her kid. A whole lot of other bullshit, sure, but not that.

And Barb seemed so down-to-earth, too. What a disappointment.

I pull up the Wilder Adventures website, wondering how

many signs I missed. Should I have known who Gabe Wilder was the moment I laid eyes on him? I did my due diligence, so how did I not recognize him the instant I saw him?

There are headshots of all five Wilder brothers on the site. Gabe's photo is the blurriest. I wasn't kidding about the amount of hair in that photo—he's a wild man. I'm sure my gaze skated right over him and on to the other brothers, all of whom are more clean cut in their photos than he is and therefore way more obviously good-looking.

None of the brothers is listed with a title, just a specialty: Gabe leads hunting trips, his brother Brody does fishing trips, and so on.

There are tons of photos of the brothers on the Facebook page, but few of them are of Gabe. I wonder if that means he's often the guy behind the camera? There is one photo of him taken over his shoulder as he sights a turkey. You can tell he's a gorgeous specimen of broad-shouldered, narrow hipped manhood, but it's not surprising I didn't recognize him from the rear view.

Although, it is a reminder that I think like a city girl, not a small-town girl. In a town this size, how many guys named *Gabe* would there be?

Obviously, too few.

I slip off my stool—Gabe's twenty more than covers both our drinks and two generous tips, because this isn't New York City, after all—and head upstairs.

I'm not nearly as calm as I want to be.

Because I had a plan, and Wilder Adventures was part of it. My plan was to do this short gig, collect the money, give notice at my job, and start my own marketing firm. Without the money from this gig, I'll have to go back to work at my old job... and I'll have to face Gennie.

After what I did to her, that really isn't an option.

I MEET my mom first thing the next morning in the hotel lobby.

"Oh, hon," Mom says, as soon as she sees me. She wraps me up in a big hug, and tears fill my eyes. Then she steps back and studies me, Mom-style.

"I know," I say. "I look tired."

We both smile at that. We have a deal that neither of us will ever tell the other one that, even if it's true.

"Let's blame jet lag," I suggest, even though we both know it's more than that. She knows the story of what happened with Gennie and Liam. Well, not all of it; I didn't get into the "O face"-level details. But I told her about the flowers and the humiliation. She is literally the only person I have told or will ever tell. My mom and I know how to keep secrets.

"But *you* look amazing," I say. It's the truth. She stopped coloring her hair when she moved from Boston to Rush Creek, and it's turned out to be the most amazing shade of silver. Her eyes are bright and her cheeks are pink, and her face, which has always been angular, almost severe, is somehow softer.

"Aw, thanks." She gets pinker. Which, if you know my mom, is hilarious. She doesn't blush. "Do you want a big breakfast? Like diner style?"

"What I really want is a breakfast sandwich and a cup of coffee."

She leads me to the coffee shop I scented last night, Morning Rush, and we each order bottomless morning coffee and breakfast sandwiches, all of which costs half what it would have in New York.

We sit at a small table near the back, where the scent of roasting coffee is almost its own high. I take a healthy bite of my sandwich. The bacon is crisp, the cheese sharp, hot, and melty, and the bagel—

"This isn't really a bagel," I say. "More like an O-shaped roll."

My mom sighs. "Are you going to be a New Yorker about this?"

"Yes. You shouldn't make things bagel-shaped if they're not bagels."

"What about donuts?"

I nod. "There's an exception for donuts."

"It's a good roll, though," she says.

"Except it's missing its middle."

She shakes her head at me and digs in. "So you're headed to the Wilder offices from here?" Her eyebrows draw together at the expression on my face. "What's wrong?"

How can she tell so easily? "Wilder Adventures," I say. "Does Barb actually *run* it? I mean, I know she owns it, but is she, you know, the decision-maker?"

"No. Her oldest runs it. Gabriel. Did I not tell you that? Did *she* not tell you that?"

I sigh heavily. "No."

Hearing his name sends a shiver through me. My attraction to Gabe is a hugely inconvenient factor here. It's strong enough that last night as I was falling asleep, I was *still* trying to convince myself that it would be okay to sleep with him. Luckily, he clearly never wants to see my face again.

So inconvenient.

My mom is eyeing me suspiciously. "Lucy?"

"I kissed him."

"You *what*?"

Because brains are a pain in the ass, mine flashes back on the feel of that kiss. As kisses went, it was pretty innocuous. You could even say it was safe for work. But it really wasn't. I wanted to grab his head, slide my tongue into his mouth, and press my body against his. And then I wanted him to sweep every item of glassware off the bar and lay me down on it, without passing go. No. Not safe for work.

"Lucy?"

"There were ducklings," I attempt. "We rescued these ducklings that were down a drain." My unhelpful brain provides a stunning, full-color close-up of Gabe's forearms, flexing as he levered the grate up. Lean muscle and ropey sinew and that forearm bulge that has always been my downfall. "And then I agreed to have a drink with him. And then he kissed me. And then I found out who he was."

"Ohhh," my mother says. "Oh, that's—"

"Bad," I say. "Very bad. I seem to be having a run of very bad luck."

She snickers at that. "But this is the twenty-first century. These things do happen. You could consult for him and also..."

Thankfully, she does not provide a verb. She trails off, but my brain helpfully finishes her sentence: *...and also fuck him*. I get hot all over. And then cold, because *nope*.

"I think the 'also' ship sailed," I say. "That cowboy rode off into the sunset, alone on his horse. Or whatever metaphor would be best for Rush Creek."

"In Gabe's case, maybe it would be that the deer took its fatal arrow? Or, hmmm. The turkey flew the roost? Is that the expression? Flew the coop?"

My mom can be easily distracted by puzzles and word games, which is one of her most lovable traits.

"I don't think turkeys live in coops. Let's go with the deer and the arrow. It's deader." Because there's no way I'm getting any more Gabe Wilder kisses now.

I'm disappointed. I have to admit it to myself. The way things started up with Gabe forced me right out of my comfort zone and into a kind of insta-chemistry and ease that would have definitely translated to orgasms. I'd *talked* to him. Like opened-my-mouth-and-words-fell-out talked.

But there's no way Gabe and I are going to be easy with each other now.

And that's for the best. Barb's job is going to pay me enough to get me halfway to where I need to be to start my own business.

Since I clearly am not a plays-well-with-others human.

Gennie's voice floats into my head. *If you'd just let any of us be friends with you like we've been trying to do, this wouldn't have happened.*

Starting my own business will let me focus on what I'm best at, without distractions. And Barb's job is the first step.

Kissing Gabriel Wilder was just an unfortunate speed bump. My last mistake before I turn things around.

I pack my attraction to Gabe into a box and stick it in the brain attic.

"Gabe Wilder does not seem to be convinced that Wilder Adventures needs my help."

My mom frowns. "Barb told me she's let Gabe do his thing for years. But it's not working. And he's... stubborn."

Oh, so Barb *does* want me to mediate a mother-son feud. Great. "I wish I'd known that. That never works. Bringing in someone from the outside to say what you should have had the courage to say yourself."

My mother sighs. "I guess she must have thought if it came from an expert, he'd listen." She reaches out and puts a hand on mine. "You'll convince him, Lucy. I know you will."

No one has faith in you like your mother.

"You're the best, Mom," I say. Which reminds me of my bad news. "It, um, turns out that the hotel room at the Depot is only for three nights. I called around last night—"

"No! I booked it for three weeks! I know I did! I'm going to call Julia. I'm sure she can straighten this out." My mom looks stricken.

I bite my lip. "I don't think she can. The woman there—I don't think she was Julia, but she seemed to know what she was talking about—she said they don't have anything after the next few days. Something about a festival." Small towns and their never-ending festivals!

"Oh, honey. I am so, so sorry. I swear I said three weeks."

"It's not your fault. I should have checked the confirmation. It's one of those mix-ups. I'll find somewhere else to stay."

I don't tell her I called every hotel in the Five Rivers area last night. No luck.

"But"—her voice is dire—"you're right. About the spring festival. I forgot about that. Everything will be booked."

"There's gotta be *something*." I say this with more conviction than I feel.

"You know what?" my mom says. "I bet Barb has an idea where you can stay. I'll check with her. And if that doesn't pan out, you can come stay with me and Gregg. The couch is very comfortable."

"I love you, Mom. And I know you love me. But if we both want to keep loving each other, I probably shouldn't come stay with you and your boyfriend and his two cats and very large dog in his Airstream *for three weeks*."

My mom says softly, "You are *always* welcome, wherever I am."

I know this to the bottom of my heart. After my dad went to prison and we found out the extent of his lies and crimes, my mom always made a place for me in her arms. She dried my tears and did everything in her power to prove to me that I still had one parent who loved me. One person I could trust. Despite her own broken heart.

"You're the best, Mom. But I bet Gregg wouldn't be so quick to agree to me staying for three weeks."

My mom wrings her hands, something she does only when she's really nervous. I squint at her. "What?"

"You can ask him yourself. I, um, hope it's okay. I invited him to join us after I got you all to myself for a bit."

"You—what?"

She looks past me, and I turn to see a man standing at the counter, ordering. He turns and waves at us.

"Don't be mad, sweetheart." Her eyebrows draw together.

"Of course not, Mom. Of course I want to meet him."

The man heads our way with his sandwich, holding his cowboy hat politely in one hand and extending the other for a shake. He's tall and broad, rugged-featured and good-looking, with salt-and-pepper hair and smile lines. "I've been looking forward to meeting you, Lucy. I've heard so much about you."

"You, too." I smile at him.

"I see she got the Spiro good looks." Gregg winks at my mom.

She blushes. Gregg does, too.

They're kind of adorable. I wasn't expecting that. I mean, I knew things were good with them or they wouldn't be moving in together, but I wasn't expecting flirting and blushing. My mom is like me, super cautious about letting people in, at least since we found out about Dad and all the crap that came after that. When she told me she was moving to a small town to be with a guy she'd met on a Hawaii vacation, I almost fell over.

She pulls up a chair for Gregg and he sits.

"Your mom says you're here for a job," he says.

I nod. "I'm doing consulting work for a local business."

He nods. My mom probably told him. "If it wouldn't be an imposition, I might ask your thoughts on mine."

"Absolutely. What's your business?"

"I own the bike shop."

I give him a second look and realize he's the guy I saw chatting with the coffee store owner last night. Right. Small town. No end to the coincidences.

"I'd be happy to help if I can," I say, meaning it. As much as I worry about my mom getting hurt again, if she loves this guy, I'll give him the benefit of the doubt.

My mom takes advantage of the moment to tell him,

"There was a screwup at the hotel. I told Lucy it would be fine if she stays with us if she needs to."

Gregg doesn't blink. "Sure thing. The couch is surprisingly comfortable." He touches my mom's shoulder and she smiles at him.

"That's so kind," I tell him. "I'll check to see if Barb knows of something, but if she doesn't have a lead, I'll definitely take you up on that."

I reach for my napkin, only to realize I don't have one. "I'm grabbing a napkin—anyone else need one?"

They shake their heads and I get up. As I come back to the table, I see they're holding hands, and Gregg leans in to whisper something in my mom's ear. She blushes again, ferociously, then tilts her face for a kiss.

I look away as fast as I can, but not fast enough.

Um, yeah. This. This is why I need a place to sleep that isn't the Airstream.

I'm happy for my mom. I really am.

But the chances of my crashing on Gregg's sofa are near zero. I can't harsh their new-love mellow, and I don't want a front row seat.

Little do I know how much I will later wish I'd grabbed that super-safe sofa option.

"You said you wouldn't interfere."

"We had a deal," my mother responds, crossing her arms and raising one eyebrow.

The Wilder stubborn streak is highly heritable. We all have it. It's just that, mostly, we don't use it for intrafamily warfare. Well, aside from the ways my brothers and I torment each other for sport.

And worse, my mom's right. We did have a deal.

"I gave you a year to turn it around your way," she says. "You said that if you couldn't, you'd let me do it my way. Well, this is my way."

I stalk across the small Wilder Adventures conference room. I made her meet me here an hour ahead of the meeting with Lucy. She wanted to know why, but I figured if she could blindside me, I could blindside her.

"You could have warned me," I accuse.

"And if I had?"

I know what she's driving at. If she'd let me know sooner that she was bringing in a consultant, I would have fought it, just like I am now. "I would have had a chance to talk you out of it."

"You would have fought it relentlessly," she says. "You would have wanted to do more of the same, and, Gabriel, the same is *not working*. More ads, expensive ads in men's magazines. More trying to reach the Portland audience. Meanwhile Portland is full of hipsters buying premium artisanal extra virgin olive-oil-flavored ice cream, not guys wanting to test their mettle in the woods. And all the while we're sitting on this huge untapped audience of girls' weekends and newlyweds and couples having sexy getaways and bridal showers and bachelor parties and wedding guests in need of entertainment. And I've been saying this to you and you've been saying—"

"I don't want to dumb it down and soften it up."

"I know, Gabriel," my mother says gently. "I get it. I really do. But you also don't want to lose the business."

She knows she has me, and not because of the business per se. Because the business isn't just a business. It's what holds our whole family together. It employs all four of my brothers, and even provides some side income to my sister, who does a bunch of office work for us. If the business goes under, there's a healthy chance at least some of us would have to live somewhere else to get work—assuming any of us could find something in the outdoors business that isn't cashier at an outdoor retailer. And I promised—*promised* —my dad I would take care of this family and keep us together.

That's a promise I'll never break.

Still, I can't help but think my dad would also be horrified by the idea of lavender sachets in the sleeping bags.

My mother recognizes my weak spot and takes a jab. "She's here now. She came all this way. At least hear her out."

"You set this up on purpose so I'd have to hear her out." I scowl.

"I recognize stubborn in my own kid. And no surprise. You're the first child of two first children. Nobody tougher, more obstinate, or better suited for turning this business around."

I close my eyes. Here's what I know. If this summer season doesn't double the revenue of last summer, we'll have trouble making payroll by winter. And if the winter season doesn't double the revenue of last winter, I'll have to let one or more of my brothers go.

My *brothers*.

No fucking way.

"Gabriel," my mother says. "I have a proposition for you."

I lift my chin to look at her. Her eyes are soft. She's still a pretty woman, my mom. Sometimes I wonder if she'll date again at some point. My dad's been gone more than fifteen years.

"Let Lucy do her job. Let her make a proposal for revamping the business to succeed in this market. Cooperate with her, give her what she needs, hear her out. You do that, and I'll give you and your brothers my share of the business, with you as the majority shareholder."

Holy *shit*.

I've always wanted to own the business. Not because I want to take anything away from my mom, but my grandfather owned it, and my father, and it feels like what I need to do. But my dad left it to my mom, and I never felt like I could take that away from her.

But here it is. My chance. Right in my lap.

And all I have to do is let her sprinkle me with lavender.

She drives a hard bargain.

Good to know my business genes are sound.

How hard can it be, hearing Lucy out? She's obviously a smart woman who knows her shit. I brace myself.

"I don't have to take her advice?"

"You have to seriously consider it," my mom says. "You have to convince me that you gave it real thought. But no. You don't have to take it."

"I still think there's another way," I say. "To keep the heart of the business as is, not turn it into—" I swallow bile. "Bachelorette parties and beer hikes and singles outings."

"And if you give Lucy's plan the consideration it deserves, Wilder will be all yours to do with as you wish."

That sounds pretty good to me.

I stick my hand out and we shake. "One more thing," I say.

"Hmm?"

"You have to tell Brody, Clark, Easton, and Kane that we're going after the New Rush Creek market. *Before* Lucy gets here. 'Cause I'm sure as hell not telling them."

"I deserve that," she says, shaking her head.

"You do."

She slumps down into a chair at the conference table.

"You reap what you sow," I tell her.

She shoots a look at me across the table, then straightens and smirks. I can tell before she opens her mouth I'm not going to like what she's going to say.

"Kath Kenney told me she saw you and Lucy at the Depot Hotel bar last night."

"Yeah? So?" I think of Lucy dissing small towns and gossip last night, and have to swallow a smile. She might have a point.

"She said you looked awful cozy."

"That was before I knew who she was."

"Been a while since you looked cozy with anyone."

"Cozy's not my thing, Mom. You know that."

She eyes me thoughtfully. "Maybe it's time to think about changing that."

I roll my eyes. "Don't push your luck. You won the important battle."

She smiles at that—and then frowns, because we can both hear my brothers' voices outside, and these next few minutes are going to be no fun at all.

For her, anyway.

"I'm gonna go take a stroll," I say. "Enjoy yourself."

The Wilder property is a few miles outside town. The low buildings of the town give way to ever-greens and houses, and then, as I follow Barb's directions, to a road that winds past ranch land dotted with sagebrush and portioned off by split-rail fences. It's beautiful, wild, and lonely, and I miss the straight lines and hard edges of my city.

Then nerves take over as I pull into a long dusty driveway on the Wilder family property. The way things ended with Gabe yesterday—even though I think I handled the situation pretty well—I'm wary about what comes next. And I know I have to talk to Barb about giving me all the info I need to do my job well.

There are two buildings at the end of the driveway, the house to the left and the barn—home of Wilder Adventures —to the right. I park Marshmallow, the butt-ugly rental car, alongside a Jeep in the small dirt parking lot. I always name my rental cars, along with all the other technology in my life

—phone, laptop, even my alarm clock. I learned it from my dad. It's the only thing about him that I kept.

The Wilder house is a Northwest contemporary, lots of glass and wood, all horizontal siding and unexpected peaks. It's beautiful.

The barn looks older. I'm guessing this land was once part of a ranch, and that the barn was original to that setup. It's painted red and has a long, pitched roof and small, scattered windows. The barn door has been remade into a business entrance with swinging glass doors.

Against my will, I'm charmed.

I grab my coffee and my Hobo bag, take a step out of the car, and breathe in the cool mountain air. Here, outside of town, the air smells totally different—sage and juniper. I catch my heel in the dirt and stumble.

For a frantic split-second, I wonder how much coffee and dirt will end up on me. Then someone steps out from behind the Jeep, grabs my arms, and rights me. Someone with big, warm hands who's strong enough to effortlessly ease me to standing.

My coffee didn't even spill.

"You should have left those shoes in New York," Gabe says, eyeing them with a scowl. The scowl gets even deeper. "How many pairs did you bring?"

"Five," I admit.

He rolls his eyes. His long-lashed, intense, dark brown eyes. He's still holding my arms. I don't want him to stop. I didn't dress warmly enough, because apparently Western Oregon in May is not like New York in May. Research failure. But the heat pouring off Gabriel Wilder is sunshine-strong and welcome, even if he won't stop scowling.

Meanwhile, something is licking my hand.

I tear my attention off his show-stopping face and realize that the culprit is a big dog that's at least part German Shepherd, along with something more playful and fluffy.

"Is this the guy you were buying dog food for yesterday?"

He nods in a way that manages to convey that we're not ever going to mention yesterday again. At the same time, he finally seems to realize he's still holding onto me and drops his hands. "This way," he grunts.

Apparently, the guy who was chit-chatting with me in the bar last night will *not* be attending this meeting. Which, fine. I get it. He doesn't want me here. I bury a tiny twinge of regret and follow him into the barn.

Which, when we're inside, more than anything makes me think of a big-box sporting goods store. Racks prickle with skis, poles, and paddles; the walls are covered with bikes and all manner of small watercraft; and cubbies and bins bulge with life preservers, helmets, boots, foam sleeping pads, sleeping bags, and tents. You name it, the gear's here. It's orderly but chaotic. And it smells faintly like a ski lodge.

I can't spend too long taking in my surroundings, because my attention is snared by the men—and two women—seated around the big conference table in the center of the room.

The Wilder brothers.

It's a sea of slightly-too-long hair in shades of brown, broad shoulders under flannel shirts, khaki hiking pants bulging at the thighs, and gorgeous sun-golden forearms arrayed on the table for my visual feast.

I think I've been reading too many why-choose romance novels, because my heart is totally pounding.

"Lucy!" a woman's voice calls, buoyant with pleasure. A

fair-skinned woman with a short silver bob and green eyes finds her way to my side. She starts to open her arms like she's going to hug me, then apparently thinks better of it and extends her hand to shake mine instead. Probably good, because I'm not feeling altogether kindly toward her at the moment.

"You must be Barb," I say.

"It's such a pleasure to finally meet you," she says. "Everyone, this is Lucy Spiro. She's here to give us some ideas about how to get more customers."

This announcement is met with eye rolls and exchanged glances. I stiffen my spine. I remind myself that none of them knew I was coming until last night at the earliest—and probably not until this morning. They'll get used to the idea. I'll win them over.

Although they're not looking like a crew likely to be won over. They're staring at me with matching scowls and identical unwavering glares.

Including the one staffer who isn't a member of the Wilder family. She's a young, sturdily built woman with tanned skin and short, dark hair. I vaguely recall there was a sixth trip leader on the website, Kane's partner for ski trips. This must be her. Hanna, I think.

Apparently, she won't be my number one cheerleader. I make a note to myself to see if I can change that. I know that just because she's female doesn't make her my automatic ally... but it's worth a try.

"Let me introduce you to everyone," Barb says. "This is Brody."

Brody is the lightest-haired of the crew. He's not wearing flannel, but instead, a black leather zip jacket over a short-sleeved copper-colored t-shirt that at first I think is covered with bugs—ew. On closer examination, they turn out to be fishing lures. Right. He's the fishing charter brother. Tattoos peek out of the sleeve of his jacket and the neck of his shirt. He looks like trouble waiting to happen.

"Hi, Brody," I say.

He gives me a sullen look and a flat-palmed wave of acknowledgment and doesn't stand to greet me. Okay, then. Maybe I'm not going to win Brody over first.

Clark's next—the survival trip leader. His hair's shorter and darker than Brody's, but his facial hair is longer—more beard than stubble. Based on the market research I did, I'm sure that the thin half-zip shirt clinging to his sculpted chest is made from wool to protect him from the elements. He's a little more friendly than Brody. He gets up and greets me with a handshake, maintaining steady-gray eye contact all the while.

Then it's Kane's turn. He runs backcountry ski trips, though we're out of season for that now. His hair is streaked with all his brothers' shades of brown, and his eyes are a pale sky blue. He's polite, and his handshake is strong but not aggressive.

He gives me a nod and gestures to the dark-haired young woman. "This is Hanna. She's my co-leader."

She nods in acknowledgment, but makes no move to get up.

"Hi, Hanna. Nice to meet you," I say.

"Hi."

If it's possible to imbue that short word with scorn, she's managed it.

Easton's last. He's the youngest, I'm pretty sure. The

baby. If I remember correctly, he does whitewater rafting trips. When his mom says his name, he stands and saunters over. Takes my hand, holds it a little too long. Winks at me. His hair is between Clark's and Brody's, in shade and length —just long enough to suggest curls. He's too pretty to be believed, with his mom's green eyes and a perfectly sculpted nose and jaw. Think Sawyer on *Lost*. Except even hotter.

He's a very different kind of trouble from Brody, but trouble no less. But he's also the chink in their armor. The place to start winning them over. He seems like a man who'd be perfectly happy to have more women on his trips—and to make them feel safe and catered to.

"And Gabe. Who you've already met."

For some reason, when I turn back to Gabe I expect his spell to be broken. After all, I've been staring into the sun for several minutes now. But unfortunately, that's not the case. Instead, he looks even better, like he's soaked up his brothers' light and is reflecting it back at me. He's the biggest of them, for one, and the only one with those dark, dark brown eyes that bore into me. And even stacked up against these intimidatingly handsome men, there's something about him that stands out.

I realize that even when he's silent, he conveys that sense of command. It's a kind of stillness and watchfulness that makes it clear that he's attentive to everything going on and ready to act if the situation calls for it. *I've got duckling rescue tools in my vehicle and I won't hesitate to use them.*

I want him in charge of me, I think again, even though that's the last thing I want. I'm in charge here. Today. I want to call the shots. I *should* be calling the shots.

He steps forward and greets me with an impersonal handshake and a clipped "welcome."

It's probably the least welcoming welcome ever uttered. I try not to feel disappointed that this is how it's going to be.

"Lucy, I'll let you take it from here," Barb says.

I survey the table—so much testosterone, so much glower!—and then decide I'm not going to let any of them throw me off my game. I came here to do a job, and I'm going to do it. So I leap right in with my spiel. I tell them who I am, where I'm from, and why I'm qualified to help them move forward. I explain that some consultants come right in with PowerPoints and answers, but I'm the other kind, the kind who wants to see how things operate now before I tell them how things should run in the new order.

I can tell that at least a few of them appreciate that. Clark gives a nod of approval when I say it, and Easton gives me a thumbs up.

Gabe's expression doesn't change at all.

I tell them some of the same things I told Gabe last night. That data shows us that woman make a disproportionate number of buying decisions, including booking trips. Trips taken by male-female couples are almost always booked by the female partner. Girls' weekends out and spa trips have become a hundred and seventy-five percent more popular in the last five years. And weddings have continued to become more elaborate and more destination-oriented, a trend that started in the nineties and hasn't stopped.

"You can have those customers," I say. "They will take your trips. If you make them trust you. If you cater to their preferences. If you make them feel safe—"

Six identical grimaces.

"Safe," Hanna says. She is the scorn master. People journey from far away to be trained by her in the fine art of cutting through bullshit with one icy word.

"—which doesn't necessarily always mean physically safe," I add hastily. "In this case, it means they know what to expect and what they're getting, and they believe in your ability to provide it."

I take a deep breath. Here's the tough part to sell to this crew. "And sometimes it means emphasizing a different aspect of adventure in your marketing. The human side. Finding yourself, finding a new friend, finding love—"

"Wilder, Sexier Adventures," Easton says, eyes on mine, a quirk at the corner of his mouth.

Gabe makes a sound that might or might not be a "stand down" growl. My body *definitely* hears it as that... and tightens. Oh, so he doesn't want Easton flirting with me. Isn't *that* interesting.

I sneak a peek at him. His jaw is rigid. If anything, anger makes him even more still. It freezes him.

He's disturbingly yummy, this marble statue version of him. It makes me want to poke him, just a little, to see if anything will splinter the veneer.

"That can be your specialty," I say to Easton, and am rewarded by the sound of Gabe's knuckles cracking as he grips the edge of the table.

I'm going to strangle Easton.

With my bare hands.

But I can't really blame him.

Lucy's hair is in curls today. Long, soft, buttery curls that I know take a lot of work. I know this because one time I touched my sister's hair when it was curled and she nearly hauled off and smacked me, then gave me a lecture on how many minutes it took to get it like that.

I want to wrap one of Lucy's long curls around a finger and tug. Or bring it to my lips and test its softness.

She's wearing a pair of black pants that hug her ass. And a long-sleeved blouse-thing in a color that only women know the name of. It isn't pink and it isn't brown. It probably has a name like taupe or mauve. It has slightly puffy sleeves that are buttoned at the wrists, and a high neck with a big button right where her pulse would beat hardest in her throat. Right where I'd dip my tongue and taste her.

It's ten times sexier than if she were wearing a low-cut blouse, because all I can think about is that big white button and how much I want to unbutton it. Or, better yet, rip it open.

There is no sign of the woman who let her makeup run down her face, who knelt in muddy water to save ducklings, or who accepted an invitation for drinks from a stranger. This woman is self-contained, professional, practiced. She uses her hands to gesture as she speaks, but the gestures are restrained. Deliberate. I get the feeling she doesn't do or say anything she hasn't planned ahead of time.

I want to undo her.

"...convince people that these trips are about something amazing that could happen to you. Something unexpected. Something new and delightful."

"So we're selling the trips differently, but we're not changing the trips themselves," Clark says, with a note of relief that I'm pretty sure we all feel.

Lucy bites her lip. "Well. That's part of what we're going to take a look at. Because branding, to be effective, has to pervade everything you do. It has to be part of the promise and part of what you deliver. Or it won't work."

Everyone slumps in their seats then, except my mother, who beams at Lucy like she painted the sky blue.

"What are we talking about here?" Brody demands. "Am I going to host bachelorette parties instead of fishing charters?"

"Brody," Barb says sharply.

"Because that's bullshit."

He's only saying what we're all thinking. And it needs to be said. I pick up the refrain. "For fifty years this business has been all about the real outdoors," I tell her. "The land. Caring for it, responsibly enjoying it, understanding how to work with it—what you can take from it without stripping it bare. How to leave no trace. How to find peace and quiet. How to test yourself against nature. I think what Brody's asking is, how much are we going to have to sell our souls, here?"

Lucy's eyes meet mine, soft and blue and curious. I feel like she might have actually heard me, which isn't at all what I expected from a city girl. Then she turns back toward the rest of the team, and I miss her attention. *Look at me that way again.*

"I like to tell clients that good branding is about figuring out where the market meets your strengths."

And my heart sinks because, after all, it's just a line. She doesn't really get it. Of course she doesn't. How could someone like her understand what Rush Creek and the land around us mean to people like me and my brothers? How could someone who likes to be anonymous, to go for days without running into anyone she knows, understand how much this business and this family matter to me?

"You haven't answered the question," Brody says. "How much compromise does that mean?"

He's angry, and I don't blame him.

Kane puts a hand on Brody's arm. "Let's hear her out, Bro, huh?" he asks.

That's Kane for you. He's the peacemaker.

Lucy says, "Let me ask you something. If you knew you would lose the business, but you could keep it exactly as it was, would you do that?"

Brody slowly shakes his head.

"If you know you could shutter the business and open a wedding venue, would you do that?"

"Hell no."

"Well. We're trying to split that difference. We're trying to figure out how you get to keep the business and not have to change everything about how you run it. What I'm hoping," she says, "is that as much as the season will permit, I can get a chance to experience all of your trips so we can talk about how to rebrand in a way that works for you *and* the market."

"Absolutely," Easton says easily, the duke of charm. "I can get you on a raft as soon as the weather warms up a few degrees. Which it's supposed to do next week. Is that soon enough?"

That bastard. He's like a shark with chum. Fresh blood in the water and he can't help himself.

"You can't wear those shoes on one of my trips," Clark says. He's staring at her spike heels and slim, pale ankles, visible below the high hem of her pants.

"I'll wear whatever I need to wear to be safe," Lucy reassures him.

I don't let myself stare at the way her silky top clings to her just-right curves. But that leaves me staring at her wide, soft, glossy mouth. Nothing Lucy wears would be safe.

Clark gives a tight, hard, nod. "There's a survival trip coming up that's not fully booked."

I don't want Lucy alone with Clark in the woods any more than I want her alone on a raft with Easton. Clark's not a manwhore like Easton. In fact, I'm not sure what he's been doing for female companionship since his wife died a year ago, but it definitely isn't anything like Easton's sex-o-rama. But Clark is—

Let's just say I saw how Lucy's eyes flared when I told her when and where to meet me. I heard and felt her response when I went in for the kiss.

I think Lucy might appreciate Clark's strong, silent forest warrior routine a little too much, and Clark needs action even worse than I do.

I don't trust either Easton or Clark not to sell out for the sake of a pretty girl.

This is rapidly starting to feel like it's getting away from me. All of it.

And then Brody says, "I can get you on my boat ASAP. It's good timing. The summer bookings are starting to come in, but I don't have anything this weekend."

Damn it. Not him, too. Given how much Brody hates being told what to do, I was sure he'd be the last holdout. But maybe doing what Lucy asks doesn't chap his ass like following my instructions.

"Perfect!" Lucy says, like they're volunteering their services purely out of the goodness of their hearts and not because she's smoking hot and a breath of fresh air in a stale meat market.

"I'm going."

They all turn to look at me. Lots of raised eyebrows.

"If there's a consultant going on our trips, gathering information, making decisions about the future of the business, I'm going to be there."

My brothers grumble. I'm pretty sure I hear Easton mutter, "Control freak." But I'm not going to defend this decision. I promised my father I would take care of this family and this company.

And they don't fight me on it. They know me well enough to know I won't back down.

When the meeting's over, I approach Barb and ask if I can speak to her. She leads me to a small office area at the back of the barn. I suspect it was built out of what used to be stables, because instead of cube walls, the area has horse head-high wooden dividers, now painted a clean, bright white. I follow her into her office.

"You didn't mention that Gabe is the primary decision maker."

"*A* primary decision maker." Barb emphasizes the A.

"Is that how he would describe himself?"

Barb's gaze dances away from mine.

"I can't do my job if I don't have all the information," I tell her quietly.

"I'm sorry. I just—I knew that you'd want to talk to him, and I knew if you talked to him..." She trails off.

"You knew he wouldn't be on board. He wouldn't have even agreed to talk to me."

She closes her eyes.

"Why *did* he agree to talk to me?"

For a moment I think she's going to lie to me—her eyes once again flick to the corner of the room. "Because I told him I'd give him my share of the business if he heard you out."

I nod. I'm not surprised. I knew something big had to be on the line to get him to be as cooperative as he'd been today.

Not that he'd looked happy about it. His face had kept its grim lines through the whole meeting, getting even grimmer when his brothers started inviting me on their trips.

I'm going.

I couldn't decide how I felt about the fact that he was going to trail me everywhere I went. On one hand, I wasn't looking forward to being watched like a hawk.

On the other hand, I had to admit that I liked the feel of his eyes on me. Way too much.

"This won't work if he hates the idea."

"He hates it now," Barb says. "But I think he'll come around. No. I know he'll come around."

"I don't know. That speech he gave about the land and their souls didn't sound like a man on the brink of being convinced."

Barb looks away, then back. Her eyes glisten. "You have to understand about Gabe. His father died when he was fifteen. And then as if that wasn't enough, I was diagnosed with breast cancer less than a year after that." She winces, just a hint of the grief and fear I know she must be remembering. "Gabe stepped up like you wouldn't believe. He held down the fort while I was going back and forth, getting chemo. Never flinched. Since then, he's been running the business and taking care of his brothers. He was a serious kid even before that, but since then... he never really got to be a teenager, never let himself be anything but head of this family. He doesn't make a move unless it's the right one for all of us. But if he sees that it is—he'll be the first to jump in with both feet."

Something in my heart cracks for a fifteen-year-old boy transformed overnight into the serious man that Gabe is now. I know a thing or two about growing up too fast. But I'm also a businesswoman. I know better than to pour weeks of work into a lost cause.

She must see it on my face because she says, "I'll double your fee."

My eyebrows shoot up to my hairline. "You'll—what?"

"If you go on those trips with the boys—with my sons— no matter what the outcome turns out to be, I'll give you a bonus equal to the amount we're already contracted for."

Now we're talking about enough money for me to launch my own agency, nearly debt free. I wouldn't have to go back to work at Grand Plan. I wouldn't have to face the looks and the whispers.

"I thought the business was hurting."

"Don't worry about where the money is coming from. I have personal savings."

"You'd—"

"You have no idea how important this is to me," Barb says.

I don't really understand, but I tell myself it doesn't matter. I tell myself that it's none of my business what motivates Barb, not unless it directly affects the job I'm doing for her.

"Draw up a contract," I say. "Make sure it specifies that the money isn't contingent on outcome, only on going on the three trips that were mentioned."

"Four," she says.

"I don't ski."

She waves that off. "It's not ski season, anyway. But you have to go hunting with Gabe."

"I—what?"

"Four trips. Charter fishing with Brody, survival camping with Clark, rafting with Easton, hunting with Gabe."

I open my mouth to say I'm not a fan of hunting, then close it again. She's offering me enough money not to have to walk the halls of Grand Plan with a scarlet A on my chest. Enough money to have a real fresh start.

My heart lifts at the thought. I can manage four outdoor adventures. I'm a big girl. "You've got yourself a deal."

"You'll have to get new shoes," she says, giving my black-and-silver pumps the side-eye.

"What is it with you guys and my shoes?"

"I don't really think I need to answer that," Barb says, with a small snort. "Also. Your mother texted to say you need a place to stay."

I wince. "Yes. Between us, we botched the hotel situation pretty badly. And I've called every hotel within reasonable driving distance of Rush Creek. All booked starting this weekend for at least a week."

"The loft upstairs is set up as a guest room," Barb says. "You can stay there as long as you need to. It'll save you a bunch of money, too. No hotel costs."

"Wait. Upstairs here? In the barn?"

She nods. "Can't get more convenient than that, can you?"

I blink. "No. Er—is there a bathroom up there?"

"Not up there, but there's a bathroom down here. No shower, but you can use the shower at the house."

I'd forgotten this part of small-town life. People's willingness to welcome you into their homes. "That's—that's very kind of you," I tell Barb. "That will be a huge help. It's not the ideal time to crash with Mom and Gregg right now."

"Oh, it's not even a matter of kindness," Barb says. "It makes absolute sense." She puts a hand behind my back and leads me out of her office, back into the big central area. "I'll give you Gabe's cell number so you can text him when you're heading over."

"When I'm heading over—?" I'm super confused now.

"To shower. Just so you don't catch him at a bad moment."

"Wait. Why would I catch him—?"

"He lives in the house."

Oh. No. No, that is a bad idea. A very bad idea. "He lives with you? I thought you lived there."

"I used to, but it didn't make sense anymore. I moved to an apartment in town and now I can walk everywhere, and Gabe is right here since he's in the barn all the time anyway."

"I don't think Gabe would appreciate—"

"Oh, don't worry about Gabe."

"Don't worry about Gabe what?" a deep, rumbly voice asks.

The man himself. Looking as pissed as you'd expect. Glowering at both me and his mother like we're in cahoots—which I guess we are, even though I never intended that.

I hold his stare, not willing to yield ground to Mr. Glower. Except, whoops, I'd forgotten about Gabe's eyes. Dark and intense and locked on mine. A wave of warmth sweeps through me, and I'm overwhelmingly relieved when he looks away first, turning his ire on his mother.

"I told Lucy she could stay in the loft while she's here, and shower at the house."

"You told her *what*?" Gabe roars.

"I'm going to run to the restroom," I squeak.

I think Gabe and his mother have a few things to talk about.

"No."

"Gabe, be reasonable. She needs a place to stay. She called every hotel in the Five Rivers region, and there wasn't anything."

"Which is a sign from God that she needs to go back to New York."

My mother heaves a deep sigh. "Gabriel Wilder. I raised you to be better than this."

"What version of raised better involves having a defenseless woman shower in a home with a predatory single man?"

I know I'm being a toddler, but I have to nip this ridiculousness in the bud.

"Don't be absurd, Gabriel. I'm not even sure which of those stupid sexist stereotypes is less accurate."

"Seriously, Mom, it's _not_ a good idea."

Because I don't trust myself. Because the idea of Lucy standing under a stream of hot water in my house, totally naked, is already working its way into my spank bank. I don't need the next three weeks to be an epic battle for self control.

I picture myself standing outside the bathroom, hand on the door handle, then turning away. It's disturbingly believable.

"You're way too much of a hermit, Gabe. It'll force you to interact with another human occasionally. And it's only a couple of weeks. This'll be over before you know it. You'll save her a fortune in hotel bills."

I resort back to the simplest tactic. "No."

She raises her eyebrows. "Hmm. Okay, then. If it's a problem, she could probably stay with Easton. He has a lot of room."

"No fucking way."

The words are out of my mouth before I can stop or modulate them.

My mother presses her lips together. I can't tell if she's stopping herself from threatening to wash my mouth out with soap or trying not to laugh. Unfortunately, I'm pretty sure it's the second one.

She knew mentioning Easton in the same breath with Lucy would get to me.

She sees way too much.

"I'll figure something out," I growl.

"You do that," she says. "And we can have Easton as a fall-back plan."

I leave her side to begin a much-needed inventory of some of the camping equipment. I pull down a big bin from one of the shelves that lines the walls. Cooking gear. As I open the tote, I'm assailed with the smells—the lingering odor of iodine-treated water, clean forest dirt, the distinctive smell of sweaty nylon straps and slightly musty cloth. Every time, it's like getting hit in the face with memories of childhood.

With memories of my dad.

Even when I was little, he brought me here and we did inventory together. Checked equipment, like Easton and Lucy are doing now. He was so patient, so good at explaining things. And all the smells locked up this equipment are the smell of safety and childhood and him.

I'll find some way to save Wilder Adventures, Dad. I promise. Even if it means following Lucy's plan.

I look up and spot her across the room, making a beeline for where Easton is carefully inspecting life jackets for wear-and-tear. She asks him a question, and he leans close and shows her the places she has to look for damage: seams, straps, hardware. They look cozy together, bent over the neon green-and-black vest.

It's taking him way too long to explain the basic concept of checking your gear before you go out on the water.

She peeks up at him with those big blue eyes through long lashes, and I know she's not doing it on purpose, but she's this perfect, disturbing combination of innocence and absolute, one-hundred-percent competence.

I close my eyes, which doesn't erase the image in the slightest. If anything, she shines brighter in my mind's eye.

In my imagination, it's me she's looking up at like that. And she's on her knees.

Gabriel Wilder, you are so, so screwed.

What I know is: She will not be showering, sleeping, or... anything... in Easton's house.

My mother is watching me from across the room. She knows what I'm going to say even before I stride to where she's standing and admit defeat.

"She can stay here," I say. "She can shower at the house."

I'll find some way not to pounce on Lucy if she showers in my house. I'll remind myself that she wants to transform my adventuring business into a book club, and that'll kill my sex drive.

My mother is a smart woman. She doesn't say anything except, "Sounds like a plan."

11

LUCY

I can't hear the conversation between Gabe and his mother because it's conducted in whispers (his mother), growls (Gabe), and hisses (Gabe). But I get the gist. He is not keen on having me around.

I get it. I really do. I'm a nuisance to him. And now I'm a threat to his business *and* infringing on his personal space.

He heads my way, and I brace myself for his anger and frustration. But if he's feeling either of those things, it's not evident as he approaches. His face is doing that Roman statue imitation, where whatever he's feeling is buried under marble.

Easton's still talking to me, but his voice has receded—like the sound's been turned down. Even blank-faced and silent, Gabe fills up more space in my head than Easton in motion and at full volume.

Gabe stops in front of me and opens his mouth to speak, but I jump in. "Look. It's probably not a good idea, for a number of reasons, for me to stay here—"

He cuts me off. "It's fine."

Easton is suddenly alert. "You need a place to stay?"

"She's staying in the loft here," Gabe says. Not quite a growl this time, but still, a thrill rolls through me.

"Keep your friends close and your consultants closer?" Easton jokes, but Gabe doesn't laugh. He gives Easton a warning look that perversely makes me want to bare my throat to him.

That said, I so don't love being talked about in the third person. "I'm perfectly capable of finding somewhere else to stay if it's not convenient for me to stay here," I tell him.

"It's convenient." Gabe's tone is final.

I'd push it further, but I sense there are many battles ahead of me, and this one is going to be the least of my worries.

I vow that I'll try to time my showers for when he's not home, which, if his mother's characterization of him as always in the barn is true, shouldn't be too tricky. We'll be two ships passing in the night.

And I won't have to listen to my mother having super quiet sex in the Airstream behind the thin veneer door.

"Let me give you a tour," Gabe says.

"Sure."

He shows me how the main room breaks down by type of expedition—water, land, snow, and so on—and where all the equipment is stored. There are two types of gear for trips, he explains—group and personal. Sometimes people provide their own personal gear, but Wilder rents it for people who can't or don't want to.

He shows me the small kitchen, with its microwave and coffee maker, and the office supply closet. Then he points me toward the back office area. We're headed that way, when he calls out, "Where's the fire?"

I turn to realize I'm four or five paces ahead of him, moving at my usual city clip. I stop and he catches up with me at a slow lope, unhurried.

"It's not going anywhere," he says.

"This is how fast I move."

"Try slowing down."

I try, but it feels weird and unnatural, like talking quietly in a library. A strain. He laughs at me, a chuckle that's rough from lack of use. It scrapes over my nerve endings like a calloused palm, and I shiver, hoping he doesn't notice.

I've seen Barb's office, but he shows me his, and I could have guessed what it would look like. A desk, a chair, a computer, everything else hidden neatly away in drawers or cabinets, except for a few family photos. All five brothers at the top of a snowy mountain, surrounded by even taller mountains. All five in a raft together. And one from when they were small, ranging from Easton at seven-ish to Gabe as a gawky teenager. He's smiling, more tentatively than his brothers. This must have been not too long before his father died.

He sees me looking and picks up that photo. "Camping at Loon Lake," he says. "One of our favorite spots. Easton was a pain in the ass on that trip. Moaning and complaining about how much weight he was carrying. I think he had about ten pounds. I had forty."

But he's smiling tolerantly, even a little nostalgically, and I decide that Gabe smiling is even more troubling than the marble statue version.

"You don't really want to go on those trips, do you?" he asks.

I wrinkle my nose at him. "What do you mean?"

"Charter fishing: Fish guts stink. Rafting: Ass stuck to wet vinyl all day. Survival camping: You and ten pounds of gear against all of mother nature. And you—all put together the way you are. Pretty clothes, hair, makeup."

The word *pretty* strikes a sweet chord in my belly, but I know he doesn't mean what he just said—*all put together*—as a compliment. Not the way he says it. He means it the way Darren, my ex, meant it when he broke off our three-year relationship. Closed. Cut off.

I force myself past it, though. I'm not here to impress Gabe Wilder with my mountaineering skills. I cross my arms and frown at him. "This is why you aren't making any money."

He draws back, startled. "What?"

"Talking about your trips that way to me. You're anti-marketing the trips. You're dismissing me as a possible customer. Pretend I'm a paying customer. What would you say to get me to go on the trips?"

"I'm trying to convince you not to go on them," he says. "I'm trying to convince you you're barking up the wrong tree. I'm trying to convince you to go back to New York, where your shoes make sense and you can walk as fast as you want."

Another small pang of hurt vibrates through me. After we rescued the ducklings together, I felt like we were, if not friends, then *something*. People who saw the good side of each other. But to him, I'm just an overdressed city girl rushing through life.

At the same time, I appreciate his bluntness. With Gabe

Wilder, what you see is what you get. There will never be any bullshit.

I give him the same. "I'm not going back to New York. I'm not going anywhere until I finish this job. But that's not the point. The point is that the New Rush Creek isn't going anywhere, and long after I'm gone, whether you've chased me away or I've finished my work, Rush Creek will be what it is. You're going to have to learn to live with it."

Nothing in Gabe Wilder's whole marble self changes, except his eyes. They darken, the way they did last night in the bar, right before he kissed me.

"Lunchtime!" a voice calls, and I look up to see a woman who can only be the last member of the Wilder clan.

THE LAST WILDER comes toward us, her arms full of a big tray of what looks and smells like lasagna. She thrusts it toward Gabe, and he takes it without question.

"Who's this?" she demands.

She has the Wilder eyebrows, dark slashes, which in her case have been carefully plucked into almost-arches. She has the Wilder eyes, intent, long-lashed, and deep set. She has the soft mobile Wilder mouth, and the bone structure that makes her strikingly beautiful and her brothers ridiculously hot.

But she's not dressed like a Wilder.

She's wearing skinny jeans, a Christina Economou slip top I recognize from Stashd, and a pair of low-heeled boots.

"I love your outfit," I tell her.

"I love yours," she tells me.

"If the love fest is over," Gabe says darkly, "I was going to introduce you two. Lucy, this is my sister, Amanda. Amanda, this is Lucy Spiro. She's a consultant mom hired."

"Mom did?" Amanda repeats.

"Mom wants Wilder Adventures to get with the New Rush Creek program and become more—" He hesitates.

"We're trying to reach a broader market of adventure-minded vacationers," I supply.

Amanda purses her lips. "You mean women," she says. "I told Gabe he needed to join the twenty-first century."

"I do market to women," Gabe says. "It doesn't work."

I give him a look. That's the first time he's owned up to that. It would have been a handy thing for him to have said sooner, if only so I could address the big, pink, lavender-scented, be-ribboned elephant in the room. "Marketing your existing trips to them doesn't work," I remind him. "Not the way you're positioning them."

A knot of muscle forms in his jaw, which is weirdly hot.

"I'm glad you're here," Amanda tells me. "I've been trying to talk some sense into these guys for years. Not that it's my business. I'm just the lunch lady."

"She's not *just* anything," Gabe says. "Hardest working woman I know. She's got two boys at home, and her own business."

I raise my eyebrows at her, encouraging her to tell me about it.

"I'd been slowly trying to figure out what I wanted to do with myself now that they're in school some of the time. Lasagna wasn't my plan, but I started cooking for these assholes, and somehow word got out, and now I have a lunch delivery business."

"That's fantastic!" I say.

"It's working well for me," she says. "I'm trying to figure out if I can expand into dinners, too, without cutting into my time with the kids after school."

Amanda gestures to Gabe to set her lasagna down on the center table and starts unloading a bag with all sorts of side dishes and drinks. Immediately, we're flocked with Wilders reaching for sodas and filling their plates. The Wilder brothers load up like eating is going out of style. Huge portions of lasagna, big scoops of salad, and garlic bread, whose scent fills the whole room and makes my stomach growl.

"They started eating like that when they were teenagers and never slowed down," Amanda said. "Mom said they'd outgrow it, but they're mountain men."

They wear it well. Not an ounce of fat on five brothers. Not that I'm looking.

Gabe and Amanda and I wait for our turns, behind Hanna.

"So, Lucy," Amanda says brightly. "Where are you from?" She looks me up and down. "Let me guess. New York? D.C.?"

"That obvious, huh?"

She shrugs. "You're not from Portland or Seattle, that's for sure. Way too fashion-forward."

Hanna snorts, turning around to give me a once-over filled with signature scorn. She's pretty, too, dark eyes, long lashes, pixie hair. I wonder if I could pull off that haircut.

"New York."

"I've always wanted to visit," Amanda says. "Someday. When the kids are older. I want to see the new World Trade

Center and go up in the Statue of Liberty. And see *Hamilton* on Broadway."

"Those are good ones," I tell her. "I always tell people to get pastries in Little Italy, eat dim sum in Chinatown, go walking on the High Line, and shop in SoHo."

"Shopping," Hanna editorializes glumly, like we've brought up cannibalism. She loads up a plate with a Wilder-brother-sized portion of food.

It's Amanda's turn at the table. She takes smaller servings of everything; I actually feel relieved that I won't be the only one who's not eating like a bear.

Gabe and I reach the table. "After you," he says.

Amanda nudges me. "He's saying that so he can stand behind you and check out your ass."

"You don't need to say everything that comes into your head," Gabe tells his sister.

"I'm saying everything that comes into your head," Amanda says.

He gives her a playful shove, and she shoves back.

There's the Gabe from last night. I knew he was in there somewhere. I just get the feeling he doesn't come out very often.

It shouldn't matter to me whether Gabe is playful or serious, as long as he lets me do my job. And it definitely shouldn't matter what he thinks of me.

"Hey, Lucy," Amanda says. "Anyone show you around town yet?"

I shake my head.

"Hey, Han," Amanda says. "Let's introduce her around."

Hanna frowns.

"Come on, Han."

The dark-haired woman hesitates.

"I promise, no shopping," Amanda says.

"I've heard that before," Hanna grumbles. "You say no shopping, but then you see something in the window and you have to try it on. Or we're 'just looking so it doesn't count' and before I know it we've been in Silver Rings or wherever for an hour and a half."

"You know you love it," Amanda says. "Hanna is one of the guys," she explains to me.

Hanna nods. "When I was in college at Portland State, I spent a semester at Mount Holyoke, and everyone joked that I was spending a semester 'as a broad.' It was only a little bit of a joke."

I laugh, and she does too. "Four brothers," she explains.

"So basically, you fit in perfectly here?" I ask.

Hanna nods. "As long as Amanda follows the rules."

"What are the rules?"

Amanda rattles them off. "No talking about clothes, makeup—what were the other things?"

Promptly, Hanna recites, "Netflix series based off romance novels, *The Bachelor*, jewelry, or nylon stockings."

I'm ninety-five percent sure she's not joking. I'm also relieved because it seems Amanda got distracted by the rules and forgot about her invitation to town. Simpler that way. I mean, what's the point? I'm only here three weeks. I can walk into town by myself and get a feel for what I need to know— what's making money in Rush Creek, who the tourists are.

I load up my plate and Amanda leads us to the table. Hanna hesitates, looking from us to the cluster of laughing Wilder brothers.

"Come on, Han, be a broad," Amanda says.

They grin at each other fondly, and Hanna plops down next to her.

Hanna and Amanda are both watching me, and it takes me a second to realize they're watching me chew, waiting for my verdict on the lasagna.

"Oh, my God," I say, finishing my first bite. It's quite possibly the best lasagna I've ever had. Tender noodles, rich, hearty meat sauce, tomato-y flavor, and soft, creamy cheese. "That's amazing. No wonder you're in demand."

"Right?" Hanna cries.

"Aw, thanks," Amanda says, blushing. She waves a hand. "Anyway, Luce, we'll show you around today. We'll meet you outside Oscar's at four."

My old instincts kick in, a horde of butterflies in my stomach—wondering if Amanda and Hanna are women I can trust.

Some women get nervous around guys.

I get nervous around prospective friends.

When all the stuff went down with my dad, and we found out who he really was, I found out who a lot of other people really were, too.

That's why it took me almost the whole four years of college to settle into best-friendship with my freshman roommate Annie—who's still my BFF even though she lives in San Francisco and we're both so busy that we barely ever have time to chat. It's also why I never went to any of those Friday night happy hours at work. I kept telling myself I would, once I had the lay of the land, once I knew who was easygoing and who was cutthroat, who had an agenda and who genuinely wanted to be friends. Who could keep a secret, and who couldn't. And maybe I would've.

I didn't get a chance to find out.

I open my mouth to say four won't work for me. That I need to unpack my stuff and settle in. Make some phone calls, nail down some work stuff.

Wash my hair.

"Oh, and you forgot one rule, Amanda," Hanna suddenly interjects. "No one is allowed to start a sentence with, 'My therapist says.'"

"Which is basically like a gag rule for me," Amanda says, tilting her head my way in a plea for sympathy.

Except, I realize, I *like* Amanda and Hanna. A ton. For once, I don't want to be my usual cautious self, the one people mistake for an ice queen.

I think of Gennie. Not angry, but hurt.

I mean, I'm only here three weeks. I can afford to take a chance, right?

I push aside the nervous flutters and say, "Sure!" like I'm the kind of person who says "Sure!" a lot.

12

LUCY

I head into town late in the afternoon to meet Hanna and Amanda.

It's earlier than when I got here yesterday, and everything's in full swing. Pairs and groups of tourists—lots of women—stroll up and down the street, stopping to look in windows. They dart in and out of shops, many carrying paper shopping bags with store names in fancy script and pretty tissue paper peeking out of the tops. Pink. Lavender.

I think of Gabe's tirade and laugh to myself. Then I slam on my brakes because a gaggle of tourists has wandered into the crosswalk without looking. They seem totally unconcerned when they spot me, too, and I have to suppress my NYC-bred desire to glare and honk.

I guess the spas and hot springs are working their relaxation magic on people.

I park in the Depot Hotel lot and stroll down to Oscar's Saloon & Grill, soaking up tourist laughter and chatter. Here and there, I spot people who are unmistakably locals—a pair of cowboy boots here; a cowboy hat there. Lots of hiking boots, too, and running shoes.

I'm starting to grasp how out of place my footwear really is.

I reach the salon before Hanna and Amanda. The smell of onion rings and char-broiled burgers makes my mouth water. I peek in the window. Buffalo, moose, and elk heads adorn the walls, along with a few saddles here and there. There are swinging saloon doors. A Western-style font proclaims, "Please Wait to Be Seated" on the hostess stand. A mural on the back wall, painted in earth tones, depicts a much older Rush Creek—dry goods store, post office, blacksmith, and cowboys on horseback. It's gorgeous.

"Lucy!" The voice comes with an arm slung around my shoulder. Amanda. "We'll grab a drink there when we're done. And then we'll drop you at your hotel. Are you at the Depot?"

I explain the hotel room situation—that I'll stay there tonight and tomorrow night, then move into the Wilder barn loft.

"Why aren't you staying with my mom?"

"She—this was what she suggested."

"Does that mean you're showering at Gabe's? The shower at his place is epic," Hanna says.

Amanda and I both turn to stare at her. Amanda's eyes are huge.

"What!" Hanna says. "No, God, no! I can't even remember anymore why I showered there. I think I had to meet my dad for birthday dinner and I had, like, three minutes to turn it around after a day of skiing, and Gabe wasn't home, so Kane let me in."

"So you and Kane showered at Gabe's house." Amanda manages to make *showered* sound like wild monkey sex.

Hanna rolls her eyes at Amanda. "You are not making a good case for marriage, girl," she says. "If you're so hard up you have to imagine sexytimes where none could ever or will ever exist."

Amanda sighs. "I just want my brothers to end up married with kids, so I have sisters and my kids have a whole passel of cousins."

"Don't look at me," Hanna says.

They both turn to look at me.

"Seriously?" I demand. "I just got here. And I'm not a long-term prospect. I'm here three weeks and then going back to New York."

I don't add that I have tried the long-term thing a couple of times, but I'm not cut out for it. I don't know how to do the give-and-take and opening-up that all nice guys who are serious about relationships seem to want. Learning that all of life was basically a long-con for my dad killed my ability to trust that way.

You're totally self-contained. You don't need me. You don't need anyone, Darren said. *I keep telling myself you'll let me in, but it hasn't happened, and I can't keep doing this to myself.*

I touch my bare left finger. There's still a slight groove from the six months when that engagement ring carved into my flesh.

"Don't hold your breath on the passel of cousins thing," Hanna tells Amanda. "Your brothers are not on that track."

Amanda heaves a sigh. "I know."

"None of them?" I ask.

Hanna and Amanda exchange glances. "I mean, Clark

was," Hanna says. She casts another look at Amanda, asking her something with her eyes.

"Clark was married," Amanda tells me. "His wife died."

I wince. "I'm so sorry."

"Yeah. It sucked. Sucks."

Her expression tells me it wasn't only Clark's loss. That she loved Clark's wife, too. I surprise myself by reaching out and squeezing her hand, and she gives me a sad smile.

"And Brody has a kid," Hanna says.

This shocks the hell out of me. Bad Boy Brody has a *kid*?

"It was a Rush Creek scandal," Amanda says. "They were engaged and then Brody called it off because he wasn't ready for the commitment. See above: Wilder brothers are not long-term prospects."

I want to ask if this goes for Gabe, too, but I keep my mouth shut. Because it doesn't matter, does it? I'm here for three weeks, and then gone.

What's true of Gabriel Wilder's love life is none of my business.

"By the way, when you see the inside of Gabe's house, don't judge," Amanda says.

"Oh, yeah," Hanna agrees.

I tilt my head inquiringly.

"It looks like he decided to move to Australia, held a yard sale to get rid of his earthly possessions, and then changed his mind."

I'm about to ask why that would be when Hanna says impatiently, "Are we going to stand here all day shooting the shit?"

Amanda rolls her eyes at me. Then she loops an arm

through mine and one through Hanna's. "C'mon," she says. "Come meet my people."

WE START Amanda's official tour at Rush Creek Bakery, a cozy glass-front store nestled between Gregg's bike shop and a smokehouse. The front windows are partially steamed up, and as soon as we step inside, I'm floored in the best possible way by the smell of fresh baked bread and cookies, tinged with a woodsmoke scent from next door.

"Hey, hon!" a voice calls out from behind the counter. It comes from a tall, slim, fair-skinned grandmotherly woman whose silvery cotton-candy hair is pulled back in an approximation of a bun. She's wearing a white apron; flour coats it, her hair, and her clothes.

"Hey, Nan!" Amanda tosses back.

By the time we reach the counter, Nan has produced three small plates, and the first question she asks me is, "Gluten free?"

I shake my head.

"Dairy free?"

I shake again.

"Thank God," she says, and sets a thick slice of buttered French bread on my plate. The butter is melting, the bread still steaming. My mouth waters. I don't hesitate. I bite into it. It's warm and tender and so, so delicious.

"God, that's amazing," I say, when I can.

She beams at me as if I was the one who made the unbelievably tasty bread and sets out two more for Amanda and Hanna, no questions asked. She puts three cookies in a bag and rings them up for Amanda, who won't let me pay for myself.

"Where you from, dressed so fancy?" Nan asks, eyeing my blouse.

"This is Lucy," Amanda says. "She's visiting from New York."

Nan looks me up and down. "Oh, right! I've heard about you."

My stomach tightens at the reminder of how fast news travels in small towns.

Nan narrows her gaze. "You want the boys to shut down their business and make pillows instead."

"Er," I say. "No. I—"

"You can't believe everything you hear, Nan," Amanda says. "She's trying to help the boys get with the New Rush Creek program."

Nan makes a face. "'New Rush Creek,'" she intones darkly. "Gluten-free. Dairy-free. No white carbs. Ironic beards and man purses. I wish they would all go to Carol's Cake Shop."

"You do *not*," Amanda says.

"Carol has vegan brownies," Nan says.

"You could have vegan brownies too," Amanda says. "I bet you'd make kickass vegan brownies."

Nan begins rearranging the front glass case, moving the remaining delectable cookies and cupcakes forward so they're more visible.

"So you're from New York? The city or the state?"

"City."

"Flew there once. Saw *A Chorus Line*. And went to the top of the Empire State Building." She gets a faraway look in her eyes. "It was 98 degrees and I hated the shit out of it." Her eyes refocus sharply on me. "But it had the best cannoli I ever tasted."

I grin. "Yes."

"I've tried cannoli," she says sadly. "Can't make 'em like they make 'em in Little Italy, no matter how hard I try. Bread is my thing. Did you hear the news about Mack downsizing?"

"The tack shop," Amanda explains to me. "No," she says to Nan. "But I'm not surprised."

Nan leans over the counter. "And he's seeing someone. Someone he met on one of those *dating sites*."

Amanda raises her eyebrows. "Is that so?"

"She's twenty years younger than he is."

"Yeah?"

"And she's *not from around here*. She lives in *Seattle*. How're your brothers?" she demands of Amanda and Hanna, with no segue.

"Mine are good," Hanna says.

"The Wilders are good, too," Amanda says.

Nan frowns. "Not Brody."

Amanda and Hanna exchange a glance.

Nan's blue gaze is piercing. "I was supposed to make the cake. And even if I wasn't, everyone's talking about the wedding getting called off. And I hear what they're saying."

The whole time she's been talking, a feeling has been building inside me: I want to get away. It's the small town gossip, the sense that there's nowhere to hide. Sure, this isn't me in the spotlight, but I remember too well what it felt like.

"Brody's okay," Amanda says. "Not everything happens the way you hear it."

"I don't believe the gossip." Nan plants her hands on the counter. "Brody's a good boy."

"You don't hear *that* sentence too often," Hanna mutters. "I wouldn't bet my sister's virginity on it."

"You don't have a sister," Nan says.

Hanna shrugs. "Just sayin'."

"If it didn't happen the way people are saying, how *did* it happen?" Nan demands.

Amanda opens her mouth to speak, but just then the door's electronic chime sounds and customers step in behind us. We turn to look. Two couples, the men in flannel shirts, slim-fit pants, and expensive shoes, sporting neatly trimmed, definitely ironic, beards. We step aside and let them order.

"Do you have any gluten-free cupcakes?" one of the women asks.

Nan raises her eyebrows at us. I feel an unstoppable laugh bubbling up in me, and apparently Amanda is similarly afflicted, because she grabs Hanna's and my arms and yanks us towards the door.

Which has just closed behind us when we burst out laughing.

"That's Nan," Amanda says, as we catch our breath on the sidewalk outside the bakery. "She's a national treasure."

"How long you think you can get away with not telling her the story?" Hanna asks.

Amanda shakes her head. "Forever, possibly," she says, "because even I don't know what happened between Brody and Zoë."

I'm... twitchy.

Lucy left with Amanda and Hanna a couple of hours ago. Everyone else has gone home.

I'm looking at upcoming registrations for the umpteenth time, hoping the numbers will look different this go-round.

They don't.

I jump on some of the outdoor discussion boards where people post asking for recommendations for fishing, hunting, and hiking trips. I answer a bunch of questions. I never try to sell my business on those sites, but my signature does make it clear that I run trips, and sometimes that fact comes up in conversation. We get quite a few bookings that way.

Not enough to move the needle though.

I reply to all the comments on Wilder's Facebook page, and update my own Facebook profile with some photos from Easton's and my last hunting trip.

Then I go on Instagram.

The business has an Instagram account, but I basically never look at it. All of us are supposed to post photos there, but none of us ever does. Amanda and my mom yell at us about it, but it doesn't change our behavior.

Truth, though: I am not looking at the business's Instagram or trying to figure out how to be more strategic.

I am looking to see if Lucy has an account.

I discover that she does.

I'm not at all surprised to discover that it's curated and flawless.

She sets up her Instagram in those nine-square puzzle patterns. There are two whole nine-squares that look like a trip to San Francisco, including several pictures of her beaming beside a curvy redhead, who she identifies as her bestie, Annie. There are all kinds of artsy pictures of New York, including a few selfies of Lucy. Made up. Dressed up. Every hair in place.

Those kinds of selfies take a lot of work—I know because every once in a while, Amanda or my mom makes me take one for some reason. Then they make me retake it until the lighting's right, I'm looking at the camera, I'm not squinting, and my arm isn't in the picture.

There are also pictures of her apartment. Her apartment is spare, and the decor is elegant and clean, like buttoned-up Lucy. Everything is mostly white, with splashes of color. Each photo looks staged—her desk, with an expensive looking pen and a leather-bound notebook; her kitchenette, with meals plated restaurant style.

I'm not going to learn anything about her this way.

I swallow disappointment that makes no sense.

I'm about to stash my phone when an impulse makes me look at Amanda's Instagram. Sure enough, there are two photos there from this afternoon. One is of her, Lucy, and

Hanna standing outside of Nan's bakery, big chocolate chip cookies in hand. Amanda's beaming. Hanna's scowling. Lucy's expression is unreadable.

The next photo is from a few minutes ago. I recognize the setting immediately, from the elk head visible on the wall behind. It was taken at Oscar's Saloon & Grille, in one of the booths. Hanna, Lucy, and—

Easton, turned toward Lucy and saying something, both of them smiling.

Something primal inside me howls.

I'm heading toward my car before I can reason with myself.

I SLIDE into the booth next to Amanda, who turns to look at me with undisguised shock.

"What the hell are you doing here?" she demands.

"Can't a man get a drink with family and friends?" I ask.

She raises both eyebrows. "Um, he *can*. He just never *does*. What, are you afraid Lucy is going to make plans to redecorate the office pink while you're not watching her?"

My eyes meet Lucy's. Hers flash amusement. She thinks Amanda's right, that I'm checking up on her.

I am, just... not in the way she thinks.

"It's not Lucy he doesn't trust," Hanna says, tipping her head toward Easton.

"Who, me?" Easton asks, all innocence.

Amanda rolls her eyes. "Yes, you, Easton, melter of panties."

"Easton the Panty-Melter," he muses. "It has a nice ring to it."

"The fact that you think so really says it all," Hanna says with disgust.

"Hey, hon," says our waitress, Jill Cooper, a petite brunette I went to high school with. Jill and I are friends with occasional benefits. Right now, she's seeing someone seriously. Last time I ran into her, she told me she and her boyfriend were waiting to hear on a promotion he was anticipating and that she thought a proposal was in the offing. I'm happy for her. She deserves good luck.

"Hey, Jill," I say. "How's Matt?"

She grins. "Really good. He got a promotion to manager."

I fist bump her. "He gonna put a ring on your finger?"

"Your mouth, God's ear," she says, grin getting bigger. "What can I getcha? And you guys, how about some appetizers?"

I order a pitcher of beer for the table and a few rounds of wings, potato skins, and cracklings, mostly because I bet you good money they don't have those in New York, and I want to see how Lucy will react. My goal is to figure out how to leave with Lucy and saddle Easton with the tab. Okay, not really, but it's satisfying to picture.

"How was your tour?" I ask Lucy.

"Really fun!" She's still wearing the blouse with the single button at the throat. She's drinking something from a martini glass that might be a lemon drop. She looks like someone photoshopped a slice of big city into our small-town bar. I wonder how she sees Oscar's. The swinging saloon doors, the mounted animal heads, the mural—does she think it's all camp? Or can she see what I see, which is that Rush Creek is where the West meets the Pacific Northwest, a place all its own?

"It was Amanda's tour of her favorite stores," Hanna grumps.

"My favorite shopkeepers," Amanda corrects.

"I liked everyone I met," Lucy says. "People were super welcoming."

Hanna frowns. "That's because we're a tourist town and newcomers are money."

"Nah," Easton tells Lucy. "It's because you're charming."

"Do you ever worry about becoming a cliché of yourself, Easton?" Amanda demands.

"Too late," Hanna says.

Lucy tries to hide a smile. She lifts her eyes to meet mine, the smile fading when she sees the expression I can't keep off my face, the murderous rage toward my younger brother. She looks away.

Fuck. She thinks my furious expression was aimed at her.

"Who was your favorite?" Amanda asks eagerly.

Lucy thinks for a sec, then says, "I think Kiona at Five Rivers Arts and Crafts."

"You know her story, right?" Easton asks her.

Lucy nods. "She told me her people are Wasco, and she bought the shop from the previous owners, who were basically selling anything vaguely-native-flavored and now all the artisans are actually Native American. So that's one good thing to come out of the New Rush Creek, right?"

I'm still not ready to concede anything good has come out of New Rush Creek. "She was turning that place around before the hot springs showed up."

"Right," Lucy says. "Gotcha."

Once again, I've knocked the smile off Lucy's face. I can't hold back my asshole tendencies tonight. I should've stayed home where at least I wouldn't have made things worse. At this rate, I'll have driven her into Easton's open arms before my drink comes. And the look Amanda gives me—*you idiot!*—says she knows it.

"Mack's Tack is downsizing from two storefronts to one," Amanda informs me.

"The feed store's hours are down to nine-to-five, Tuesday through Saturday," Hanna adds.

Amanda traces a finger around the rim of her wine glass. "Krandall's Outdoor Outfitters is now selling gifts, which mostly seem to be bachelorette party favors and girls' night games."

Hanna wrinkles her nose. "And Wagon Wheel Sandwiches changed its name to Spa Day Sandwiches. The wheel's still out front, though. Which is just dumb."

"Yeah, but what would you put there instead?" Easton asks. "A giant pump bottle of massage oil?"

"A huge bridal veil," Amanda suggests.

"A basketball-hoop-sized garter," Easton counters.

"A lavender eye pillow for an elephant," Lucy mouths to me.

I snicker, and she bites her lip, hiding a smile. She hasn't totally given up on me. My grinchy heart grows a half-size, because that's about what I can manage.

"Did any of you ride in the rodeo?" Lucy asks.

Easton shakes his head. "Nope. Too busy skiing, fishing, hunting, you name it. But we all miss going. There are rodeos all over Oregon, but Rush Creek's was part of our growing up."

"Could it come back?"

I shake my head. "No. It'd been hanging on by a thread. Losing money in the last couple years. When the hot springs surfaced, it was a miracle for the town. Just—"

"Hard for some of the businesses," she says. "Including yours." Her voice and expression are soft. Sympathetic.

"Yeah." My voice is hard, even though I want my better self to accept her kindness.

But she doesn't look away this time. The warmth in her eyes does something messy to my chest. And I think she might know it, because her eyes soften even more.

"Well. I know you guys are all broken up about the rodeo, but I'm excited for the spring festival," Amanda says. "I finished my dress." She gets a look on her face. I recognize it. It's the prequel to mischief. When we were kids, I used to love that look because it meant something fun was about to happen. Now it scares the shit out of me.

"Lucy!" Amanda says. "You can be my model for the trashion show!"

"Trashion show," Lucy says slowly. I'm torn between amusement at her confusion and irritation with Amanda for blindsiding her.

Hanna squints at both of them. "You didn't ask me. I'm hurt." She lays the sarcasm on "hurt" with a trowel.

I love Hanna.

"I mean, if Hanna wants to do it, she should definitely do it." Lucy clearly has no idea what a trashion show is but knows she's being roped into something she wants nothing to do with.

Amanda rolls her eyes. "Hanna's totally messing with you. You couldn't pay her enough."

"This is true," Hanna says.

"Besides, even if Hanna actually wanted to model the dress, she and I don't have the boobs for it," Amanda says, unfazed. "Lucy has way better boobs. And a waist. Lucy, you're like a perfect hourglass. You're like who I designed the dress *for*."

I try hard not to make a sweep of Lucy's body to confirm the boobs claim, but my eyes betray me. Amanda is absolutely right; Lucy is a natural for the job. On the upswing, of course, I catch Lucy's eye. Damn—busted. Lucy raises her eyebrows, and the corner of her mouth twitches with amusement. This sign of feistiness, along with the visual feast I just enjoyed, strikes enough sparks in me that I have to judiciously adjust my position.

"I have boobs," Hanna insists, scowling. "You just can't tell, because sports bras." She turns to Lucy. "But I get it. And, okay. Before you agree to anything, you should know the dress is made of Tillamook cheese bags."

"Tillamook cheese bags?"

Hanna nods. "The ones the shredded cheese comes in."

"That really doesn't clear things up," Lucy says, shaking her head, laughing.

I've had enough. "Are you seriously trying to talk a woman fresh from New York City and dressed to kill, into putting on a dress made out of cheese bags? Does she strike you as someone who would wear repurposed cheese plastic?"

"She has an excellent sense of fashion," Amanda says. "She would carry it off with panache."

"Um," Lucy says. "I still have no idea what you're talking about."

"Every year, as part of the spring festival, there's a fashion show of garments made exclusively from recycled materials," I explain.

"Is that, like, a New Rush Creek thing?"

I shake my head. "It's an Old Rush Creek thing. Oregon is the third-greenest state in the U.S."

"Well," Lucy says. "I appreciate the show of faith in both my... boobs and my fashion sense, but I'm probably not your girl."

"Is it the cheese bags?" I murmur and am rewarded with another trying-not-to Lucy smile.

"Bummer," Amanda says. "But I'll find someone."

Jill brings my beer and the appetizers. We dig in. The cracklings are fresh out of the fryer, crisp, hot, and flavorful.

"These look unhealthy," Lucy says, nibbling on one. "Oh. Yum. What are these?"

"Cracklings," Easton says.

"Pork rinds," Hanna bluntly adds. "Pig skin."

Lucy pauses midchew. She's tough, I'll give her that; her facial expression barely changes. But I notice she switches to potato skins after that.

She doesn't touch the wings.

Too messy, I'd bet. She doesn't strike me as the type to lick sauce off her fingers.

Great, now I'm picturing it. Those soft, plump lips tugging along the length of her finger, savoring.

I'm tempted to reach out and squeeze her hand. Instead, I move my foot to nudge hers. I'm trying to say, I see you.

Her gaze flicks to mine, and I feel a gentle pressure back against my foot.

The sensation buzzes up the whole length of my leg and

lodges itself in my groin. And we're talking two layers of shoe leather here.

It's not very well-lit in here, but I can see every last tiny freckle on the bridge of her nose. The pale parts of her eyelashes that mascara hasn't touched. The faint translucency of her eyelids. I want to run a thumb lightly over that eyelid. Across her cheekbone. Over her plump lower lip.

That lip.

I have to look away and get my thoughts under control.

"So Lucy," Easton says, "Tell us about New York. What do you do there?"

Lucy gets a deer-in-headlights look on her face. I know from our disastrous drinks date that she hates talking about herself, and I want to kick Easton under the table.

But she's a trouper. "I work for a marketing consultancy called Grand Plan. I work on a team that specializes in marketing to women."

"Do you live in the city?"

She nods. "A studio in Manhattan." Her voice flattens.

Easton doesn't notice. "Wow! In Manhattan! The marketing gig must pay well."

For a charmer, Easton can be dense as brick.

"It was my grandmother's. I inherited it when she died." She bites her lip, like even that information reveals too much.

"Is your life like *Sex and the City*?" Amanda asks. "Do you have glamorous friends and Tinder hookups—?"

Quit it! I try to will Amanda to leave Lucy alone.

"They didn't have Tinder back when *Sex and the City* was made," Easton says.

Amanda nods. "I wish they'd do a remake, because I feel like I need to know how they would have dealt with Tinder."

"You need a whole episode devoted to dick pics?"

"No one needs to devote any time to dick pics."Amanda scowls. "But seriously, Lucy, what's it like? Living in New York City?"

Why can't Amanda see that Lucy hates answering questions about herself? It's all over her face. She wraps her arms around herself, self-protective, and I suddenly want to yell at them all: *Leave her alone!*

She waves a hand. "Oh, you know. All the takeout you could ever want. Lots of nightlife. Nonstop fun."

Amanda opens her mouth, but I jump in. "Amanda. How are things going with the dinner option?"

Amanda is easily distracted, and starts telling us about the challenges of expanding a catering business from lunch to dinner, and the conversation moves on from there without circling back to Lucy and New York.

Jill checks in to see if we want dessert, and we all groan and say no. After she leaves, Lucy excuses herself, asking Easton to let her out of the booth. When she stands, she sways a little. "Oh," she says. "I think those drinks were stronger than I thought."

"Oscar's is notorious for that," I say. "No one warned you?"

She shakes her head, then sets out for the restroom, unsteady on those heels. Easton watches her go. When he turns back, I accuse him, "You let her order two and didn't say anything."

He shrugs. "So sue me."

"Asshole."

"She looked like she needed to relax."

"Not your way, she doesn't."

Amanda and Hanna are watching me curiously. "To be fair," Amanda says, "we didn't warn her either."

"Yeah, but you're not going to try to walk her back to her hotel afterwards and get in her pants," I say.

"Who says—?"

"Don't bother, Easton," Amanda says.

Easton sulks. "I'm so maligned."

"Sure you are."

When Lucy reappears, she says, "I should probably head back." She pulls out two twenties and drops them on the table. "Is that enough?"

"It's on me," Easton says, and hands her back her cash. "And let me walk you back to the hotel. I should have warned you Oscar's makes strong drinks. Plus we're at 3,000-plus feet here. Alcohol works faster."

"I'll walk Lucy."

They all turn to look me.

"She and I have business stuff to talk about."

I see the faint surprise bloom on Lucy's face. This is news to her. Her eyes meet mine, and I see a hint of the naughty shine that was there the other night in the Depot Hotel. My cock twitches in answer.

"Gabe's right," Lucy says. "He and I have things to talk about. Thanks for the offer, though, Easton. Some other time."

"Like in your dreams," Amanda murmurs.

I turn away before anyone can see my grin. No one likes a winner basking in his victory.

G od *damn* those drinks were strong.

Easton and Gabe were having some kind of penis-waving fight over walking me back to the hotel. And if any penis is going to be waved in my direction, I definitely want it to be Gabe's.

Let me clarify:

I would very much like Gabe's penis to get waved in my direction.

But I'm pretty sure that's the alcohol talking. It would be epically awkward to have to face him over that Wilder Adventures conference table knowing that we'd—to borrow Gennie's very apt phrase—seen each other's O faces.

Plus, I have no idea where Gabe's head is on this. He gives so little away. Only, sometimes, what's in his eyes. I thought I saw anger.

But then later, we had a funny moment over the giant lavender sachet joke, and I thought maybe there was still something between us. That ease, that charge that lit up both of us last night when we were saving the ducklings, and afterwards, when he kissed me.

That kiss. I can't stop thinking about it. Once you've had someone's mouth on yours, it's impossible to see their face the same way. Gabe's mouth just looks like something I want to kiss. I know that he's forceful and gentle at the same time. Just the way I like it.

Also, I *know* he changed the subject so I wouldn't have to talk about my life in New York. Is that because I told him something bad happened there?

He's a good guy. I'm not wrong about that.

I am swaying in his direction, I realize. Trying to feel the heat of his arm against mine. Catch his scent—woodsy and male.

Of course, that means I'm not paying attention to my feet. And my ankles tend to give out after a full day of wearing heels. So I'm not surprised when I stumble over a rough bit of sidewalk.

I pitch forward, bracing myself for a fall, but Gabe catches me and sets me upright again.

"You need real shoes," he says, his breath ghosting across my cheek.

He lingers, hands on my arms, giving me time to study how good-looking he is. Strong nose, slashed cheekbones. A day of scruff along an iron jaw. His lips full and well-defined. But his eyes are definitely the most striking part of him, dark and intense and fixed on mine.

His gaze drops to my mouth. My whole body goes hot. He's going to kiss me. He's going to—

He releases me and moves back to my side.

Disappointed, I walk in silence beside him. The caramel

scent of cooked sugar wafts in my direction from a candy shop, and my mouth waters. We pass the bookstore, a couple of women's clothing boutiques, the coffee shop, the bike shop, Nan's, the smokehouse, and an all-purpose gift shop.

The Depot comes into view, and we amble up the front walk, side by side.

Should I ask him in? Ask him up?

Common sense screams no. My body, warm and tingly with lemon-drop goodness, howls yes.

"I'll walk you in," Gabe says.

My breasts tighten with anticipation. My sex, primed with alcohol, softens, melts, and clenches around the empty space I want him to fill.

He walks me as far as the elevator, asks me for my floor, and pushes the button. We stand there, facing each other. He's studying me. In the dim elevator lobby, his eyes are so dark I can't make out the pupils. Just the heat in his gaze.

The elevator comes, slides open. He puts his hand on the door, holding it open.

"I want you—"

My imagination goes wild.

Naked on the bed, legs spread.

On your knees in front of me.

At least three times before the sun rises.

"—to sit down tomorrow with each of my brothers and let them tell you about how they run their trips. You'll get more out of that than out of me trying to mansplain all their individual models to you. Some stuff's centralized, like the booking system. But almost everything else is specific to the type of trip."

I'm nodding like I understand what he's saying, but my brain is still trying to come back from where it went.

"Brody's going to take us fishing Friday. We'll go out with Clark sometime next week, and then Easton after that. I have to see if I can get a tag or two so I can take you turkey hunting."

It's sinking in that my alcohol-pickled libido is not going to get what it wants.

I have to remind myself that I'm not in Rush Creek to get myself in more trouble because of sex. I'm in Rush Creek to do exactly what Gabe was talking about: go on outdoors trips so I can earn the ungodly amount of money that Barb promised me. So I can remake my New York City life as a solo operator.

Solo. Simplest, and safest.

"Sounds good," I say.

The elevator makes some kind of beeping noise, griping about the fact that Gabe is still holding it open. I step in. I brush by him to do it, and my body soaks up his heat. His forest-floor, bear musk, all-male scent.

He lets the door go.

It is almost closed when I see him drop his head into his hands.

He was feeling it, too. He might have been pretending to be all business, but he was torn. He wanted me as much as I wanted him.

I shouldn't be so glad, but my drunken tingly bits are ready to celebrate with confetti.

15

GABE

Wednesday afternoon, two days after Lucy's arrival, she's back in the office, interviewing my brothers. Right now, she's sitting with Kane and Hanna at the big table, and they're talking her through the backcountry ski trips.

Earlier, she sat down with me and I walked her through our whole marketing strategy. I sincerely hope I made sense, because I was having trouble concentrating with her that close to me. I could smell her shampoo, like the Hawaiian vacation my family took when we were kids. On that trip, my mother couldn't stop sniffing the air (and secretly, neither could my brothers and I).

I hope I didn't actually sniff Lucy this morning.

I wish Kane would sit further away from her. I don't want him to know that Lucy smells like an island in full bloom.

She's wearing a low-cut black silky blouse. It's the first time she's worn something low-cut, and I want to make her go home and change. It's totally professional, of course, but when we were sitting together earlier, I had to work hard not to see the edge of black lace peeking out from under the scoop of her black silky blouse. That edge cupped the creamiest, softest curve I've ever laid eyes on.

I know that because I snuck a peek at lunch time while she was loading up her plate. I let myself imagine replacing black lace with my own palm, cupping her. Shaping her, plumping her—and then dipping my head to lick.

I was hard in seconds flat. I walked away from the lunch table and into the bathroom, where I had a long discussion with myself about all the good reasons not to jerk off in the family workplace.

To be honest, I've been a hot fucking mess since Monday night, when I walked Lucy back to the hotel.

I wanted to follow her into the elevator. Slap my hands against the stupid gold-plated interior walls on either side of her and kiss her until she whimpered.

But I was trying to be a decent human being, and I was pretty sure sober Lucy wasn't going to look at me the way drunk Lucy was looking at me, like I was the perfect fit for her Instagram nine squares.

Kane says something and Lucy laughs. I want to make an excuse to remove Kane from the meeting. But it won't help. Another brother will take his place. And they all seem smitten with her, except Brody. He can be counted on to stay hostile.

Kane and Hanna finish up, and Kane goes to get Clark, who's up next.

Lucy glances over and catches me staring.

I should look away, but I don't. I can't.

She doesn't either. She stares right back at me. I'm aware of every breath she takes, even though my eyes stay on her face. Her lower lip softens, and I have to discipline myself not to move, not to cross the fifteen feet between us, take her face in my hands, and suck on that soft flesh. Her hand comes up to tuck a non-existent strand of her hair behind her ear. Her fingers briefly touch her cheek before she drops her hand again, and I feel the softness of that cheek like it's my hand.

I'm hard again, mouth dry, heart pounding.

And then Clark steps between us and breaks the spell. I drop my gaze, and when I look back, she's chatting and laughing with him, tossing her hair without any self-consciousness.

I hate Clark. And Easton. And every guy who has ever kissed or touched Lucy Spiro or, worse, made her laugh.

Pure fucking insanity.

"Gabe."

My mother, of course, because there is no justice.

"I'm working on a new ad campaign for *Outdoors* magazine. Lucy gave me some ideas, but I wanted to run them by you."

"Shoot."

"She wants us to drop the emphasis on speed and risk and survival and pushing limits—"

"Of course she does."

"She's not wrong, Gabe," my mom says softly. "Look." She shows me the ad mockups she's done.

Get out of your comfort zone.

Learn how strong you are.

Meet your people.

The images are different, too. People hiking side by side. Standing at the top of a ski slope together. Beaming at each other around a campfire.

"I don't hate them," I say. "Except this one." It's two women, bundled in faux-fur-lined-hooded parkas, drinking cocoa during a break from snowshoeing. "We don't do snowshoe trips."

"Yet." My mom beams at me.

"No."

"Oh, yes."

"Has anyone told Kane and Hanna about the snowshoe trips?" I demand.

"The snowshoe trips were Kane's idea, as a matter of fact."

I groan.

That makes my mom smile. "Oh, Gabe," she says. "I would apologize, but it's really a sorry-not-sorry thing. Lucy's pretty awesome, isn't she?"

I hazard a quick glance across the room. Clark is showing Lucy something on his laptop, their heads bent together.

I close my eyes.

"You know what?" my mom says. "Don't answer that. Yet."

16

The next morning, I slap a hand down on my alarm and look over to discover I've somehow managed to oversleep. I must have been sleep-snoozing. Damn it. I told Lucy I'd be at work early this morning so she'd have the house to herself for a shower. Last night was her first night sleeping in the loft, so this morning is her first shower at my place.

I stagger out of bed and into the shower, telling myself that there's no way she'll be exactly on time—five minutes from now—so if I shower fast enough, I'll be out before she gets here.

I crank the hot water high and step under it, soaping myself up. My mind immediately jumps to the subject it cannot leave alone, Lucy. I slide my hand down my belly and fist my cock.

My offer to vacate the house wasn't a pure act of selflessness. It was an attempt at self-preservation.

You're supposed to be showering fast and getting out of here.

Lucy will be here any moment, Common Sense and Decency say.

I ignore them and give myself one fast, hard stroke.

I'm thinking of her in that blouse she wore the first day in the office. The one with the single button at the throat.

In my mind, I touch her face. Cup her cheek. Let my hand slide down so the soft pale cream of her throat is against my palm. I imagine the startled look on her face when I let my hand slip down to undo that button. She gasps, exactly the way she did when I leaned in and kissed her. Her blouse falls open to reveal her breasts, plumped up to spill over the top of her lacy bra. I duck my head and lick.

In this fantasy, she's wearing a short little skirt, and my hand finds the hem, pushing it up to discover she's not wearing panties. I tease into her wetness, find her clit, and work it until she begs me to fill her.

"Gabe?"

My hand stills. The pressure in my balls is insane.

She's at the end of the hallway—she must have come up the stairs toward the bathroom and then heard the water running. I don't lock the door at night, and I told her she should be able to come right in.

"Do you want me to come back?" she calls through the door. "Sorry—I saw a light in your office and thought you were in there."

It was probably one of my brothers; when Clark can't sleep, he sometimes comes into work early.

"I'm almost done," I call back.

I turn away from the sound of her voice. Lean my forehead against the cool wall of the tile. For a split second, I almost find the self-control to stop.

Then I jerk myself off with four more long, harsh strokes, thinking of her out there, only ten feet away. I come so hard I strain something in my low belly. I make myself stay absolutely silent, mouth open but wordless, soundless, as pleasure grips me, tight as a fist. Then I watch the strands of cum wash down the drain, not feeling nearly as ashamed of myself as I probably should.

I mean, it's better than the alternative, right? Coming out of the bathroom with my cock tenting out my towel?

But of course when I finally exit the bathroom with a towel around my waist, she's nowhere in sight. I retreat to my bedroom, yank on jeans, and head downstairs.

She's perched on the edge of the couch, but stands up quickly when I walk into the living room.

"'Morning," I say, an effort to act like a normal human and not someone who just jacked off thinking about her.

"Good morning."

Her eyes go straight to my chest, then quickly back up to my face. And my cock, which should be down for the count, gets heavy again. Because she was definitely checking me out.

Sober Lucy, in full possession of her faculties, was checking me out.

She has a shower caddy in one hand and her hair piled on her head in what I know from Amanda is a "messy bun." It looks like she just kind of tossed it up there. There are lots of escaped strands, curling around her face. Small, real curls, like they couldn't help themselves.

I know she doesn't want me to see her like this, any more than she wanted me to see her with her makeup streaming down her face the first night, but I see her.

For a split second I think that maybe I'm the only one

who does. Who sees past the carefully curated surface to the woman who'd ruin her hair, her clothes, and her makeup to rescue ducklings.

Don't be ridiculous, Gabe. A woman as beautiful as Lucy has had lots of relationships. Men who've seen her far more vulnerable than you have.

I yank myself out of my own head and back to reality.

She's wearing—

Oh, *God*.

What is she *wearing*?

PJs, obviously. And not anything special. Just a pair of pants tied at the waist and a pale pink t-shirt.

But *nothing* else.

And holy mother of God, look at her. Look. At. Her. The pale pink shirt clings to her tits, and I can see the hard tips of her nipples, spiking the fabric.

I want to do more than look. I want to mold my hands over her and see what happens if I use my thumbs to stroke those peaks.

"You're cold," I say, idiotically. "Would you like a robe? Let me get you a robe." I basically flee upstairs. I need to get a grip on myself, and not the kind I had a few minutes ago.

I come back down with my navy terry cloth robe. I hold it out, and she looks at it, and then at my face.

"It's clean," I say. "I never wear it. Like, I literally have never once worn it since Amanda bought it for me for Christmas..." I have to think about it. "Two years ago."

She takes the robe and puts it on, which allows my brain to work a little more effectively.

"I'm really sorry," she says as she knots it. "I thought—"

"No, I'm sorry. I totally screwed up. I must have been snoozing my alarm in my sleep. I'll get out of your hair now."

What I won't do is reach out and touch one of those willful, escaped curls. I won't brush them all back from her face, cupping it with both hands so I can bring her close to me and taste her.

She bites her lip. "I mean, don't rush. If you have to eat breakfast or whatever—do what you need to do. I'll shower and scoot out of here."

"Uh, okay."

Brilliant, Gabe. The lip-biting has made me even less functional than I already was.

My eyes fall to her shower caddy, which contains a surprisingly meager number of items. I can see soap, shampoo, and another bottle that is probably conditioner. Deodorant.

"Don't you need your makeup bag and your hair dryer and your curling iron?"

Her mouth moves like she's edging toward smiling, then thinks better of it. "I'll do all that back in the loft."

"You can do it here if it's easier." I think of her in the cramped office bathroom. No counter space there. Not that my bathroom, a nineties-tastic, tiled monstrosity, is anything to write home about.

"Thanks," she says.

She starts upstairs, and I turn away so I'm not watching her fantastic ass, clad in those soft pants, recede up my stairs. I do need breakfast, so I head into the kitchen and make myself a bowl of oatmeal.

While I'm eating, I hear the water come on.

She's in there, under the hot water.

Which version of her?

Neat and self-contained? All business?

Or messy? Tilting her head back to let the water pour over her head, abandoning herself to the pleasure of the wet heat, letting it run down over her breasts, until it's dripping off those hard nipples....

In the end I have to take my oatmeal over to the office and eat it there, because that's the only way I can be sure I won't unzip myself and go for round two.

I stand in the shower, trying to pull my thoughts back together while I wash my hair. The washing is going pretty well. The pulling together, not so much.

Gabe without a shirt on.

Gabe without a shirt on is...

Pretty sure I counted at least an eight pack before I realized that I was edging over into gaping, and raised my gaze back to eye level. But it took me a minute to get there because between the eight pack and his oh-so-serious, intense face were these gorgeous, golden just-right pecs, with a perfect smattering of hair.

I wanted to look back down, to check out the matching trail to paradise, but I got stuck again on his dark gaze, which was...

Hungry.

On my nipples.

I'm pretty sure, anyway. They definitely thought so, at least, hardening to demanding points. My breasts felt tight and full, and the tug shot straight down to my core.

Which was around the moment my brain kicked back in and yelled, *Lucy! Quit it!*

Can you get any more unprofessional than this?

I was supposed to be in his house when he *wasn't* there. He wasn't supposed to see me with no makeup, my hair looking like something the cat coughed up, and my three-year-old boring PJs.

More to the point, I wasn't supposed to be ogling my client, and I wasn't supposed to be standing still like a diva in the spotlight's glow, savoring the fact that he was eye-licking my nipples.

When I woke up, hungover, on Tuesday morning, I was well aware that Gabe's self-control was the only thing that had stood between me and—

Well, a few things.

Being filled with Gabe's cock.

I get a little breathless at the thought.

But also deep and abiding professional regret. He saved me from that, too. For better or for worse.

I had a love-hate relationship with Gabe's self-control for most of Tuesday morning, but then over the next couple of days, something happened.

I kept catching him not-looking at me. Every time I surfaced from a conversation with a Wilder brother, there he was, not-looking at me with every ounce of himself.

Once I caught him actually *looking*. That was the best of all. Every nerve in my body aligned itself to the hungry expression on his face. I stared right back. Neither of us was going to turn away first, and it went on and on until I was breathless.

From a look.

Imagine what would happen if it weren't just a look.

With hot water pouring over me, I fantasize that he is downstairs, as hyperaware of me in the shower as I was of him. He is standing in the kitchen, eating his breakfast, but all he can think about is me, washing myself. Hands on my breasts, belly, hips, cupping my pussy.

In my mind, he pushes away from the counter, sets his bowl down, and starts up the stairs. He can't help himself.

Because this is fantasy, I've foolishly left the door unlocked. Rookie mistake. Of course I don't want him to walk in on me. I don't want him to quietly open the door. Shed his clothes. Step into the shower.

I would gasp, surprised. *What are you doing here?* Maybe I sound outraged, like, *how dare you?*

I couldn't stay away. That's what he'd say. Grating it out, like it hurt him to admit it.

Alone, in the shower, I slide my finger into my folds, finding my clit.

His finger would be thicker. Rougher. He would hold me from behind, pinning my body against his. His cock wedged between us.

Gabe's shower has a detachable head, because apparently there is a God.

It's a really good shower head, too, not too weak, not too strong. Just right.

I make short work of myself and come, swallowing gasps and cries. In the fantasy, he covers my mouth with his hand, and I nip him, but he doesn't let go.

In reality, I'm alone in the shower, feeling breathless and

foolish. Because Gabe is obviously not here. And I wouldn't want him to be. That would be complicated. I'm supposed to take my trips, give my best effort to fixing his business, and make my money. I'm supposed to go back to New York and start up my own consulting company.

Sleeping with your boss's not-exactly-boyfriend by accident because you didn't know who he was, that's a mistake.

Sleeping with your client, that's a bad decision.

Also, doing both of those things? That would be a pattern.

I finish washing my hair and get out of the shower. I head downstairs, not sure whether I want to find him there or not.

By the time I get to the bottom of the stairs, I can tell he's not there. The house feels not-Gabe.

I'm developing finely honed Gabe sensors.

I take advantage of the emptiness to poke around a bit. Not outright spying, just glancing around at what I can see as I head out.

Amanda wasn't kidding about the house looking like someone sold everything off in a yard sale. The living room has bare hardwood floors, a plain heather-gray sofa, and a matching armchair. No throw pillows, no rug, nothing on the walls. There's a bookcase, but it's only half full. No end tables, no lamps, just overhead canister lighting.

If Amanda hadn't alluded to the fact that there's a story here, I would think that Gabe just doesn't care about stuff. That he hates throw pillows—like any self-respecting guy. That he spends most of his time in the woods, in a tent, with a sleeping bag, and doesn't give a shit about rugs or books or, well, anything.

But Amanda made it sound like there's more to it than that.

I guess I want to know. I want to know why the house is the way it is.

I want to know why Gabe is the way he is.

18

"**N**o."

That's the only word that will come out of my mouth. I have just seen what Lucy thinks she's wearing to go out on the boat, and *no.*

It's early on Saturday, and she and I are scheduled to meet Brody and his best friend, Connor Perez, at the Green Will Lake Campground launch. We're angling for trout, but mostly we're trying to give Lucy a feel for what a fishing trip is like. And fact number one: It's a fuckload messier than she thinks it is.

She stops in her tracks and looks down at her clothes. "I'm wearing jeans. And a t-shirt. And comfortable shoes."

She's wearing expensive-looking tight jeans, a pale-gray t-shirt, and those flimsy, lame shoes I think women call ballet flats. They're basically slippers.

"You're going to ruin your clothes, freeze your ass off, get eaten alive by bugs, and crack your head open slipping on the deck, not to mention impaling your foot on a hook."

"Sounds like fun," she says dryly. "Can't wait. Have I mentioned you don't know how to sell your trips?"

I glare at her. "I don't sell. I tell it like it is. And you're changing your clothes."

She opens her mouth and shuts it again. Then: "This is the least dressy outfit I've got."

"I was hoping you weren't going to say that." I cross my arms. "How can it be that the future of my outdoor adventuring business is in the hands of a woman who doesn't know how to go outside? What size shoe do you wear?"

She looks down at my feet. "A lot smaller than yours."

I can't resist. "You know what they say."

Our eyes meet.

"I do know what they say."

And I instantly regret having gone there. All the heat we've been trying to tamp down is between us again. She looks away first. Thank God.

"What size?" I repeat.

"Eight."

I text Hanna and Amanda. They'll be awake—Amanda because of the kids, and Hanna because she's Hanna. *Pls tell me one of you wears a size eight shoe.*

Hanna texts back right away: *I do. Lucy?*

Yup.

😊 *Wanna stop by and grab 'em?*

Do you have some grubby clothes she can wear?

Do I have any clothes that aren't grubby? she shoots back.

Have I mentioned how much I love Hanna?

My pants are going to be short on her. But yeah I've got stuff she can wear.

"We're stopping off at Hanna's," I tell Lucy.

"I don't care if these get ruined," she says.

"You can't wear those shoes, so we're stopping at Hanna's."

"Do you boss everyone around?" she demands.

I think about it for a second. "Yes."

"And they put up with it?"

"No." I open the the Jeep's passenger door for her and close it carefully behind her. I jog around to the other side, climb in, and start 'er up. "My brothers give me constant shit. And Amanda mostly ignores me."

When we get to her house, Hanna leads away an unwilling Lucy and soon returns her in sturdy hikers, a pair of hiking pants that leave a couple of inches of ugly brown wool socks showing, a long-sleeved wool base-layer shirt, and a sweatshirt that swallows Lucy whole. Hanna has also pulled Lucy's hair back in a high ponytail.

Lucy looks absolutely miserable. And I have to admit, the effect is pretty unflattering. Except for the high ponytail. What is it about ponytails? This one makes Lucy look both uptight and cute.

Which is pretty much straight-up Lucy.

Also, Lucy in unflattering clothes is still hot. I know she's under there, and now I'm supplying the contours of her gorgeous body in my head. Thinking about sliding my hands under the baggy sweatshirt and outlining her with my palms.

"If you're going to keep going on these trips," I say to her, "you're going to need some clothes that actually fit. Hanna can take you shopping."

"Like hell I can," Hanna says. "I don't shop."

"Where do your clothes come from?"

She shrugs. "Christmas presents?"

"I'll take you shopping," I say, even though there are few things I hate as much as shopping. Seeing Lucy in outdoor-wear that fits would make it worth it, though.

We're half an hour behind schedule when we finally leave Hanna's. We drive in silence for a bit, until she says, "You know what we need?"

I have a lot of answers to that, but luckily she answers her own question. "Music."

I snort. "Oh, yeah? How do you think that's gonna go? I predict zero overlap in our musical tastes."

She crosses her arms. "You think you know what kind of music I like?"

"I think I have a pretty good guess."

She snorts. "Okay, go ahead. Guess."

"If I can guess three songs on your phone, I get to choose the music."

"No, wait. I get to guess, too." She thinks a minute. "How about this. If you guess three on mine, I get to take a shot at yours. If we both guess right, we have to find music we both like."

I give her side-eye. "Which we've already agreed is zero overlap."

"I didn't agree to that. I bet we can find music we both like."

"That's because you're an optimist."

She makes a sound at 'optimist.' "What gave you that idea?"

"You assumed I'd help you save the ducklings even though you'd never met me before. You agreed to have a drink with me even though I could have been an axe murderer."

"It was a public place."

"Still. And you assumed my brothers would listen to you, even though what you're proposing to them is ridiculous."

"But tell us how you really feel," she mutters.

"Also, you thought you could go fishing in those clothes. Optimist. I rest my case."

"I'm not an optimist," she says. "Optimists think people are basically good and well-meaning."

"Exactly. And that's you."

She shakes her head. Hard. "It's really not."

I don't believe her, but I don't try to argue with her. She's the worst kind of optimist, the kind who thinks she's a realist, but I'm not going to win that fight. Instead I say, "Shakira, 'Try Everything.'"

"That's low hanging fruit," she says grumpily.

"But I'm not wrong?"

"You're not wrong."

"That's one." I think for a minute. "Walk the Moon, 'Work This Body.'"

"I bet a lot of women have both those songs on their phones. Those are both on my workout playlist."

I shrug. "Yeah, so? That doesn't disqualify them. The deal was, I had to guess three."

"Okay, but pick at least one that's not a pump-up song."

I frown. "How about, Plain White Ts, 'Hey There, Delilah.' That's not a pump-up song. It's from the 'I love you/have sex with me' subgenre of pop."

"Wait, what? That's not a thing."

"Sure it is. Songs by guys singing about how much they

love her so she'll give it up, already. It's, like, three-quarters of pop. Am I right?"

"No! It's a love song!"

I sneak at look at her, pink-cheeked and outraged. She's fun to rile up. "Suuure it is. But you're avoiding the real point here. Am I right that 'Hey There, Delilah' is on your phone?"

She grunts.

"Well?"

"Okay. You won that round."

I resist the urge to crow. "Now you."

I discover I really want to know what she's going to guess.

"Hmm," she says. "Okay. John Mellencamp, 'I Was Born in a Small Town.'"

I roll my eyes. "Speaking of low-hanging fruit."

In my peripheral vision, she brings a knuckle to her mouth and nibbles it. It's distracting. Like, really distracting. I'm thinking about other things I want her to do with that mouth. It doesn't help that I know exactly how soft and warm it is, and how eager and responsive she is. I wonder how, exactly, she feels about oral sex. Can she let herself get the kind of messy that leads to the best, hottest sex?

I really want to find out.

"Mark Knopfler, 'Money for Nothing.'"

Well, shit.

"Ha!" she says, seeing the expression on my face.

"That's only two. You need one more."

She makes a *mmmm* thinking sound that for some reason I can feel in my skin. All over. Then I realize that she made a very similar sound when I kissed her. And now I'm thinking about it again. That kiss.

"Got it! Alison Krauss and Brad Paisley. 'Whiskey Lullaby.'"

I don't say anything. She nailed it. And I'm torn between irritation at losing and feeling weirdly pleased.

She does an outrageous little victory dance, wiggling in the seat. My mouth goes dry.

"And here's the best part," she says. "That song's on my phone, too."

"Seriously?"

She shrugs. "I like country. Roots. Americana. Bluegrass."

My mouth falls open. "You—what?"

"My mom lived most of her life in a small town. I was born in one. Country genes die hard."

I'd forgotten. "But you hate everything about small towns."

"I like the music," she says simply.

I reach for my phone and press my thumb to the home button. "You heard Joss Ebert? Like Miranda Lambert and Margo Price had a love child?"

"Nooo." Her voice is full of wonder. "But oh my God I want that."

That exclamation roughs itself over my nerves. I want to give her what she wants, and not just in the pressing Play way.

I want to push all her buttons.

And lick and suck a few of them, while I'm at it.

I play the song for her.

She listens carefully, not talking, through the whole song. I like that. No one does that. You play something for them and then they talk at you while they're supposed to be listening. But Lucy listens.

"I love that line," she says, at one point. "*Home's the place you can't forget.*"

"You feel that way about New York City?"

"Not really."

"Where, then?"

She thinks about it a minute. "I don't really feel that way about anywhere."

For some reason, that makes me sad.

The lake where we meet Brody and his friend is nestled deep in the national forest. When we get out of the Jeep, it's ten degrees cooler than it was in Rush Creek, and I suddenly get why Gabe wanted me in warmer clothes.

The lake's beautiful, surrounded by mountains, some of which are still snow-capped. There's a campground in the woods behind the boat launch, where people have set up tents and RVs. I'll have to ask if Wilder Adventures owns an RV. They could set it up as a glamper. I bet that would appeal to some honeymooners.

Out here, I still smell sage, juniper, and evergreen like I did at Wilder headquarters, but there are other notes in the air, too—the clean water scent, and something that must come from the damp earth and the tangle of reeds and grasses around the edges of the lake.

A different kind of woman would be thinking about taking her shoes off and digging her toes into the soft mud.

The kind of woman Gabe and his brothers probably date.

The boat is already in the water, next to the dock, Brody standing beside it. In the bright sun, he seems less broody than he did inside the Wilder Adventures offices, but he still looks like he's got a solid dark streak. Maybe it's the tattoos, or maybe it's the leather jacket, but I think it's the fact that he never quite meets my eyes.

He helps me into the boat. It's a decent-sized fishing boat, but I still hate the way it feels under my feet. I've never liked boats.

I was always the one who stayed home from waterskiing even though I loved the actual skiing part, because I hated being in the boat so much.

I'm hoping it won't be an issue today. I'm pretty sure fishing is mostly floating.

"This is Connor," Brody says, and his friend steps forward and shakes my hand. He fits right in with the Wilder brothers. He's over six feet, olive-skinned, dark-haired and dark-eyed, dressed in fishing overalls that shouldn't be sexy but somehow manage it.

"Hey, Connor," I say. "I'm Lucy."

"I bring Connor along because his mom makes the best Cuban sandwiches in the Five Rivers region and she can't stand for anyone to go out on the water without bringing a full picnic."

"He's full of shit," Connor says. "He brings me because he doesn't want to clean the boat alone after."

"Yeah. That, too. But the Cubanos don't hurt."

Gabe sits down and gestures for me to sit too, which I do a second before Brody unwinds the rope from the dock and pushes off. A moment later, we're moving slowly across the water, and I release a breath. I can handle this.

But I've forgotten how much I hate the bounce of the boat as it crosses another boat's wake. And the gasoline-and-oil smell of a boat motor.

I'm determined not to let anyone see how much I hate it. I sit very still and try to breathe deeply through my nose, but I have to stop, because the gas smell is making me nauseated.

After a moment, I rest my head against my hand.

"You okay?" Gabe asks.

I nod. If I hold very still and breathe through my mouth, I will be.

As we motor further onto the water, Gabe gives me a little background about the lake—that it didn't use to be accessible from the forest road, but now it is; that if I look carefully I'll spot elk, all kinds of waterfowl, and close to shore, pikas, which are sort of like what you'd get if you crossed a rabbit and a mouse. "And bald eagles and osprey," he says, gesturing at the sky, which is a bright blue so vivid it hurts to look at.

We find a location that Brody likes. This part of the lake is mostly deserted, except for one other boat. Brody, Connor, and Gabe set up their rods, while I watch. Gabe offers to let me have a rod and bait my own hook. I say no thank you with more force than I mean to, and Connor laughs, but Brody and Gabe don't. I wonder what they're thinking.

I try to make Brody tell me what he's doing. I've been thinking maybe some of the wedding groups would like to learn to fish. I want to see what Brody's like with a newbie.

What I learn: He's like Gabe when he doesn't want to talk. He grunts answers.

"Don't make Brody teach," Connor says. "Brody doesn't teach or give tours. He only works with anglers who already know their stuff."

"You'd have to talk more," I say. "If you want to broaden your audience."

Brody stiffens.

"Lucy wants to make Wilder Adventures more appealing to the wedding and spa tourists," Gabe explains to Connor. He says it almost neutrally, just the slightest edge in his voice. I'm making progress.

"People would like this," I say. "Just this. Just a boat ride out to a quiet place, with a picnic. Maybe Brody giving basic fishing lessons, explaining the wildlife."

"Huh," Connor says. "Sounds like a good idea, right?"

"I also picture some small girls-weekend groups. Maybe photography? Landscape painting? Bottle of wine, a manicurist and pedicurist, or chair massage, on board."

Heads swivel and all three men aim looks of disgust at me.

"Not in the forest," Brody says.

"There must be other bodies of water, not in the national forest, where you could do something like that."

"There are," Brody says irritably. "I could. But I would rather have my own fingernails and toenails pulled out one by one."

"Than be surrounded by pretty tourists in a good mood?" I ask.

Gabe snorts.

"Tourists are assholes," Brody snarls.

"Brody." The warning in Gabe's tone catches me off guard. Brody glares at his brother, and Gabe stares him down. Brody ducks his head and goes silent.

Connor jumps in, obviously the smoother-over here. "She

makes an excellent point about pretty and in a good mood," he says.

Brody and Gabe don't say anything. But Brody doesn't repeat his throwdown, either, so that's a good sign.

"Just don't fuck with my fly fishing trips," Brody grunts.

I tilt my head.

"I lead river fly fishing trips, too. They're sacred. I'm not turning them into tourist traps."

"Noted," I say, and sit myself down for a while. I'll harass Brody more about my ideas when we're off the water.

It's crazy peaceful out here. The sun is higher now, warm, sparkling off the surface of the water. I watch an eagle flying overhead, its bald head white against the dark of its body. It's so beautiful and fierce.

The guys relax again, joking around, ribbing each other about fishing technique and other stuff. Gabe's so mellow, I almost don't recognize him. He's giving Connor shit about the garbage trout he's been catching, and Connor's dishing it back.

Brody's quiet, though. I think of the back and forth between him and Gabe and wonder.

"How's Rachel?" Gabe asks Connor. "That's his little sister," he tells me.

"She's coming home next week to spring ski with us," Connor says.

Brody freezes. I'm the only one who notices. Connor and Gabe are focused on rebaiting and casting.

Connor adds, "For my mom's birthday." He casts and sets the rod back in its slot. "She moved in with her boyfriend."

"I didn't know she had a boyfriend."

Am I the only one who can tell how studied Brody's

nonchalance is? If he tried any harder to pretend to be disinterested, he'd fall backwards out of the boat.

Connor grimaces. "Yeah. And she hasn't let us meet him. I don't know yet if I need to beat the shit out of him."

I sneak a look at Brody. He's schooled his face to blankness—but I see the furrow between his brows.

Interesting.

"So she'll be in town next week?" I ask, because I know Brody can't. "For how long?"

Brody shoots me a look. I can't tell if he's pissed at or grateful for my interference.

"A week," Connor says.

"Is she bringing the boyfriend?"

Connor frowns. "No. I'm going to have to go to Boston to check this dude out. Make sure he's good enough for her."

Brody winces.

Yep. There's a story to Brody and Rachel.

The good news is, Connor doesn't seem to pick up Brody's weird vibes. "How's Justin?" he asks Brody.

"He's good." Brody turns to me. "Justin's my kid."

"Hanna mentioned him."

"Yeah. Well. You stick around here long enough, you're going to hear plenty about it. It's Rush Creek's favorite topic." Brody's voice has hardened even more.

Gabe puts a hand on his shoulder. Brody doesn't look at Gabe, but his jaw relaxes a notch.

Something warms in my chest.

Gabe's a good guy. A good brother.

I like him so much more than I wish I did.

I like him so much more than is convenient for this situation.

"Pika!" Gabe calls, pointing, and sure enough there's a cute critter sitting on the shore with its hands up to its face, nibbling on something in its adorable paws. It looks like a tiny rabbit with mouse ears.

No elk, yet, though. I'll have to wait on that one.

Every once in a while, one of the guys brings in a trout. Some get thrown back—too small—some go into the cooler. I can't watch while they're removing the hook. I try not to even think about it. The good news is, with the boat anchored and the motor off, my motion sickness has ebbed. There's a small amount of gentle rocking with the wind, but it's not bothering me.

After a while, Connor breaks out the Cuban sandwiches, and holy shit, Brody wasn't kidding. Pork, ham, melted Swiss, mustard, pickles, all on toasted bread that has somehow managed to keep its crispness despite being wrapped in waxed paper and aluminum foil.

It's about as good as it gets, eating out here on the water with the sun shining down.

Tourists are going to love it.

Mid-afternoon, Brody pulls up anchor and we head back to the dock. It's okay at first, but then the boat picks up speed and we cross paths with a few other boats. The sun is glaring off the white plastic of the boat's interior, blinding me. And the gasoline odor is back, filling up my senses like I can hear it and feel it, not only smell it. We're bouncing up and down and I'm suddenly not okay. Not okay at all.

"Lucy?" Gabe asks.

The world tunnels. I put my head between my legs. My mouth has filled up with saliva and everything is gray and staticky.

"Brody, stop the boat," Gabe says, in a voice of absolute authority.

Brody obeys, and I lean over the edge and throw up. I grip the hull, miserably sick and embarrassed. So unprofessional. So unlikely to convince any of these men that I'm equipped to help them come up with a new direction for their business.

I feel a hand come around to cup my forehead, and then there is a body behind mine, bracing me. It's the most comforting thing ever, even better than when my mom held my hair back when I was a kid.

When I'm done, I straighten up. Gabe backs away, taking his warmth and strength with him. Silently, he hands me a small bottle of water. Then he takes off his sweatshirt and gives me that. To wipe my mouth, I realize. I stare at him in disbelief. "No way."

"Better than Hanna's sweatshirt, right?"

He's got a point. I sip the water, swish some and spit over the edge, and clean myself up. Then I fold the sweatshirt and keep it in my lap. "Unless you want it back." I give him the cheekiest grin I can manage, trying to show that even if I get seasick, I'm not one to give up.

"You can put it straight in the washer," he says gruffly.

Brody takes it slow back to the dock, and I notice he goes out of his way to avoid wake.

"We're going to need some ground rules," Brody says, as I climb onto the dock, painfully relieved to be on steady land.

"Ground rules?" I ask.

"Before I take anyone out, they have to sign a contract saying they won't puke."

Pretty sure he's not joking.

s I pull into the driveway, Lucy, who has been asleep with her head resting against the window, stirs.

She's a good sport.

She totally could have bowed out of that trip, knowing she gets sick on the water, but she didn't. I saw her go green when we first set out from the dock, but she didn't say anything. She didn't complain.

I have to admit, I was rooting for her. Hoping she'd make it back to the dock without losing it.

I'm not the kind of guy who jumps in when there's vomit involved, so I don't know what made me leap to help her out. Just this wave of protectiveness. I couldn't stand back while she was suffering. I had to do whatever I could to help.

This is another bad sign. I have done pretty much whatever I could in life to avoid feeling this way about people other than my family members. At least since Ceci.

"Luce. You, um, want the first shower?"

I watch her take a moment to figure out where she is and

what the hell is going on. When she remembers, she makes a face and reaches for the soiled sweatshirt, which is folded in her lap. "You can have the first one. I have to grab my stuff anyway."

I nod. "I'll make it quick. If you text me when you're ready to come over, I'll head to the office."

"You don't have to do that. You've already seen me at my worst. Soaked and muddy. Barfing over the side of a fishing boat. Heck, you've seen me in my PJs."

What Lucy doesn't understand is that I like her at her worst. Not more than I like her at her best, because Lucy at her best is also a thing of beauty. Lucy at her best is long ringlet curls and glossy lips, silky clothes all buttoned up and waiting for someone to undo them. And Lucy at what she calls her worst is Lucy when she's unsure. When she isn't wearing armor and putting on a performance. When she might make a mistake, and you might see it.

But I don't say any of that.

I say, "Give me that."

She holds the vomit-y sweatshirt away from my grasp. "No."

"Do you want to keep it as a souvenir?"

She glares. "It has to go in the wash. I don't want you to have to touch it. Bad enough I ruined it."

"You didn't *ruin* it," I say. "You temporarily soiled it. Give it to me."

But she's insistent. "Show me where the washer is, and I'll put it in there so you don't have to touch it."

It's easier not to argue—and it's not like I *want* to touch it —so I let her follow me into the house. Buck greets me like I've been away for a year instead of just for a day, jumping up and licking me and butting my hand with his head. "Hey, buddy. Sorry I didn't bring you today. Next time."

He turns his attention to Lucy, giving her similar treatment, just a little warier. She smiles and scratches him behind the ears, the way he likes. He catches wind of the nasty shirt and tries to tug it out of her hands.

"No, bud," I say. "Give me a sec, I'm going to let him out." I coax him to the back fenced area.

I show Lucy through the kitchen and into the pantry/laundry room. She drops the shirt into the front loader. I point her to the laundry sink, and she washes her hands quickly and dries them on the towel hanging there.

"I'll give you, what, ten or fifteen to take your shower?"

I nod, trying not to think about the last time I was in the shower with Lucy in my house.

She leaves, and I let Buck—who's scrabbling at the back door—inside. He follows me upstairs and settles himself on the carpet outside the bathroom while I strip off my clothes and get in the shower.

For a minute, I'm content to rinse off the scum of the day, but once I'm clean and the water is falling warm over my skin, I think, *What if...*

What if she came up the stairs, and this time she didn't stop and call out my name? What if she dropped her clothes on the floor outside the bathroom, slipped through the door, and joined me in here?

For a moment the fantasy is so vivid that my breathing stops. Her skin, satiny and warm against mine, the slickness of the water falling over us mingling with the slickness of her sex as I slip a finger between her legs. To seek her clit and stroke it. To find her wet heat and thrust into it.

This could become a bad habit, I think, as my hand reflexively reaches for my aching erection.

I make myself stop. I wash my hair and body, not lingering to stroke myself, even though the temptation is stronger than ever.

I pull on clothes and head downstairs, followed by Buck. I'm thinking breaded and fried, with lemon butter. I pull out the panko.

I'm squeezing lemons—the citrus fruit kind—when I hear her on the front porch. She hesitates at the door, and I can feel her trying to decide if she should knock or just come in. In the end, she knocks.

I open the door to find her carrying her shower caddy and a small tote bag. She's wearing my robe and a pair of flipflops. Her bare legs are visible beneath the hem of the robe.

Does that mean she's naked underneath?

The urge to reach out and tug that stupid blue terry tie is strong.

My restraint in the shower is now seeming like a really stupid choice.

Her eyes meet mine like she knows what I'm thinking. Like she's thinking it, too.

Like she wants me to do it.

I'm reaching out my hand to grab the tie where it's knotted. I'm going to tug her forward. Kiss her breathless.

Except Buck has insinuated himself between us and nosed into her crotch.

"Buck, quit it," I say, grabbing his collar, trying not to laugh. Dogs, man. They are all id. I use my knee to push Buck out of the way, and Lucy slips around me and into the house.

Moment lost.

I follow her in, head into the kitchen, and call out, "Beer?" I come back into the living room with two and hold one out to her.

She waves the beer off. "I should probably have some food first."

"I'll start dinner while you're in the shower."

"Dinner—"

"It's too much fish for one person."

"Sometimes people ask, Gabe," Lucy says, but she's smiling. "Like, 'Hey, I've got all this fish, wanna stay for dinner?"

"Hey. I've got all this fish. Wanna stay for dinner?"

"Sure." Her smile gets even bigger. "You, um, know how to... cook?"

"I'm a thirty-five-year-old bachelor. I'd be pretty screwed if I didn't."

"You've got a lot of family. Including a sister who makes a mean lasagna."

"Go shower," I say.

Still smiling, she turns and goes upstairs. A few minutes later, I hear the shower running. I break a couple eggs and grate some parmesan cheese. Keeping my hands busy seems like a really good idea. I turn on some music, too, so I can't hear the water running upstairs. That keeps me from wondering what she's doing in there.

She comes back down when I'm dropping thin spaghetti into the pasta water and heating the oil in the pan to fry the fish. I've sautéed some garlic and red pepper flakes, and now I add spinach.

"Oh, my God, Gabe, this is amazing," she says. "You're amazing."

"You're not going to flatter me into liking your ideas for Wilder."

She laughs. "You and your brothers will like the ideas for Wilder when you see how much money comes in."

"My brothers and I will *never* like the ideas for Wilder."

Her face falls, and I feel bad. The thing about Lucy is, she really believes in what she's selling. She meant what she said when she explained how she'd try to find a way for us to build the business without sacrificing our vision.

I just don't think it's possible.

Oh, God, the competence porn! Is there anything this man can't do? He's cooking with both hands, flipping the fish, then testing the pasta, stirring the spinach. Everything smells amazing, like butter and lemon and garlic. My stomach growls.

Plus the dog adores him. Buck is lying at Gabe's feet, gazing up at him like Gabe... well, like Gabe wields the can opener. But also probably the frisbee and the ball launcher and the treat jar and the soft fleecy bed. Gabe squats for a moment and gives Buck's head an affectionate ruffle.

Honestly, I kind of get it. After today, I want to sit at his feet and stare up at him adoringly, too. Especially if he'd stroke my hair.

Instead, I ask if he needs any help. He says, "No. But I want to show you something."

"I want you to show me something, too," I say.

Whoops! I meant to think them, but the words fell out of my mouth, husky and suggestive.

I'm rewarded by a full-on Gabriel Wilder smile, which is rare and beautiful. He has a dimple in one cheek and laugh lines at the corners of his dark eyes. "Don't tempt me."

That's it, though. He doesn't look at me the way he did at the door, or take me up on my not-at-all-subtle come-on.

At the door, he'd stared at me like he wanted to get me out of his robe as fast as possible. My whole body got hot and melty. I was going to let him kiss me, and I was going to enjoy every minute of it, and I wasn't going to stop with kissing. I would worry about the consequences later. Life is short.

And then Buck got in the way.

"Look," he says. "You see how it's translucent here, but not here?"

I'm leaning in close to see the fish, and yeah, I see it.

"That's how you know it's done, when it's no longer translucent. People overcook fish in the worst way. You have to have a visual. You can't do it with a thermometer. By the time you get the guideline temp, it's way too late."

He takes the fish off the heat, drains the pasta, heaps the spaghetti onto two plates, and arranges the spinach and fish on top. It's even pretty to look at.

Meanwhile, I'm trying not to feel rejected because I basically told him I wanted to have sex with him and he showed me how to cook trout perfectly.

He sets two places across from each other at his kitchen table. Nothing super fancy, just plates and cloth napkins and silverware. But then he gets up again, goes and gets two wine glasses and a bottle, and comes back. "You okay with white?" he asks. "Red's too heavy for trout."

"Who *are* you?" I demand.

He laughs at that. "Just a guy who loves good fish, cooked right, and served with the right drink. Believe me, it's not like I know wine pairings for everything. Okay, reds with steak. And beer with everything else. Especially Chinese and Indian."

The food tastes as good as it looks. The trout's flaky and buttery and crispy and lemony and oh my God I have to close my eyes so I can fully enjoy it. When I open them, he's looking at me, and *that's more like it.*

"Lucy," he says, all dark and intent. "You have to stop that."

We're both frozen, me trying to figure out if he means it in that bossy, intensely hot way it sounds, and him—

"Oh, *shit*," he says suddenly, and then I hear it, too. The sound of someone—well, something—heaving and retching in the next room. He's out of his seat in an instant, running for the pantry.

I get up to follow—to see if I can help—but he calls, "Stay out there. You don't need to see this."

"What—?"

"He got my sweatshirt out of the laundry and chewed it, and—well, you got the rest."

He's gone a long time. When he comes back, he sinks into his seat, looking exhausted.

And then suddenly I'm laughing, because poor Gabe. "That's a lot of barf for one day," I say, between gasps, and, "I did ruin your sweatshirt. In the end."

For a second, he stares at me, and then he starts laughing, too, the two of us belly laughing, getting control for a second, and then setting each other off again. It feels so good to laugh, and I can't think how long it's been since something really set me off.

When we both stop, we sit down and manage to finish our now mostly cold but still delicious meal. I'm still feeling the afterglow of laughing with him, seeing and hearing him laugh, him letting go and enjoying himself. I know it doesn't happen often, because even on the boat today, he didn't laugh or smile a ton. I don't think he lets himself. I think he cares too much about making everything run smoothly and taking care of everyone.

"What's it like growing up with five siblings?" I ask.

"Lots of fun. Never quiet. Never boring. There's always someone to do something with. Throw a football, go swimming or fishing or hunting, accidentally burn down a deserted shed."

"You did that?"

"Uh-huh," he says. "No one got hurt. Brody and I had to earn the money to pay back the owner. We learned our lesson. Sort of. We weren't very good at generalizing, so we didn't see setting off firecrackers in the Haverill's barn as an instance of the same dumbass thinking. Luckily, we were able to put out the fire before we had to earn the money to rebuild the barn, because that definitely would have set us back. You have siblings?"

I shake my head. "Only child."

"Just you and your parents?"

Now we're into territory I stay away from. "Yup." That's the simplest version. "And a few pets. Mostly cats, guinea pigs and hamsters. I always wanted a dog." I reach down and scratch Buck's head, and he gives me a toned-down version of the adoring-Gabe look.

"You getting a chance to hang with your mom while you're here?" he asks.

"Yup. I had breakfast with her and Gregg, and then dinner night before last. Gregg seems like a good guy."

Gregg had grilled up chicken breasts outside the Airstream, and we'd talked about his marketing issues with his bike store, among other things. I'd made a few suggestions for how he could tweak his approach. He'd been super grateful.

My mom had beamed most of the night, like she could imagine nothing better than watching Gregg and me chat while she sat back and sipped her wine.

"Gregg's great," Gabe says. "We get a lot of referrals from him, and vice versa. The bike touring crowd and the adventure crowd overlap."

I steer the conversation back to Gabe. "So all your brothers work for you?"

Some of the light goes out of his face. "Since we lost my dad," he says, matter of factly, but I know the tone hides a lot of pain.

"I'm sorry," I say.

"It was a long time ago."

"You sure take good care of your family."

His eyes fly to mine, surprised.

"I see the way you watch out for them. Amanda, Brody, even Hanna. You're fierce. In a good way."

He turns his head away, but I can tell he's pleased.

"You done?" he asks, reaching for my plate. I nod, and he stands and clears for us. I start to fill the sink to do the dishes, but he waves me off. "Fill the sink with warm soapy water and leave everything," he says. "Let's go watch a movie."

"What makes you think we'll be able to agree on a movie?" I ask, teasing.

"Oh, we're not going to agree," he says. "We're watching *A River Runs Through It*."

Okay, I totally picked *A River Runs Through It* to get Lucy's goat. But I'm learning that with Lucy, everything I do to get under her skin comes back to bite me in the ass.

In this case, it's the maddeningly slow pace of the movie. The long, contemplative fly-fishing scenes, the dialogue with stories unfolding at the same pace.

It leaves me immense stretches of time to be hyper-aware of Lucy.

She's sitting close enough that I can smell the floral of her shampoo and feel the warmth of her body. Her thigh is not quite close enough to touch mine, but in some ways that's worse. I *want* it to touch mine. I want it like I want my next breath.

I edge my thigh closer and closer to hers. And I think she's doing the same, because the gap is definitely narrowing.

In a quiet moment, I hear her breathing.

It's ragged.

So is mine.

"Lucy," I say.

"Mmm-hmm?"

She turns to look at me.

I reach for her, sliding one hand behind her head, her silky ponytail slipping between my fingers, the smoothness of her hair against my palm. She makes a surprised needy sound that shoots straight to my balls. I cup the back of her head and guide her face to mine. Just before our lips touch, she whimpers, and I lose control. I let myself take her mouth, not gently. I plunder her. I lick into her. I slide my tongue against hers. And I consume all the little noises she makes, the hmmms and whimpers and pleas. She consumes me right back. Not at all restrained, not at all polished. Hungry and messy and real. Her hands are in my hair. On my face, curling around my ears, my jaw, insinuating themselves into the kiss itself, so I'm kissing her lips and sucking her fingers at the same time. She cries out when I do that, and my cock surges hard against the restraint of my jeans. I glide my fingertips down her throat, finding the vee of her shirt. I tug it down and slide a hand against the satin of her bare chest, still kissing her desperately.

She pulls away, breathless. "Oh my God. This is—crazy."

"Crazy—bad?"

"Crazy good."

We're both panting. Even in the mostly-dark, the flickering glow of the screen, I can see how red her lips are, soft and open, the bottom one still inviting me back.

"Lucy—"

I can tell she thinks I'm going to call a halt. She bites her lip and looks uncertain. I don't want to stop. But I want her to understand how it is in my world, so there aren't any misunderstandings.

"I've wanted you since that first night."

Something shines in her eyes in the flickering light thrown off by the TV screen.

"If I hadn't found out who you were, and if you'd let me, I would have fucked you."

A tiny sound escapes her parted lips.

"You okay with that word?"

She nods, big-eyed. She's more than okay with it, I realize.

"You like it."

"Yes," she whispers.

I file that away, my cock swelling hard where it's trapped against my fly. I hope I don't have to file it away for too long, because I love the idea of talking dirty to Lucy. I love the idea that Lucy, of the buttoned-up clothes and the neat hair and makeup, the smart plans and the rehearsed speeches, might fall apart to my words.

But I have this thing I need to say, still.

"I wanted to fuck you that night, but then I found out who you were, and it felt like it would be way too complicated. And I don't do complicated, and I don't do relationships."

"I don't either," she says. "I don't do either of those things. So that's good, right? We're in heated agreement on that point."

She reaches up, pulls out the ponytail, and for a hopeful moment, I think she's taking her hair down for me. Moving us forward. Then she wraps her hair in a tight bun and secures it with the elastic. Locking it down. Taking all the swerve out, all the possible mess.

She's shutting us down.

I was only trying to say that I still wanted her. To let her know that I could deal with a little bit of complicated if it meant getting to follow that insane, hungry kiss where it was leading us.

I'm not sure how much longer I can stand jerking off in the shower and craving her every minute of every day.

I want to reach out and yank the elastic out of her hair. Cup her head and lower my mouth over hers. Feel that wet heat and her fiery, needy response, go where it takes us. And I know where it would take us.

It would take us both there so fast, I'm not sure either of us would know what had hit us.

That thought finally snaps me back to rational thinking.

There's a reason I don't do complicated. I don't do relationships. I don't do this, this... out of control lust. I don't do anything except tourists who are leaving town in the next few days and women I've known for years, who want nothing from me and have just about that much of themselves to give. It's because the last time I did, I got my heart broken and it hurt worse than the one time I took buckshot in the bare calf—and for a hell of a lot longer. And I don't think any sex, no matter how good, is worth the risk of that again.

So what about Lucy makes me want to break those rules?

What about Lucy makes me want to argue with her? To tell her that this isn't crazy, it's the sanest thing I've done in years. To tell her it's not confusing, it's simple, the equation of wanting each other this bad. To tell her it's not complicated in the slightest: We just need to get it out of our systems.

I don't though. I don't argue. I lean back on the couch and let my breathing slow down. I let my erection, which was straining at my fly, subside. I let Robert Redford's Montana landscape and the peace and quiet of the river wash over me.

But I'm listening. To see how long it takes her breathing to slow down.

And I can't stop feeling her, warm and alive next to me.

Or smelling her. Her arousal, salty and beckoning and so, so much more real and fierce than all the florals that she wraps around herself.

I'm not watching the movie.

I don't think she is either.

I CORNER LUCY after work the following Tuesday. She hasn't been around as much the last few days. She finished asking us the questions she needed to ask, and she's been out and about, visiting the hot springs, spas, and wedding venues, and trying to get the lay of the land. Maybe gearing up for the next outdoor adventure we push on her.

I'm in awe of how thorough she is. She wasn't kidding when she said she wasn't going to make recommendations without understanding our business and the market first.

But right now I'm worried about another aspect of her research—Clark's survival trip, which we're joining this weekend. She still doesn't have the clothes she needs.

She's been re-breaking in Hanna's hikers since the fishing trip Friday, wearing them around the office. Which is hilarious, because she hasn't changed anything else about the way she dresses. Today she's wearing high waisted, slim-fitting cream-colored pants, a copper-colored tank top, and a cream blazer. The hikers are completely incongruous.

But scratch the word "hilarious," because there's actually nothing funny about Lucy's outfit today. She took her blazer off at lunch because Amanda's chili was blazing hot—temperature and spice-level—and we were all sweating. That left her shoulders and arms bare. The tank itself was just a scrap of silk. If you'd slipped those spaghetti straps off her shoulders, the whole thing would puddle at her waist. Or on the floor.

And, when she stood up to go to the restroom, I noted no panty lines under her cream-colored pants.

So of course I can't stop wondering: thong? Or nothing at all?

I set this question aside and tell her what's on my mind:

"We need to get you clothes for this weekend."

She raises her eyebrows, then looks down at her outfit. "I was planning to wear this."

"I wouldn't put it past you."

"I know you wouldn't." She grins at me, and I can't help it; I grin back.

"I'll drive you into town. You can get stuff at Krandall's."

"Sometimes, Gabe, we ask people what they want. Like, 'Lucy, would you like me to drive you into town? Krandall's is a great place to shop, if you're interested.'"

"Sometimes we do," I agree. "But in this situation, it's a safety issue. You need clothes that are going to protect you from the elements."

"In May."

People make this mistake all the time. "Closest I've ever come to dying was in May," I say. "People think it's safe because it's spring, but the nighttime temps are brutal, and you can always get wet or even just sweaty and bam, you're hypothermic."

This time, she doesn't gripe at me about how I'm not selling the trip well. She says, "Okay, let's not do that. I have no desire to get close to dying."

That decided, she follows me to the Jeep and we head into town.

As we approach the shops, she's gazing out the window and I wonder, again, what she sees. It's been a decade since I set foot in New York, and all I have left are vague impressions —speed, noise, smells, and steel-and-glass. We must seem slow as molasses to Lucy, with our one- and two-story buildings. And maybe a little old-fashioned, too, with the flower barrels and railed saloon porches and gas lamps.

"What do you think of Rush Creek?" I ask, without meaning to.

"Hmm," she says. "You know? I think I like it. And I like the old and the new. I know I'm an outsider, so I don't feel the history the way you do. But I like the rugged West meets lavender sachet vibe."

For some reason, that makes me smile.

In Krandall's I explain what she'll need: at least two base layers like the one Hanna lent her the other day, top and bottom, wool socks, a wool hat, wool gloves. "We've got enough outer layers between us to get you set for that. But you'll need a pair of hiking pants. Unless you want to wear those."

We both look down at those creamy slacks of hers. Our eyes meet on the return trip, and she looks away, but not before she blushes. I may have given away how hot I think she looks in that outfit.

I leave her to her shopping and strike up a conversation with Joe Kahn, Krandall's current owner. He's the guy who called to me the night Lucy and I were saving the ducklings, the one who asked who my friend was. He raises his eyebrows in her direction, but keeps his mouth shut on the subject. I ask him how business has been, both of us knowing I mean in the New Rush Creek.

He shrugs. "I'm getting used to it, man. It takes a while, but I'm figuring it out. Once upon a time you could outfit yourself for a real trip here. Now if I keep all that stuff in stock, I'll be out of business in ten minutes. People have to haul it to Bend and go to REI. But you can get yourself a hell of a bikini, and a variety of massage oils."

"Do you hate it?" I ask.

He shakes his head. "I like that there's more money coming in now than there was. More tourists, more tourists with money. And to be honest, I actually am enjoying the variety we can carry now. I was stubborn, Gabe. Took me too long to accept that things had changed. I almost lost the store."

I sigh. "Those words could be coming out of my mouth."

"Most any of ours here in town. That your girlfriend?" he asks, curious. Because even Joe Kahn, who's little more than a friendly acquaintance, knows "girlfriend" is not a Gabriel Wilder thing.

I explain about Lucy, and he says, "That so? I could use a chat with her."

"I'll let her know you're interested."

His gaze skirts me and settles. "Well, well, well," he murmurs.

"Shut it, Joe," I say, because friendly acquaintance or no, this is Lucy we're talking about. I turn to check her out.

Lucy, I learn, can make hiking pants look good. These ones are gathered up the side seams and snug in the ass and thighs. And she's wearing them with a cranberry-colored base-layer half-zip that is molded to her tits. Which would be heart-stopping under any circumstances, but I can see the lace of her bra through it, and something about that, about Lucy in lace and base, goes straight to my cock.

I push off from the front counter and stalk toward her.

She takes a quick step backward, and I wonder what exactly she sees. If the expression on my face contains half the hunger I feel for her. I follow her to the back of the store. The fitting rooms are behind a divider wall, and I chase her to where we're out of view of Joe.

"What?" she demands. "Do I look like a total poser?"

"You look fucking hot."

She giggles. Actually giggles.

"Jesus, Lucy, do I look like I'm kidding?"

She takes in my face, and then her gaze drops and she surveys the rest of me.

"No," she says quietly. "You don't."

I spin us into the fitting room, pull the door shut behind us, back her up against the wall, and kiss her. Her mouth is ready, willing, and eager, her tongue licking into my mouth and driving me wild. Her hands clutch at my hair, my clothes. She rubs herself against me, her sex hot through the hiking pants, against the thick muscle of my thigh, so, so good. She whimpers and pulls my head down, clutching me, pressing her breasts into my chest. I'm so hard it hurts, my cock throbbing against her belly. I drop a hand between her legs, cupping the heat, and she hikes her hips against it.

I could get her off like this. Here. In the dressing room. Watch her fall apart, practically in public.

Except I'm pretty sure she'd take me with her.

We pull apart at almost the same moment, stepping back. Eyes on each other's faces.

"God," she says. "We have almost no self-control when it comes to each other."

I like that she says it like that. Not a question and including both of us. We're in this together, and I like that she knows it.

"No," I agree. "We really don't."

She glances down at her clothes. "Well," she says. "I guess I'm buying the hiking pants."

23

LUCY

L ate that afternoon, I get a text from Gabe.

I'm making dinner. Want some?

I'd been about to order something for pickup, but hell, yes, I do want some. Some of whatever Gabe is cooking. Some of Gabe.

Some *answers*.

I hadn't gotten any in the car on the way back from Krandall's. He'd put on Alison Krauss and we'd enjoyed *Forget About It* together in silence. I think neither of us was willing to put words to what was going on, for fear we'd have to back away from it again.

I meant what I said last night, when I agreed with him about keeping things simple. After Darren said he was calling it quits, I realized I'm not cut out for relationships. Relationships are for people who know how to trust. They're for people who know how to open up and give back. I'm way better off sticking to casual sex and flings.

That said, I'm pretty sure the insane chemistry between

Gabe and me isn't going to disappear. I've never been as turned on in any public place as I was in the outdoor store fitting room. A big part of me wants to know what it would feel like not to stop. To slide right into that heat and tension.

And maybe I can?

There's an end date on whatever happens between me and Gabe. I'm only here for another two weeks. So as long as we keep it casual, it should be okay to enjoy what's happening.

As long as we keep it casual.

Yes, I text back.

Come over any time.

Buck practically knocks me over when I show up at the house. Luckily, I'm wearing dark jeans and not the cream-colored slacks I'd had on earlier, because Buck, even at his cleanest, tends to leave paw prints. I kneel and rub Buck thoroughly behind the ears, and he pants and rewards me with lots of licks that I have to dodge because I don't want him to ruin my makeup.

"Hey," Gabe says. He's standing over me, watching me. I know him well enough now to know that's not irritation on his face. He's just watching, the way he does, like a sheepdog at the top of a hill, surveying 360 degrees of territory. Like he's in charge of a big flock and has to make sure everyone's safe.

And now, somehow, I'm one of the flock... and it's scary how much I like the feeling.

"Hey," I say back, straightening up. I want to hug him, but I'm still a little afraid of what will happen if I do.

He leads me into the kitchen.

He's made steaks and baked potatoes and asparagus. Simple and delicious. I don't comment on the fact that he's clearly bought and cooked enough for two, even though he asked me to join him only a few minutes ago. We sit down to eat. Neither of us says anything. But he's looking at me in a way that makes my skin feel like it's on fire.

I am wound so tight from the way he kissed and touched me this afternoon, that look on his face is like fire held to a line of gunpowder. My breath is fast, light. I wonder if he can tell.

I think he probably can, because his eyes get darker.

Are we going to keep going like this? Drawn together like magnets, stepping over the line, then pulling back?

"Depot has a room for me starting tomorrow night," I say.

"You don't have to feel obliged to stay there. You can stay above the office as long as you need to."

"And shower here." I say it flatly.

"And shower here." His eyes—dark, hungry—search my face.

I lose patience, suddenly. It feels like too many days of game playing, too much pent-up frustration. "Gabe. We can't pretend nothing's happening."

"No," he says. Rough, definite. "We can't."

My heart is pounding. This is a line, too, and if we cross it, I don't think we can pull back.

"I think we want the same thing." This is still new to me, having to spell out the terms. I did it with Liam: *just tonight, nothing serious; I don't do serious.* For all the good it did me. Remembering the outcome of that night gives me a moment of pause. But this is different. Gabe isn't a stranger. And this has an expiration date, less than two weeks from now. I trust Gabe, as odd as that is to say. And I think maybe he trusts me.

We trust each other not to ask too much. To meet each

other's needs without becoming needy. After my relationship with Darren, I know what I can and can't promise. I can be good company. Great in bed. But not the kind of person who opens up emotionally. No promises there.

Gabe watches me, as intently as if he could hear the words forming in my head. I want to look away, but I can't, and my body heats in the flame of his gaze.

"I want—" he says. His voice is dark as coffee and twice as hot. "I want you moaning my name. I want you thrashing in my arms. I want you coming so hard you forget everything you ever thought mattered."

I make a shocked, small noise, and he's around the table, pulling me to my feet, taking me in his arms, supporting me as my knees give out at the heat of his body and the scent of his skin. I cling to him, and he kisses me, so fierce and deep and needy. I whimper, and he swallows it, and then my moan, too, his tongue sliding against mine, teasing my lips, sending tingles everywhere it touches. My breast is plumped up in his hand, my nipple between his fingers, his other hand sliding between my legs, and then up, finding the button and zipper of my jeans, undoing me. He slides that palm down, cupping me, and I groan and rub, trying to get traction, biting his lip because it's there and I need to bite something. He bites back and I squeak and he makes a dark, gravel sound in his chest that winds the tension in my belly even tighter. He feels so good against me, so muscly and hard, his thigh helping support me, thick and strong and pressing where I need him. His fingers work my clit, sliding down to tease and play with my wetness, easing his way, until everything feels slick and needy and I can't tell where his fingers leave off and I start.

Except I know the tingling clenching feeling is me, rising and spiraling, and I follow it, like a line to an unknown deep dark place, until I'm coming like he said, moaning his name, thrashing, so lost all I can feel is the tightness, the sparks, and the letting go.

24

GABE

I'm still holding her, because I don't trust her to stand. My knees are liquid from her climax. I can't even imagine what she feels.

I'm so hard it hurts, my balls drawn up tight.

"Lucy," I say hoarsely.

She drops, suddenly, and I try to catch her, but she's done it on purpose. She's on her knees. Reaching for my fly. She unbuttons and unzips me, frees me from my boxer briefs with a warm, soft hand. Then she's nuzzling me, velvet lips on my cock, opening to let me into her wet heat.

"I'm not going to last," I warn her.

She hums against me, her tongue circling. It feels like it's everywhere—around the head, down the shaft, twisting and twirling. "God, Lucy. Yes. God, yes."

She puts a hand on my hip, slides it around to my ass, and tugs me closer. And that's what does me in. "Lucy!" I try to pull back, but she won't let me, and I come in her mouth, hips jerking toward her as she finishes me off with long, draining pulls. She holds me there until I draw away, and then she looks up at me, licks her lips, and grins.

I drop to my knees and kiss her, deep. Her mouth is all soft and yielding, hungry.

"That was so good," I tell her.

Her grin gets even bigger. Her lips are bright red and slick. Messy. I know her pussy is messy, too, because I had my hand there a few minutes ago, and I know how wet she is.

Messy is so good on her.

What I really want right now is to scoop her up, carry her to my bedroom, and keep her there all night. But our dinners, mostly uneaten, are still on the table, and with one urge (temporarily) satisfied, I'm realizing how hungry I am.

I see the moment she spots our uneaten food, too, and starts to laugh. "Our steaks are probably cold."

"Worth it," I say.

"Totally," she agrees.

We zip and button ourselves and return to our seats. The steaks are cold, but still really good.

Although I realize I'm eating fast. Because I want to finish and kiss Lucy again. More than kiss her.

Which is when I remember a thing I forgot to do.

"You want to know something bad?"

"What's that?"

"I don't have condoms."

Her eyebrows go up. "You totally destroyed my image of you."

"What exactly was your image? I'm not Easton."

That makes her laugh. "No, I got that. But you're so—" She looks me up and down in a way I really like. "Hot. I assumed you got a lot of offers, and okay, this is a dumb stereotype, but I always figure guys mostly say yes when the opportunity arises."

"No complications," I remind her.

"Right. So that makes the pool smaller."

"Yup. I'm definitely not a monk, but I'm cautious."

She gets a look on her face like she wants to say something, but she doesn't.

"So the condoms ran out and I forgot to get more."

"See, that right there. How does a single guy in his thirties forget to get more condoms?"

"You want the truth?"

"Of course I want the truth." She takes a sip of wine.

"It got kind of boring."

Her mouth drops open. "Boring?"

"I had some friends with benefits, but no one I really had great chemistry with. And I hook up with people who are passing through, but hookups are super hit or miss."

"Amen to that," she says.

"Do you hook up?"

"Sure," she says. "When the opportunity arises." A shadow crosses her face.

I'm trying not to think too hard about Lucy hooking up with random guys. A big part of me wants this to be unusual for her, something she did because I'm different. Not her usual pattern of, I don't know, itch scratching, or whatever.

Because what I'm saying, very badly, with all this stuff about being bored, is that she *is* different for me. Not just an itch, even if it's short-term and keep-it-simple.

"Anyway," I say, knowing I'm not doing a good job, but not knowing how to fix it, "sometimes it's easier to DIY it."

She laughs. "You could show me that later. How you do that."

"I'll show you if you show me."

"Deal," she says. "And that's one of the nice things about not having condoms. Because you know what? Once we have sex, we'll have a lot of sex. So we should do all the other stuff first, so we don't miss anything."

I push my plate, cold steak and all, to one side. "One more thing."

"Mmm?" she teases.

"We should start as soon as possible."

M onday afternoon I'm at the Wilder barn, trying to wrangle ideas about how to diversify Brody's boat-based offerings.

It's not easy. My mind keeps going back to last night.

I was up late. In the best possible way. It's all Gabe's fault, and I have nothing but warm feelings on the subject. And stubble burn on my chin.

That man can kiss. And unlike many men I've been with, he likes doing it. A lot. I haven't made out that much with anyone in years.

Which means I'm thinking about it. Non-stop. Wondering if tonight, maybe, he'd be up for another round.

That's when Amanda appears at my shoulder. Breathless. Frantic.

"Lucy," she says. "I know you said no to modeling in the trashion show, but my model is in the hospital with a broken leg and I don't know who else to ask."

I start to gather excuses and denials.

And then, for reasons I will never totally understand, I say, "Sure."

I don't even really feel like I'm faking it this time.

"Oh, man, Lucy, I love you so much. You are a total lifesaver. It's at six. Can you meet me backstage at five to make sure the dress fits and I don't need to do any last-minute alterations?"

"Absolutely."

Which is how I find myself, less than two hours later, in a very small, curtained backstage area, surrounded by other women in equally crazy getups. I'm being very gently oiled with cooking oil so the cheese-bag dress will slide over my skin and not catch.

I try not to think about how much the operation reminds me of condoms and lube.

"Blow out your breath," Amanda says. She's already made a few tucks and other alterations, while I gaped in wonder at how fast she could sew.

I do as asked, and she fastens several hooks at my back. Then we both examine me in the mirror.

The dress is remarkably pretty for something with the Tillamook cheese logo all over it. If it were made of blue fabric, I'd want one. It's made of cheese bags stitched together, like a quilt. It nips in at the waist and fits like a (plastic) glove over my hips and butt. And Amanda's right about my boob situation. The dress has straps, but the bodice is generous. I have to admit, I've worn designer dresses that didn't flatter my breasts as much as this one does.

"You are a woman of many talents," I tell her.

"And you look hot in my dress," she says. "Gabe is going to lose his ever-loving *mind*."

Startled, I turn to look at her.

"Oh, hon," she says. "I knew the second he showed up at drinks the other night. That man doesn't come anywhere near an open-ended social gathering without good reason. And then when he told me he was going to be *at the trashion show* tonight? I was like, either he's the fourth horseman of the apocalypse, or he's caught feelings."

"It's just—we're just—" I try not to think too hard about the idea of Gabe Wilder catching feelings for me, because I might like the idea way too much. "I'm going back to New York in a week and a half. It's just a fling."

Her eyes flicker to mine, then away, and I see the small sigh. "I know," she says. "But you can't blame me for getting my hopes up. At least that someone would talk him into buying a coffee table."

I think of the bare living room and my sense that there was a story behind it.

"Yeah, so, what's up with the sold-all-his-possessions look?"

She sighs. "He did, literally. Or gave it away, mostly. After Cecilia left."

"Cecilia?"

"His ex-girlfriend."

She gives me a look, like she's appraising me. Deciding if I need to know this story, if I can be trusted to know it. Then she pulls me away from the fray, to a corner of the backstage area, and tells me.

"She was here taking care of her aunt, who was dying. It was always going to be temporary. She was going to stay to sell the house and then she was going back to Chicago. Gabe knew it. We all knew it. And it was like watching a slow motion train wreck, him falling for her anyway."

She watches me for a moment, that appraising look again. "I think you probably know by now that Gabe isn't someone who falls easily or gets over it quickly."

I nod.

"She kept telling him it was temporary. He kept doing everything in his power to convince her to stay. He let her decorate the house. Even then, she kept saying, *As long as you know this isn't because I've changed my mind about staying.* She told him every way she knew how that she couldn't stay. In the end, she left, like she'd said she would. She did ask him to go with her. But he wouldn't. Because of Wilder. Because of us.

"After she left, he tore out everything she'd done. He left the furniture, but he got rid of the rugs and the pillows, the posters and art and stuff. Sold it. Actually, mostly, gave it away."

My heart hurts, thinking of Gabe in that house, systematically tearing Cecilia out of it. Like Amanda said, it's almost impossible to imagine Gabe, Mr. Hyper Competent, Hyper In-Charge, letting himself fall like that.

For a moment, I'm jealous of Cecilia, and furious with her for not understanding what she had.

Amanda looks down at her watch. "Oh, man, time to line up."

I insert myself between someone whose mermaid dress is made of white plastic mailing envelopes and someone wearing a loose jumper made of bubble wrap and fashion magazines. The dresses are amazing. I'm in awe of the inventiveness and talent that goes into them.

I try not to think about the fact that in a minute, I'm going to have to walk down a makeshift runway in front of most of the town of Rush Creek, old and new. Amanda says the trashion show draws more audience than almost any other spring festival event.

"Did you make yours?" I ask the woman in the mermaid dress.

She nods. "This is my third year."

"Carina's dress last year was made of pages torn out of books discarded by the library," Amanda says from behind me. "It won first prize."

"There's a photo on the website if you want to see it," Carina says. And then it's her turn, and she disappears between two curtains. I can hear the applause. My heart is pounding.

"And, *go*," Amanda says, and I'm promenading down the middle of the aisle between two sets of chairs, showing off her creation.

There's lots of applause, and some hoots and whistles. I take my turn across the stage and then it's over.

"You look stunning," a familiar male voice says, rumbling with amusement.

"Are you mocking the cheese bags?" I murmur, as he dips his head to brush his lips against my ear, my neck, and then a small, sensitive bit of bare shoulder.

"I might be," he says. "Or I might be admiring the way you wear them." His eyes move slowly, appraisingly, over the exposed tops of my breasts. My breathing speeds up, just from that.

"Do you want me to show you around the festival?"

"Be still my beating heart," Amanda says, appearing from

nowhere and giving her brother a curious look. "Gabe Wilder, enjoying the spring festival. Will wonders never cease?"

"I go to the spring festival," he protests.

"What, when you were twelve? C'mon, Luce, let's get you out of that thing and I'll turn you over to Gabe for the evening."

We make the rounds of the crafts booths together. Lucy treats every booth, no matter how heinous, as if it deserves her full attention and respect. She touches the crafts, oohs and ahhs over them, and asks their creators to talk about methods.

And Rush Creek's craftspeople and artists are *more* than happy to talk. She learns about some art techniques, scumbling and alla prima, from Tricia Spooner, wet collodion process from a photographer I don't recognize, and Scandinavian flat-plane wood carving from Bob Woe. But she spends the most time with Kiona from Five Rivers Arts & Crafts, listening to her talk about how she achieved her weaving techniques—and about the importance of buying Native designs only from Native artists.

I half listen while I stand in front of a woven wall hanging. It's a geometric design, a series of strips of individual patterns, pale greens and mustard yellows and cream, and for some reason I can't stop looking at it.

I want it.

I put my hand on my back pocket, touch my wallet.

And then I remember that the last time anyone hung anything on the walls in my house, it was Cecilia, and I get a small shock of pain.

I don't think about Cecilia very often, because when I do, I still feel all the same hurt and loss. And anger, at myself, for deluding myself into thinking that even though her words told me she was leaving, she might stay.

I will never make that mistake again.

Lucy has pulled out a credit card to buy a small basket from Kiona. She says she's going to put it in her new office, when she starts her own business. She says it will remind her about the importance of integrity and being true to herself and her clients.

Kiona, who is normally reserved, comes out from behind the table and hugs Lucy.

"I love Lucy," she tells me.

Everyone loves Lucy, I think, but I don't say it out loud. Instead, I make a note to myself to ask Lucy later about this new business of hers. This is the first I've heard of it.

Then I drag her off to the music-and-wine bop.

The bop is a tour of the town's restaurants—really, the whole Five Rivers region's restaurants—but we're on foot and doing the Rush Creek thing right now. So we go from Royal Pizza to Casa del Oro to Jane's, a bistro-style fine-dining restaurant. At each location, there's a different Oregon wine and a different local band.

Everywhere we go, the food smells are mouth-watering— peppery grilled meats and garlicky wood-fired crust pizza, fresh-fried crisp corn tortillas, burnt sugar.

We drink a lot of wine, and somewhere around the third glass, Lucy wants to dance.

So we dance.

We dance to a talented bluegrass trio, and then to a not-so-talented blues band, and then to a really, really bad classic rock five-piece. Lucy is a great dancer. She kicks off her heels and lights it up. She is flushed, her hair still up from the trashion show, but bits and pieces curling around her face like the first time she came to shower at my house. Like she's coming undone bit by bit. Like Rush Creek is softening her up and having its way with her.

We end up at Oscar's with pretty much everyone else I know. Amanda and her husband, Heath, are there, so I'm guessing the kids are with my mom. Hanna's there, throwing darts with Kane and Easton. Clark's there, drinking by himself at the bar. The only one I don't see is Brody.

I'm suddenly conscious of how much I've had to drink. How much Lucy's drunk. I still want to pull her into my arms and dance with her. There's a good roots group playing, and I know she likes the music because she's swaying to it as we stand near Amanda and Heath and work our ways through yet another glass of wine. But if we dance again now, my siblings and everyone will make something of it.

And it's not *something*.

It can't be.

So we chat with Amanda and Heath, play a few rounds of darts with Hanna, Kane, and Easton—spoiler alert, Lucy *sucks* at darts—and join Clark for a few minutes, although he barely acknowledges our existences.

And then just like that, it's last call.

"Do you have a ride home?" I ask her.

She nods.

I almost say, *Do you want to stay at my place tonight?*

It should be no big deal.

But for some reason, it feels like it would be, so I keep quiet and watch her head to Amanda's car, wishing like hell I'd let the words out of my mouth so I could mess up her hair the rest of the way.

Two miles into Clark's survival trip, on a vicious uphill, I am very, very tired. My hips and shoulders are killing me. And I am sweating in places I didn't even know I had sweat glands.

Also, I have just discovered I am totally in over my head.

"Wait," I say. "Say that part again. About how if it rains..."

"If it rains," Gabe says patiently, "we will be very wet all night."

He's behind me on the trail.

"Because..."

"Because we are sleeping in shelters that we make ourselves, and they're not watertight. But you know, Lucy, even if we were sleeping in a tent, if it rained hard enough, we'd get wet."

You know how you can agree to something, because it's kind of vague and abstract, but then when you get close to it, you realize what you've agreed to?

Yeah, that's Clark's trip.

"This isn't, like, hard core," Gabe says. "Clark does hard-core trips, too. He does several week-long trips where he gradually weans people off all their gear until they can operate with only the clothes on their backs and a knife."

I stumble and almost topple onto my ass. Gabe grabs my pack and steadies me from behind.

"Only the clothes... and a knife..."

The words come out gasp-y, because I haven't been able to completely catch my breath since we started the very-much-uphill portion of today's hike. Despite being in pretty decent shape.

Apparently, it's different with forty pounds on your back.

"That's not what this is, Lucy. This is more of a beginner's guide to surviving."

"That sounds like an oxymoron. Like, you need to have enough expertise to survive, right? Or you'll die?"

I'm trying not to sound as panicky as I feel.

Still patient, and now—I'm pretty sure—trying very hard not to laugh, Gabe says, "No one is dying. There's nothing remotely risky about this trip. We're going to get to the campsite, and then Clark is going to teach us essentials. Basic wilderness first aid, the psychology of survival..."

"There's a psychology to it?"

"Yes," Gabe says, very, very dryly. "Not panicking."

I take the deepest breath I can manage, step in a puddle, and splash mud all over myself. I groan.

"Oh, Lucy," Gabe says, definitely trying not to laugh. "Take my word for it; this is the cleanest you'll be for the next two days."

"That's what I was afraid of," I whisper. "No shower tent, huh?"

"What is a shower tent?" Gabe asks, like he's afraid of the answer.

"I've been doing some research," I say, "and there are shower tents. And privy tents. I'm thinking that maybe when Clark does glamping trips, he can add those."

There is a deafening silence from behind me. I don't dare turn around, not because I'm afraid of Gabe's reaction, but because if I quit watching the ground in front of me for even a second, I'll go down. Or more likely, heels over backpack over head.

"I want to be there," Gabe says finally, "when you raise that idea with Clark. I want to see his face."

"You don't think he'll like it?"

"I'm going to assume you're messing with me. Because that's the simplest explanation."

I decide that now is not a good moment to defend my case for toilet and shower tents. "Okay, so what else, besides wilderness first aid and *not panicking*?" I try to make it funny, like *who would do that???* but it comes out nervous.

Gabe, maybe out of self-preservation, doesn't tease me. "Staying warm," he says. "The first step of which is building shelters, then making fires without matches. And heating a shelter without creating a fire risk. Then water."

"Water," I repeat. I put my hand to the side of my pack, where there is one more quart-sized bottle full of clean water.

"How to find water sources and purify them."

"I mean, doesn't the campsite have running water?"

Gabe snorts. Loudly. "The campsite is a few flat spots in the woods where people have set up tents in the past. It doesn't have anything else, except maybe a small piece of litter that someone has forgotten to pack out."

"But there's a stream, or something, right?"

Gabe takes pity on me with a big sigh. "There's a stream about a quarter mile away. Clark doesn't draw attention to it because he wants us to be resourceful and find other sources. You'll see. He'll show you how to collect dew and rainwater and how to dig a very simple well. And then tomorrow he'll cover foraging for food. And some rudimentary fishing and trapping. But the truth is, in a short-term survival situation, it's more important to conserve energy than it is to look for food. Because you'll be rescued before you can starve. It's only if you're stranded for a longer period of time that you'll need to make food-finding a priority."

I make a small sound of distress.

"Stick with me, Lucy," Gabe says, all open amusement now. "And you won't need to worry about any of this."

CLARK ROVES the area where we've set up camp, checking on all of us as we build shelters from fallen tree debris.

I'm still working on finding two branches that will stand up and make the A of my A-frame. So far, I've toppled several pairs. I cross my arms as another duo falls.

Clark eyes my progress. "May I make a suggestion?"

"Sure," I say.

"I think you need a bigger notch here. To support the other branch. Look for something with more of a real 'Y' shape."

I go looking. My feet are killing me. My back hurts from bending over.

I'm several hundred yards from the main campsite when I

stumble into a second clearing, where Gabe is building his shelter. And all at once, I'm not tired at all. Because:

Gah, look at him.

Gabe is as competent at survival as he is at everything else he does.

I stop behind a tree and watch, hoping I don't get caught shamelessly engaging in outdoor adventure porn.

It turns out that a big man in a form-fitting base layer and hiking pants, with a day's scruff, is my jam. Every muscle in his back, shoulders, and arms flexes under the thin shirt—including the eight-pack abs. The hiking pants are loose except where they cup his perfect ass and stretch over his solid thighs whenever he squats.

Also, his shelter is almost done. And it looks like a small cabin. Okay, I'm exaggerating, but seriously: This guy has built a shelter big enough for two.

Which might come in handy later, especially if I don't get my act together.

Gabe turns around and catches me looking, raising his eyebrows and smirking at me. "How's yours coming?"

"Mmm," I say. "I'm still trying to master the fine art of finding two branches."

He chuckles. "Let me know if you need help."

"Pride won't let me accept your help."

"Pride goeth before a long, wet night."

I look at the sky, panicked—and then back at Gabe, who's laughing.

"There's no rain forecast, is there."

"Nope," he says.

"Bastard." I punch his arm. I punch it again, because *so satisfying!* And then I wrap my hand around it and squeeze.

"Your shelter looks cozy, Big Man," I say, and watch, amused, as Gabe's eyes go dark.

"If you're really nice to me, I might let you share it."

"If you're really nice to me, I might accept your offer."

I squeeze his arm one more time, for research. Then I resume my search and manage to find two branches that lean against each other and support the weight of the main spine of my shelter. I start collecting sticks and branches to line the sides.

My shelter is not the only troubled one. There are three men with us on the trip, and the one who I thought would turn out to be a pro, a big beast of a dude named Iggy, wearing flannels and sporting a beard, turns out to flail even worse than I do. We commiserate on the difficulty of getting leaves to cover the outside of the shelter without them falling through. He admits to never having camped a day in his life, and explains that he woke up one morning and decided that he wanted to start doing things that scared the shit out of him. He asks if I have a similar story.

I explain that I'm here to do research so I can help the guys tailor trips to bring in new customers.

He suggests Clark reduce the first day's hike from five miles to three.

"I had that exact thought," I tell him, "right around mile one."

We share a rueful laugh.

I catch Gabe frowning at us and decide I like it way too much.

When we're done with shelters, we move on to water. With Clark's instructions, I do my best to craft two different water-collecting devices from tarp, rope, and my water bottle, but my knots never quite... knot. And my tarps don't sag in the places they're supposed to sag.

I hope Clark's dew-collection strategy, which we'll practice in the morning, works out better for me.

Gabe saunters over. "How's it going, City Girl?"

"Mock me at your own peril, Mountain Man. If you ever visit New York, I'll find ways to make your life miserable."

As soon as the words are out of my mouth, I regret them. Partly because they contain a big assumption I'm embarrassed to have made: that Gabe would ever visit New York, and that if he did, he would look me up. But mostly because they remind me that I'm going back to New York, and all this... hotness... with Gabe will be over almost before it starts.

Gabe watches me quietly. Then he reaches over me, takes two rope ends out of my hand, and knots them with neat, efficient movements.

Damn.

This is a man who could tie me to a bed in three seconds flat. Which is not even a thing anyone has ever done to me. I've never wanted anyone to.

But right now, Gabe's body is surrounding mine, big and hard and hot at my back, and unless I'm very much mistaken, he's as happy to be there as I am to have him there.

I have to resist the urge to press my wrists together and put myself at his mercy.

I 've been giving Lucy a hard time, but the truth is, she's
doing great. She's a fish out of water, but she never
balks at anything that needs to be done, in or out of the
woods.

Right now, she's doing her damnedest to start a fire using
flint and steel, and even though she's probably struck them
together a hundred times without success, she's still doggedly
trying. Everyone else has a passable fire going, even the ironi-
cally bearded Iggy.

I kneel beside her and hold out my hands.

"I will never live this down, will I?" she asks.

"Probably not."

Clark calls from the other side of the clearing. "Luce. You
want to try one of the drills?"

Clark fashioned two drills, a hand-drill and a bow drill, to
demonstrate how rubbing wood inside a groove can start a
fire. He brings them over to where Lucy is crouched, shoulders slumped, and offers them to her.

"You want me to demonstrate again?" he asks.

"I got this," I tell him.

He cocks his head, considering me. I give him a *shut the hell up* brotherly look. He retreats, smirking.

Yeah, I know. I don't usually act this way around women. Any women. And I know I'm going to hear about it later.

But I can't stay away from Lucy. Like earlier, when I saw her struggling with the water collecting. I'm a fixer—it's who I am. And those knots needed fixing.

It was a bonus that I got to wrap my body around hers.

Double bonus that she wriggled herself back against me, just a little bit. Like we were both trying to pretend it wasn't happening.

She got away with the pretending a hell of a lot better than I did.

Here I am again, Mr. Fixer, with the fire-starter.

I still have ulterior motives, too. Not gonna lie. I like being her hero—I have since that first day with the ducks. Sometimes, like when I was cooking fish the other night, or when I was building my shelter earlier, I catch her watching me. With wonder in her eyes.

I've had women look at me that way before. But it's different with her. Having someone I admire so much look at me like that cracks me open.

I feel like I'd do almost anything for that look in her eyes.

Plus, I like to mess with her.

"So, look, you want to put the drill rod in the opening, here—" I murmur. "And then apply just the right amount of pressure."

I meet her eyes. They're wide. Her cheeks are pink, too.

"You're doing that on purpose."

"Of course I'm doing it on purpose. I'm making a point. It's all about the friction. And the technique."

"Gabe," she grumbles, but she traps her soft lower lip between her teeth, and her breath is quick.

"All that rubbing," I murmur.

I watch the flush cover her throat, and hope the way I'm squatting conceals my raging erection.

"What's basically happening here is that the two pieces of wood stop knowing where one ends and the other starts. Their molecules mix. And that's combustion. Heat. Flame."

On that note, the wood smolders and I tease it to life with my breath, adding tinder, fanning the flames.

Of course, I narrate what I'm doing, too, checking to make sure she's with me.

The flush, and the way she's torturing that soft lip, tells me she is.

"What did I say?" I tell her. "Stick with me, and you'll be just fine."

"Or dead from sexual frustration," she mutters.

I grin. "Stay patient, baby."

"You know I only brought one change of underpants, right?"

"I can't help it if you underestimated me," I tell her.

She turns a shade pinker, and I get to test out how hard it's possible to become without being touched.

CLARK HAS DEMONSTRATED a variety of open-fire cooking techniques. Because this is a short trip and there isn't enough time to cover everything, he packs in food, so dinner is way more satisfying than on most camping trips. We've stuffed ourselves on meat, rice and beans, and vegetables, and people are relaxing around the fire, two of the guys swigging from flasks they've brought with them, against Clark's explicit instructions.

Alcohol is an enemy to wilderness survival. But on the short trips Clark doesn't make a big deal about it, because no one is going to die of dehydration or heat loss from enjoying a nip around the campfire. He does give them a lecture though, and one of the guys tucks the flask away. The other one shrugs and keeps drinking.

After a while Iggy goes and stows himself away in the shelter he built. It's more of a bird's nest than a shelter, and he almost knocks it down getting into it, but it's not a huge deal on a warm, dry night like tonight, so Clark and I give each other an eyebrow and let it go.

Not too long after that, the drinkers retire to their respective A-frames.

Clark gets up and goes to his shelter. To challenge himself, he made a circular shelter, which is a little more advanced than the campers' set-ups. He disappears into it, and I have Lucy to myself.

She gets up and walks toward her pack.

"Where are you going?"

"I brought a surprise."

"What kind of surprise?"

She pulls s'mores fixings from her pack. Half a chocolate bar, a handful of graham crackers protected by a small, square Tupperware box, and a Ziploc bag with some pretty seriously squished marshmallows. My first impulse is to chastise her for wasting space. My second is to start hunting for sticks.

"I brought cocoa, too, for tomorrow morning," she says. "S'mores and cocoa are about to become an integral part of your marketing."

I roll my eyes. "Does this look like a s'mores and cocoa kind of trip?"

"It does now," she says, watching as I sharpen a stick and hand it to her. I like the way her eyes follow my hands and then flash to my forearms, my upper arms, and my shoulders, trailing down my torso. I like her looking at me. "Are you good at everything?" she demands.

"No," I say. "Just the things I need to be good at for my job."

"And rescuing ducks. And running a company. And kissing."

"Mmm," I say, leaning over and obliging her.

A throat clears behind us.

"Hi, Clark," Lucy says.

His eyebrows are in his hairline.

"Forgot my fleece," he says with a smirk, retrieving his shirt. "All makes sense now, though. Why you had to be on all the trips. Why Easton says you've been jumping down his throat."

"Shut it, Clark."

Clark's grin gets even bigger. "Just sayin'."

When he leaves us alone again, I give Lucy a sheepish look. "Sorry. Brothers. He's giving me shit because—" I stop myself. I don't need to get all confessional about this.

But she's waiting for me to finish now, and I discover I

want to. "He's giving me shit because I don't usually get like this. Possessive."

"You don't?"

I shake my head. "Nope. I want you all to myself. Long as I can have you."

Her expression gets soft. "You've got me," she says. "For the next two weeks." She wrinkles her nose. "Week and a half."

Suddenly, that feels like not enough time.

I set the marshmallow sticks down and use a couple of shovels full of dirt to put out the fire.

"What are you—?"

I swoop her up and carry her back to my shelter.

"Cave man!" she accuses in a whisper.

"Guilty as charged."

Anticipating this moment, I laid out my sleeping bag earlier. I slide her onto it and lower myself over her. She opens her thighs and I settle myself between them, feeling the heat and softness of her through the thin hiking pants.

"These are the clean underpants," she whisper-wails.

"Not anymore."

LUCY

I'm breathless, pinned between the firm ground and his equally hard body. He smells like wood smoke and pine, and the pressure, the friction, is so good. I whimper as he works his erection over my sex. The layers of fabric whisper back and forth across each other, conducting sensation. I moan, and he laughs and covers my mouth. I bite his hand and he bucks, thrusting against me. Heat surges through me and for a second I think I'm going to come, but then the sensation sinks back down, banking itself.

It's there, though. He could push me over the edge so easily.

He helps me out of my shirt and sports bra. There's a lot of rustling and giggling involved. I'm now very glad that he built his shelter at a distance from the main site.

"I wish I could see you," he says. "I'm going to grope you a lot to make up for it." And he does, his hands on my breasts, shaping me, plumping me, thumbs finding and fondling my nipples. His mouth follows his hands, and another wave of heat takes me up against my cliff.

I don't know how he knows, but he does. "Not yet," he says. "You wait for me."

"I don't know if I can."

"You will."

"Don't touch my nipples, then."

"Really? They're that sensitive?" He sounds totally amped, like he just discovered you can make fire with matches. No more bow and hand drills and flint and steel! Instant, phosphorous conflagration! "Could you come from that? Just my touching them?"

"I mean, when I'm already this close and you're between my legs like that, yes."

"So what you're saying is..." He ducks a head and licks a circle around my nipple. Not touching it. "This is basically torture."

"Mmm-hmm. The best kind of torture."

"So, like, if I—" He hikes his hips, and the stretch and pressure is so, so good. I can feel the breaking point, like a horizon.

"If you keep doing that, yup."

"Then I should probably stop."

"Gabe," I plead.

He props himself next to me—there's just enough space in this brilliant shelter for the two of us side by side—and works his base layer off. Then his pants.

"You smell so good," I tell him. Like aftershave and the woods and honest work and camping soap, which is not a thing I ever thought would be an aphrodisiac, but that was before I met Gabe.

"You, too," he says, nose in my hair, then my neck, then between my breasts. Gah. I want him on my nipple again. I grab his head to try to steer him, but he resists, chuckling. I palm him through his boxer briefs, hoping to entice. He presses into my palm.

"Can you take these off?"

He nods, and does, crawling over me, stroking the velvet skin gently over my inner thigh, then right along the seam of my sex so I feel the friction through my lips and on my clit. I whimper, and he does it again, nudging my clit with his cock's head.

Suddenly I can't wait.

"Gabe. Please."

"Please what?"

"I want you inside me."

"Can't," he says, with satisfaction.

"What?"

"I bought condoms, but I left them home. On purpose."

"Please tell me you're full of it."

"Nope. You said it was more fun waiting."

I groan. "I lied."

He's working himself on me, against the soft skin of my inner thigh, against my slick pussy, nudging my clit over and over again. The orgasm is gathering itself with the inevitability of an oncoming train. I'm totally helpless. I pull his head down, wanting his mouth on mine, and kiss him, hard and openmouthed, our tongues tangling, soft and silky. He slides his hand up over my breast and works my nipple between his thumb and forefinger, and it's just right and too much, at the same time. I come in slow motion, my climax tightening down and rolling over me, rocking my hips, making every muscle in my lower body clench.

He gives a rough cry, props himself up on one arm, and

strokes his cock until he comes all over my belly and chest. The moonlight illuminates the show: long, pretty ropes. His whole body tenses, every muscle in his torso beautiful in high definition. My pussy musters a few last sympathetic spasms.

Suddenly I'm laughing.

"Really, Gabriel Wilder?"

He's still speechless, lowering himself onto his side next to me, resting his forehead against mine, breathing hard, stroking my hair.

"We're in the middle of fucking nowhere with only the water in our water bottles, and you decided it would be a good idea to come all over me?"

"Are you mad?" he asks, sounding as uncertain as I've ever heard him.

"Are you kidding me? That was so fucking hot."

His grin lights up the shelter.

He cleans me up, using his boxer briefs, then settles back down. He lies down on his back and pulls me half onto him, urging me to rest my head in the crook of his shoulder. We're officially cuddling. I know without being told that it has been a long time since Gabe cuddled anyone, but I don't say anything, because I don't want to scare him.

Or myself.

A couple times a month we all cook together as a family—or family plus, depending on who shows up. We use my house because it's the biggest and everyone wants to get in on the cooking action.

A few days after the survival trip, it's my mom's birthday, so even though it's midweek, we all get together.

Amanda always shows up first with her husband, Heath, and the three kids, Anna, who's nine, Noah, who's six, and Kieran, who's three. "Uncle Gabe!" Anna says, throwing both arms around me.

Noah and Kieran, who worship their big sister, follow suit. I bend down so I can give them all quality hugs, then swoop Kieran up for belly kisses, because he's still little and chubby enough.

Brody shows up soon after—no baby Justin with him, I note regretfully—with Kane and Hanna in tow. Sometimes Connor and Rachel and their parents, Maria and Antonio, join us, and we cook Cuban food—lechón asado, rice and beans, tostones. Those are some of my favorite nights. But the

Perezes are on Maria's birthday ski trip, the one Connor said Rachel was visiting for, so we planned on Italian instead. A big pot of my mom's meat sauce recipe, lots and lots of spaghetti, garlic bread, and tons of green salad. My mouth is already watering.

Easton's next, and then finally, my mom, with Clark as her chauffeur.

Amanda's phone pings, and she pulls it out. "Oh, good," she says. "Lucy's on her way."

"Wait, what?" I ask. "I asked her if she wanted to come and she said no."

"Well, yeah, of course she did," Amanda says. "She's shy. But I wore her down. I said we'd go easy on her. We will, won't we?"

"Of course," my mom says.

But my brothers are all staring at me. "Say that again," Kane says. "The part where you asked her if she wanted to come to family dinner."

"If I didn't, she'd be sitting over there in the dark while we all partied it up over here."

"So Gabe was just extending Wilder hospitality," Easton says, smirking.

Clark, who is supposed to be my kind, level-headed brother, says, "Like Saturday night."

They all turn to look at me.

"She needed a place to sleep," Clark says innocently. "He invited her right into his shelter."

You never see the family resemblance as much as when they all have their mouths hanging open.

"Oh, *man*," Brody says. "That makes so much more sense. Why you let her wipe her mouth on your sweatshirt. You're fu

—" Brody looks up, sees Mom staring at him, and rethinks his word choice— "*sleeping* with her."

"None of us blame you," Easton says, shrugging. "She's smokin'.'"

"Lay the fuck off," I say tightly.

The gazes on me narrow visibly.

My mother clears her throat. Easton snickers.

"You *like* her." That's Amanda, her voice gentle. "Like, actually *like* her."

No one says anything after that. They're all staring at me like Amanda has dropped an actual bomb. And they should be surprised. They know my pattern. Nothing with stakes. Nothing with a future. Fucking the hottie who's in town for three weeks? No big deal. But telling my brothers to fuck off talking about her?

I get why they're surprised.

I'm surprised.

And more than a little freaked out.

"Hello?" Lucy calls out from the front hall, and we all freeze.

My mom breaks the paralysis. "Come in!"

Lucy comes into the kitchen, looking spectacularly Lucy-ish. Wearing a pair of khaki pants that are loose everywhere except over her curves, with a black t-shirt that has ruffly sleeves. It should be ridiculous. But it's flirty and adorable. And her hair is in those sleek curls that make me want to touch. She greets everyone, meets Heath and the kids, and compliments Hanna on her beanie. Hanna looks—shockingly—flattered.

"Gabe, if you brown meat, I'll chop onions," Kane says. He and Amanda usually mastermind the cooking. The two of them are pretty tight, I think because Amanda's the only girl and Kane's—well, Kane is Kane. I've never asked him, but sometimes I wonder if he feels like he was born into the wrong family. I think he might have been happier as a professor or an artist or something.

"What can I do?" Lucy asks.

Kane hands her a jar of beef base, a Pyrex measuring cup, and a pot. "I need nine cups of beef broth."

Lucy doesn't hesitate. She studies the instructions on the jar, fills the pot, asks me for a set of measuring spoons. When she's done, my mom puts her to work on salad fixings. I start on the garlic bread, mashing garlic and butter into a paste. We're side by side at the kitchen island, not close enough for me to feel her heat, but definitely close enough that my whole body's on high alert. Closer than two friends working at a counter. Almost like a couple.

And I like it.

Way too much.

See: What happens to Gabe Wilder when he starts to hope a woman will change her mind about leaving.

When the salad's done, she crouches on the floor, where the kids are trying to convince Buck to fetch one of his chew toys, a stuffed lamb with a squeaker. They toss it and yell *fetch, Buck!* He slouches over to it, lies down, and begins gnawing. Rinse and repeat.

"Let me try." She wrestles the toy from Buck, holding it gingerly away from her clothes. I watch her, amused.

She gets the same results as the kids, which they find hilarious. Then she starts hamming it up for them.

"Buck, please," she says. "I'm begging you. Fetch. Just this once. Pretty please. With sugar on top. With *kibble* on top. Extra meaty kibble."

The kids giggle and take up the game, inventing all sorts of dog-friendly things that could be heaped on top of the *please*. Dog treats in the shape of cats. Bully sticks. Milk bones.

"Now, Buck," Lucy says, in a teacher-y voice that makes me want to mess up her curls and peel her out of the ruffles. "You and I talked about this last week. Remember? We made a sticker chart, and I said I'd give you a gold star every time you followed instructions. But if you can't fetch when I say fetch, I'm going to have to put you in the naughty corner."

"Naughty corner! Naughty corner!" Noah chants.

For some obscure reason, Buck chooses that moment to bring the damp lamb to her and drop it in her lap. For a second, I expect her to freak out, but she doesn't. In fact, she grabs Buck around the neck, draws him close, and gives him a big smacker on the nose.

The kids are in heaven, and in a moment, they're all piled on. And Lucy, far from looking like she wants to escape, is grinning ear to ear.

My mom catches my eye and raises an eyebrow. Not at Lucy's behavior, but at the fact that I'm standing at the kitchen island, paused in my preparations to watch her. I turn away.

It makes no sense that Lucy, an overdressed city girl with nothing good to say about the outdoors or small towns, would seem to fit right into the Wilder family dinner, but there you have it.

I make my mom get mani-pedis with me. For research.

"How is this research again?" she asks. We're at Glory Day Spa, sitting side-by-side in massage chairs with our feet oiled up and wrapped in hot socks, and we're both blissed out. The aesthetician, Kathy, left us alone with stacks of magazines and cups of tea.

"I have to think like a woman on a spa weekend in order to get myself in the right mindset to make a marketing plan."

My mother—my own mother!—rolls her eyes at me. "Do you get to expense it?"

I think about that for a second. "I'm gonna guess the IRS would get persnickety about that. But I like the way you think."

"So, any insights?"

"Only that I need to do this more often," I say, with a deep, satisfied sigh. In all fairness, I have spent the last few days scoping out the town's new spas, gift stores, and wedding venues, looking for ideas about how Wilder can target its new audience. And I have some great ideas, including pretty postcards at registers advertising couples' and girls' trips "under the stars," "on the peaceful lake," "in nature," and so on. All, of course, with plenty of amenities and perks.

"I do need to figure out how to break it to the Wilder brothers that I need about two hundred percent more photographs of them on the website and social media."

"They do seem like they'd be a selling point for girls' nights out," my mother muses.

"Maybe not so much for couple getaways."

"I am sure you can segment the marketing."

I grin at her. "You've always had so much faith in me."

She turns to look at me with a mother's critical—and way too observant—gaze. "You seem... happy," she says. "If I didn't know any better, I'd say you like it here."

"I don't hate it here," I admit.

I more than don't hate a certain Wilder brother, but I don't say that. If I tell my mother about things between Gabe and me, she'll make more of it than is warranted, I'm sure of it.

"Lucy," she says.

Damn it, I know that tone of voice. It's the opening note in a mom lecture, and I'm powerless in the face of those.

"I've never thought you seemed happy in New York. Or in that job. You seem a lot more... lighthearted... than I've seen you since your father..."

She lets it dangle there. She doesn't like to say it.

"Went to prison," I finish for her. Quietly, because even though I hate that she can't even say it out loud, I don't want to be overheard. I know Rush Creek well enough by now to know how fast gossip like that would spread.

"He destroyed your sense of trust," my mom says sadly.

"Don't," I say. "You're giving him way too much credit. He may have damaged it, but you helped me build it back up."

I don't like talking about the man who fathered me. I feel like it gives him too much power over me, power he never deserved. Besides, he's gone now. He died in prison, and I don't think the world is worse for it.

"I just... feel like maybe you could give small town living another chance."

I shake my head.

"It wasn't Atwell's fault, Luce. It wasn't the town's fault that he was a sociopath and a liar and embezzled half a million dollars."

I frown, because this is the first time she's ever defended our former friends and neighbors. For years, she was the one who told me over and over again that small towns might have low crime rates, but that didn't make them safe places.

People you think are your friends can hurt you.

She'd only been telling me what I'd already seen firsthand.

"But it was the town's fault that instead of rallying around us when they found out, they froze us out."

Turned their backs on us on the street and in the school hallways. Stopped accepting our invitations. Whispered about us in stores.

Made it impossible to go on living there.

And—I don't add—it was *my* fault that they had the ammunition to do any of that. My fault that the truth came out, and that everyone knew about it.

I look at my mom's sweet face. Her life was turned upside down that day, way more than mine. It still makes me angry to think about.

"I know I said a lot of harsh things to you about Atwell. And I know you were at a very impressionable age. But I was wrong to blame the town. There were just as many people who stepped up to be supportive as ones who indicted us."

"Maybe," I say, unconvinced.

"Rush Creek is a good place. The people who are here care about each other. They like the feeling of knowing everyone and having everyone know them. And I have to admit, I like it a lot, too."

"I'm just not small town material. Like you said, the people who love it here, they're people-people. Team players. I'm—I'm not that person. I need a lot more space than that. That's part of why I want my own business, so I don't end up dependent on people again."

She frowns. "It's not about being dependent on people. It's about *depending* on people. Being *interdependent*. That's a different thing. It's about letting them in, opening up to them."

"And I suck at that."

"Darren was *wrong* about that," she says fiercely.

"You just think that because you're my mom," I say, trying to lighten the mood.

She sighs. "I think it's because I know your heart, beautiful girl. I know it's not easy for you to open up, but you have a big heart, and I think you need people more than you want to."

"I have you. And Annie." But as my friend's name comes out of my mouth, I think about how long it's been since she and I talked. Could it be six months? I didn't even call her to sob after the Liam-and-Gennie-incident. I felt too raw.

"You could have a life here," she says. "If you'd let yourself."

"I have a life in New York."

She doesn't say anything. She just kind of... nods.

But it doesn't feel like a yes. It feels like a no.

And I find myself thinking about it for a long time afterwards.

I love my apartment, the care I take with every aspect of it. I love my work. Those things feed me. I have phone calls with my mom and with Annie.

Still, could you call what I have in New York a life?

And why, for the first time in forever, does the answer matter to me?

We're lying on my bed that night. Breathing hard, limp as rags. Her hand is splayed out across my belly and mine is still tangled in a hank of her hair.

We're still playing the no-condom game, and I should be frustrated as hell, but Lucy was right: This waiting is forcing us to be more inventive than I knew was possible, and I've used just about curvy surface of Lucy's body to find release, and each time I come harder than the last.

I'm probably going to turn myself inside out the first time I get inside her, which needs to be soon.

"How was the time with your mom?" I ask her.

"It was good," she says. But she's frowning.

"What?"

"I—she asked me if I'd ever move here."

She said *move here.*

No. She said her *mother asked if she'd ever move here.* Which is completely different.

"And you said?"

"I said no."

"Well, duh," I say.

Of course she did. Girls from New York, girls like Lucy, who have New York etched into the pleats of their dress pants and stacked in the heels of their shoes, don't move to Rush Creek.

When a woman tells you she is leaving, believe her.

That is the most important lesson I have ever learned, and I will *not* forget it, no matter how adorable Lucy's freckles are, no matter how sweet the curves of cheek and breast and belly, no matter how much I love the feel of her hand in mine.

"You can't get your laundry picked up and dropped off here," I say.

"No." She shakes her head.

"You can't see any movie you want, any time."

"No."

"Although you can see the new Marvel movie in three different theaters. So that's something."

"That *is* something," she says.

"And you can't get Nan's bread in New York."

"I hate to break it to you, Gabe, but you can get bread from ten different bakeries in a ten-block radius of where I live in New York."

"So there is nothing Rush Creek has to recommend itself over New York."

"Mmm." She rolls toward me. "I wouldn't say nothing." But then she stops. "Do you know why I couldn't ever live here? *Ever*?"

I know she's joking, but the ferocity of her voice still stabs me.

She grabs her phone from the nightstand. "I was researching marketing firms in Portland. Look at them, Gabe! I could never fit in here!"

I study the screen. "They're very... Portland. Portland has a totally different vibe from New York."

"I'm starting to get that." She examines the photo. "How do they get away with it? No makeup? Gray hair? They're in marketing, which is all about appearances."

"That's the vibe here. If they were all decked out, they'd stand out. But who the fuck cares about that? I'm all for whatever women want to do. You're hot no matter what you wear."

She gives me a quizzical look, like she can't believe that could be true. Then she sets her phone aside, curls her body against mine, and rests her head on my chest. I put my arms around her. I want to block out the rest of the world and be in a cocoon with her.

"It's true, City Girl. You're hot naked and naked-faced, and you're hot in all the business clothes, all dolled up. There is no way you can look or dress that I won't want you."

"Did you want me even when I was flailing in the woods?"

"Did I not make that clear?" I demand.

"Okay, yeah. You, um, made that clear." She starts kissing her way across my chest, and damn if I'm not ready to go again.

Except that I'm still fixated on what she said. *I could never fit in here!* Did she mean that?

Is it true?

Looking at that website, I could see why she said it. One of these things is not like the other. Lucy doesn't look like a small town Oregon girl.

She doesn't belong here. In the Pacific northwest, in my small town.

In my bed.

Except she does. Having her here feels so exactly right.

She asked me if I'd ever move here.

I said no.

I feel a twinge of longing. Or maybe that's the sensation in my groin caused by Lucy slowly sliding down my body. Of all the bonus effects of "waiting," I'm loving frequent blow jobs the most.

I stroke her hair, then wind my hand in it.

She starts at the very tip, working her way lower and lower.

I can't tell if the falling sensation in my stomach is because of how very, very good she is at what she's doing.

Or because of how much I still desperately want to ask her if she's thinking about staying.

I know what happens when I start to hope a woman will stay, and it doesn't end well for me.

Gabe takes me turkey hunting.

The Jeep has a locked gun box, which he packs and inventories while he gives me a lecture on gun safety. I break it to him that I have no intention of shooting anything, and he shrugs.

"Didn't figure you would."

He drives us deep into the forest and parks the car at a gate, and then we hike for a few hundred yards and he shows me where we'll set up shop.

I find the sight of Gabe in hunting gear with a gun slung over his shoulder disturbingly hot. Of course, I would find him equally hot if he were wearing a bear suit. I've reached that point with Gabe where I'll salivate like Pavlov's dogs for little-to-no reason.

I'm wearing Hanna's camo. Apparently—who knew?—turkeys have amazing eyesight. The camo is super baggy on me, and I feel ridiculous. The orange vest and hat don't help, either. Gabe, of course, looks hot in the orange hat. Like a total badass.

He knows it, too, and gives me a cocky look that doesn't help the situation.

"We're hunting Merriams," he tells me, like that will mean something to me.

I tell him I don't care, I just hope he brought a good picnic.

He laughs and says it's Connor's mom's food.

That's all I need to know.

There are some ridiculous shenanigans involving turkey calls, which of course he can imitate. Some guys use electronic game calls, but Gabe says he thinks his way is better.

Watching Gabe make turkey calls is *not* sexy; I can't lie. It makes me want to laugh, but he shushes me because that will ruin our chances.

Ah, so in addition to their outstanding vision, turkeys have excellent hearing. Which doesn't explain why we eat almost fifty million of them on Thanksgiving.

We do a lot of tiptoeing around, trying to get in the right position, wind-wise, to where the turkeys are likely to be. I wonder whether this means they also have well-honed senses of smell? I feel like the turkeys might be laughing at us. I tell this to Gabe.

"It's possible."

He's definitely laughing at me.

It starts to rain, and Gabe curses quietly. Then it starts to rain harder. A lot harder.

He pulls me to my feet. "We need to go over there." He points. "We're going to get lucky over there."

I start after him, but the ground is muddy now, slippery, and I've taken maybe thirty steps when my foot slips out from under me and I start to go down. I grab for Gabe's hand and manage to pull him down after me. We're both breathless, laughing, ridiculously muddy.

"Is this reminding you of anything?" I whisper. "The two of us, a bunch of birds that aren't where they're supposed to be, and rain pouring down?"

"It's how it all started," he says.

Then we're kissing. A lot. In the rain. It pours down over our faces but we don't stop. His mouth feels so good, warm and certain. He cups my face and kisses it all over, then returns to my mouth with his full attention. His tongue sweeps in and conquers mine. I don't resist very hard. Just enough to make it fun.

He breaks off the kiss.

"Can I tell you something?"

I nod.

His brow furrows. "I haven't shot a turkey in a year."

"Because you secretly suck at turkey hunting?"

He shakes his head. "No. Because I shoot to miss. My nephew, Noah, you met him. He asked me if it makes me sad to kill the turkeys."

"Oh!"

He nods. "I said it didn't. Then he gave me this look. Five-year-old sad face. He said it made him sad that I kill the turkeys. I got choked up. Later, I asked Amanda if she put him up to it—she doesn't love the hunting—and she said no. I even asked her if she and Heath talk about it, like if they tell the kids that they don't approve of hunting, and she said no, they try not to talk about it because even though it's not their thing, they respect that it's mine."

Amanda is good people. All the Wilders, I think, are good

people. My heart gets wobbly. It's going to be hard to say goodbye to them. All of them.

"Since then, I haven't been able to shoot to kill. Not turkeys. Not anything, frankly."

"Oh, Gabe," I say. I can't manage any other words.

He frowns at the trees. I think there's something else. "I keep doing it though. Hunting. Because—it's what my dad and I did together. When I'm out here, I feel closest to him."

The words hit me in my already bruised heart. Gabe Wilder doesn't talk about himself. But here we are, and he is.

"Tell me about him," I say quietly.

"He was a really good man." Gabe is still staring into the distance. "He was strong and fiercely protective of his family. He laughed a lot and made us laugh a lot. He ran a really successful business. I don't think Wilder would be in these straits if he were alive."

"That's not true, Gabe. Wilder is struggling because the town changed faster than you all could. Not because of anything you did wrong."

"I just think he would have known what to do. When he was dying—"

Rain continues to fall in my face. Gabe's hand is on mine on the muddy ground. We haven't gotten up. We're sitting here in the mud, getting wetter and wetter. I'm sure we're violating a fundamental principle of wilderness safety. I can practically hear Clark losing his shit.

But I'm not going to move while Gabe is talking to me like this. I'm not going to do anything that risks this moment.

"—he begged me to take care of them. My brothers, my mother, Amanda. He said he was so scared to die, not for himself, but because he didn't want to leave them alone. He wanted to know they'd be okay. So I promised him. I can't let anything happen to Wilder, Luce. I can't."

I reach for him, pulling him into my arms, tucking his head against my shoulder, holding him. And he lets me.

"We won't let anything happen to Wilder," I whisper. I want desperately to say, *I promise*. I don't. But I think it. I think it hard.

We strip off our clothes and shoes inside the front door and are already wild—kissing and grasping. I can't get enough of her. I'm afraid I'll never get enough of her.

I swoop her into my arms and carry her up the stairs, depositing her on her feet on the bathroom floor. Kissing her again. She grabs my head, pulls my hair. Her hair is a total disaster, a messy bun gone completely to seed. Wet, muddy. I tug the elastic out and her hair spills down her shoulders.

"You're so beautiful."

I start the shower. Steam fills the bathroom, fogs the mirror. I reach out and make a heart on the mirror, with our initials inside. She stares at it, then at me. She doesn't say anything, but she has that look on her face, the one she gets when I've done something she thinks is next level. It makes me want to cover the whole mirror with hearts.

I step into the shower and hold back the curtain so she can follow. The hot water pours over me. It feels good on my cold skin, on muscles that stretched in the woods and stiffened on the car ride back. I love the first shower after being in the woods, even on a day trip.

She slides into my arms. Her hair is dirty but smells like flowers. Her skin is soft and smooth. Nothing else feels like that, in my world of rough things. I have to touch it everywhere. I have to test all the spots, to see which is softest, which makes her whimper. I have to test them with my fingers and my mouth.

She likes having the underside of her breasts touched and licked. I stay there for a long time, teasing her nipples every once in a while.

I soap her belly, breasts, hips, ass, thighs. Then I slide my hand between her legs and circle her clit. She drops her head to my shoulder and moans, hitching her hips, asking for more. I tighten the circles, getting her close. Then I stop. "I want you to come when I'm inside you," I tell her. I'm hard against her hip. She reaches for the soap, reaches for me. Takes me in her soapy fist, nice and tight. That's the best thing about waiting so long. She knows exactly how much pressure and friction I like. She twists her wrist like a pro. She gives the head extra attention, her palm slicking over the most sensitive spot, lingering there.

I make her stop, my hand on hers. "I want to last a while."

We towel off and she follows me down the hall to my room. "Here—sit here," I say, and she does. I kneel between her legs, dipping to taste her. She is so, so soft there. The softest spot of all. And she tastes so good, sweet and briny and her. I take my time, winding her back up. I slide a finger inside her, so I can feel when she's close. I don't let her come this time, either, even though she curses me out.

I guide her down onto the bed, lower myself over her. We

kiss and kiss. It's heartbreakingly good. The mechanics, yes, but also whatever this other thing is. The soul of it. I've never told anyone what I told her in the woods. I've never felt this connected to anyone.

We kiss until she's lifting her hips over and over again, seeking pressure, seeking contact. Yelling at me, telling me I'm a pain in her ass, and she needs me. I roll on the condom and settle myself between her legs, which she opens to welcome me. She's so wet and so swollen. I line myself up and ease in. Her body resists me. She's tight.

"Let me in, Lucy," I murmur.

A tremor runs through her.

"Please."

I bend my head and kiss her, working her mouth over, begging her with my lips and tongue, and she softens and blooms and opens to me, my cock easing into her tightness. And holy shit that's good. Her mouth, her pussy, the clench of her body around me, the rasp of her fingernails down my back.

I already want more. I want her around me now, and I'll want it again when I'm done, and again and again. *Stay*, my body pleads. My heart. *Stay, stay, stay, stay.*

"Let me in, Lucy."

I know he's not just asking me to relax and let him fuck me. I know he's asking for something more. And I want to give it, and that scares the hell out of me.

Like Darren said, I don't know how to do that. How to let someone in, how to open up.

But Gabe makes me want to try.

He kisses me then, like he's using his mouth to tell me what he needs. *Open for me, baby*. His tongue shows me, and my body listens.

I breathe deeply and let myself let go. Relax. Let him in.

He slides home with a groan, filling me. Stretching me. He's big and thick and very, very hard from the long time we played, and it's so, so good. Nothing has ever felt like this. Not just the sensation in my groin, hot and golden, not just the tingles racing back and forth along that secret, invisible wire between my clit and nipples, not just how much my mouth, hungry and empty, wants his kisses. But him. Gabe. So serious when he's not being funny. So bossy when he's not letting me take whatever I need. Filling a room, commanding it, loving his family like it's an Olympic sport, loyal, fierce, competent, kind.

He pulls away, watching me, and I decide I'm not going to hold anything back from him. I look into his eyes, and he meets my gaze, unflinching. Those dark eyes tell me how good I feel to him; his mouth twists with pleasure; his brow furrows as he chases it for both of us. He adjusts his weight, lowering his hips over mine, the pressure over my clit perfect. Each thrust delivers on a promise, stretch and friction, and his eyes tell me he knows exactly how much I like it and that he likes it too. We're winding each other up, totally tapped into the shared pleasure. Everything in me is lit up with Gabe, and I'm helpless, powerless, arching my back to try to get more, closer, lifting my breasts to offer him a nipple, which he takes, but only lightly. Because he knows me. He knows exactly how to play me.

Another thrust, roll of hips, surge of pleasure. His teeth on that nipple. It's like an electrical circuit. "Gabe," I gasp.

"Not yet, baby," he says. "Not yet."

"I can't help it—"

"Fuck, Lucy, you're so fucking *hot*," he says, and then he's sucking my nipple and thrusting hard, all control lost, and we go over together, clinging to each other, crying each other's names. Waves and waves of it, and impossible to tell which is me and which is him, it's all just us.

I take a long time to come back to earth. When I do, I look over at him. He's looking back, and the look on his face is—

He looks wrecked. Which is, on one hand, exactly right, and on the other, all wrong. And then he wipes his face of whatever that expression was, and smiles at me. It's an honest

Gabe smile, no faking it, but I know there's more to the story than that smile. And I know that whatever that story is, I'm going to need to know. Because I knew in the woods that I loved him, but now I know it in my body, which is better and worse. Better because this is how sex is supposed to be, this all-over, lit-up, through-and-through feeling; this is what it feels like when you're in it with all your emotions and not just your body.

And worse, because I don't know if he feels the same way, or what it would mean to either of us if he did.

"I'm starving," Lucy says after a few minutes, and we both start laughing. Because yeah, food would probably have been a good idea, first.

She puts on one of my sweatshirts and I put on a pair of jeans and we pad downstairs into the kitchen, where I start a pot of pasta.

She gets the clothes from the front hall—"because I already know where the washing machine is!"—deposits the contents of our pockets on the counter, and starts a load of muddy laundry.

I reach for my phone, reflexively, and, "Oh, shit."

"What?"

"Brody's in trouble. I have to go bail him out."

"Of jail?"

He sighs. "No, luckily, but only just. He got into a fight outside Oscar's. They separated the guys and hauled Brody back inside, but he's banged up and very, very drunk and Jill didn't want him driving, so she texted me."

"Jill—our waitress from the other night?"

"Yeah. We're friends."

"Friends with benefits?"

She sounds possessive, and I don't hate it. "We were," I say. "She's all but engaged now." *Besides,* I don't say, *you have nothing to worry about. You are in a league of your own.*

And I don't just mean the sex, although that was next-level, out-of-control, apply-the-superlative-of-your-choice.

"Want me to go with you?"

"Nah, I've got this."

"I know you've got it. But—"

There's a softness to her voice that makes me sit up and pay attention in a way I wouldn't have if she'd been sharper.

"Gabe, you're good at everything. You can take care of anything. I don't doubt whatever's up with Brody, you've got it totally under control. I'm not asking that. I'm asking if you want me there."

I do want her there. I want her there, and everywhere, in a way that scares the shit out of me.

"You're starving, though," I say.

"I'm a big girl. I can eat a power bar. And maybe Jill can get us something wrapped up to go?"

I hesitate, but she doesn't. She crosses to the stove and turns the heat off under the water.

"Let's go," she says.

"WHAT WERE YOU THINKING, ASSHOLE?" I ask my brother. His face is bloody. He's going to have one hell of a shiner, and he's lucky his nose isn't broken, although it is bleeding pretty bad —his shirt is definitely ruined.

"He had it coming," Brody growls.

"Your fighting days are supposed to be behind you, man. You have a kid. You have to be a good role model."

"You don't know what the fuck you're talking about," he says sullenly.

"I might, if you talked to me."

He sinks into silence, then, draws in on himself, and I realize how much there is about my brother I still don't understand and might never.

Lucy watches us, quiet. I have never appreciated, so much, what it means to be there for someone. To just stand there, out of the way, not intruding. Just witnessing. Her being here means so much to me.

It takes some effort on the part of Jill, Lucy, and me to get him loaded into my car. "Hey," Jill says. "Follow me back in a second."

I do, and she runs into the kitchen and comes back with a paper takeout bag. It smells unbelievably good. Thank you, Lucy, for figuring out how to get us fed in the middle of a crisis.

I head out to the car, but as I approach, someone calls my name.

I turn to find a pretty woman with long dark hair and Connor's eyes. I'd know her anywhere, even though I haven't seen her in a couple of years. Rachel, Connor's sister. The one who got Brody's undies in a bunch on the boat. Brody maybe thinks I didn't pick up on that, but I did. And I always knew, even back when we were kids, that Brody's feelings for her went deeper than "my best friend's baby sister."

"Is he okay?" she asks.

We both look toward the car. Lucy's watching us, curious.

Brody appears to be at least half asleep, his head lolling against the window.

"He'll be okay," I say carefully. "Did you see what happened?"

Rachel nods. "I don't know exactly what went down, but I could tell Len was giving him a hard time before it happened."

"Doesn't surprise me. But still. He needs to learn how to walk away." I sigh.

"Some people find that harder than others."

"Tell me about it," I say, and we exchange tight smiles.

"Tell him—tell him I said hi."

I log the concern in her eyes and nod. "I will."

I slide into the driver's seat and pass Lucy the takeout, then rest my hands on the wheel for a second, pulling myself together.

"Did she see?" Brody slurs from the back seat.

I don't try to pretend I don't know what he's asking. "Did Rachel see the fight, you mean? Yeah, she saw."

"Fuck." Brody taps his forehead against the window glass.

"If you don't want people seeing your dirty laundry, you shouldn't air it in public."

"You don't know what you're talking about," he grinds out.

I don't remind him that that's because he doesn't talk to me. He's still too riled up and volatile. I let it go.

Still, I'm wary, driving with one ear cocked to the back seat. I've rarely seen Brody this drunk, and I know that with the blood he may have swallowed and the blows to the head he took, he might be sick.

Sure enough, we haven't even gone a mile when I hear him retching in the back seat.

I pull over, fast as I can. Lucy is out of the car before I am, wrenching open the back door, helping Brody out of the car, helping him onto his knees as he heaves up his guts all over the shoulder of the road. By the time I get around the car, Brody's almost done, and Lucy's murmuring quietly to him.

I should be jealous of her hands on his shoulders, her fingers smoothing back his hair, but I'm ridiculously grateful. And so in love with her that I stand back from them for a second, in the way she stood back to watch Brody and me.

We get him back in the car, and he passes out a few minutes later. He wakes up just enough to stumble up the steps and into his apartment. Lucy helps me get him most of the way undressed, and then she leaves while I strip him out of his jeans and maneuver him under the covers. I set Advil and water on his nightstand and go out to find Lucy sitting on his couch, leafing through *Outdoors* magazine.

I drop heavily onto the couch next to her, and she wordlessly turns to me and wraps me in her arms.

"Is he going to be okay?"

"Yes," I say, hoping it's true. And then, "I don't know what's going on, and he won't tell me. He won't tell anyone."

She nods. "He will, when he's ready." Her eyes are on my face, taking me in, all sympathy and understanding. "This is how it's always been, huh? You taking care of everyone? It must have been hell when they were all teenagers."

"You have *no* idea." I lean my forehead against hers, and she strokes my hair.

"Was that Brody's kid's mom? The woman talking to you outside the bar?"

I shake my head. "Justin's mom? No. Connor's sister, Rachel."

"Ohhh."

"Yeah," I say.

"Is there something up with the two of them?"

"I don't know." *I don't know anything.*

She must hear the defeat in my voice, because she cups my cheek. Her hand is cool and soft and I could rest my face against it for hours.

We both look toward the closed door to Brody's room. "We should probably stick around a while, huh?" she says. "In case he's sick again?"

"I'll stick around. You can take the Jeep and go home. Brody'll drive me home in the morning."

She smiles at me. "You're a slow learner, huh? I'm not asking to go home. I'm asking if you want me here with you."

I don't even try to lie about it this time.

"Yeah," I say. "I want you here."

I want you here, as long as you'll stay.

WE OPEN the takeout bags and dig into the food. It's wings and cracklings. I shoot a worried look Lucy's way, but she doesn't even hesitate. She dives right in, stuffing her face with cracklings and starting on a wing.

"They kinda grow on you, huh?" I ask her, amused. "And I didn't know you liked wings. You didn't eat them when we were at Oscars."

"Yeah, well, I wasn't as hungry that night as I am now." She licks her fingers, and I watch her soft lips pull around her digits. You'd think that after a few blow jobs, the gesture would have lost any power it might have over me, but no: I can't look away, and my cock plumps, envious. Luckily, she resumes eating and digs out a napkin a moment later. Otherwise, Brody's couch would get a christening.

We eat till we feel more human; then she cleans up the mess and deposits it in the trash under Brody's sink. She comes back into the living room, smiling. My heart squeezes. It hurts.

"Thank you for coming with me," I tell her, because I don't have words for the whole big way I feel about tonight. And her.

"Of course," she says, but it's not *of course*, not at all. "It must get lonely sometimes. Being the one everyone leans on."

I don't answer. I reach out and take her hand.

There's something in her expression I can't read. Softness, yes, sympathy, but something else. "I lost my dad, too." Her voice is super calm and level, but I know how hard it is for Lucy to reveal even the smallest things about herself. And this isn't small.

"Yeah?" I ask it casually, not wanting to scare her off. *Let me in*, I said to her when we were making love, and I meant it. I needed it. I still need it. Let me in, Lucy, and not just like this in bed, but in all the ways.

"He went to prison."

I'm surprised, and not surprised. Part of me must have known there was something in Lucy's past, something to make her so good and clean and careful, when there is so much passion and energy in her that wants to get out.

"When I was twelve. Embezzling. He was treasurer of everything. Basically, one of those guys who's good at it so he gets asked to do it, like for the Girl Scouts and the school and the Chamber of Commerce or whatever. Turns out he was making a fortune off this. But we weren't getting rich. We had money troubles. All the money was going to his *other* family."

When she says *other family*, I see it. Twelve-year-old Lucy, suddenly understanding that her father wasn't who she'd thought he was.

There's losing your father, and then there's *losing* your father. "Oh, Lucy," I say.

I hold my arms out and she crawls into them, resting her head against my shoulder, exactly where she belongs. And if I felt protective of her before, I am all claws now.

"I was the one who figured it out. My friend Paulina and I. She had a Harriet the Spy complex. She was always snooping —like she would read her parents' sex books and get into their birth control. We found the keys to my dad's briefcase. There was a phone in there I'd never seen, and all these financial documents for banks I'd never heard of. I was only twelve, but I kind of knew—the way you know?"

I nod.

"I begged Paulina to keep it to herself. *I begged.*"

Twelve-year-old Lucy, just wanting to protect the people she loved from a truth that was coming for her no matter what she did. My heart hurts like fuck. "But she didn't."

She shakes her head. "I mean, it wasn't Paulina's fault. She had to tell her parents what she'd seen. But to me, it felt like a betrayal, like if she'd kept my secret, my life wouldn't have fallen apart. And once the investigation started, everyone knew. That was the part that wrecked my mom. People would stop her on the street and basically tell her she should have known what he was doing or imply that she *did* know and hadn't put a stop to his stealing from basically every charitable organization in town. We had to leave. We moved to

Boston. For years, my mom railed against 'people who can't keep their opinions to themselves' and 'people who don't mind their own business.'"

It all makes sense. How much she hates small towns. How much she hates talking about herself. What Amanda said offhandedly about Lucy resisting every gesture of friendship.

"That's why you don't talk much about yourself."

She nods.

"Where's your dad now?"

"He died in prison. Had a heart attack."

"I'm sorry."

"It was hard to even know what to feel about it. I mean, I was sad. Of course I was. And it's hard not to have closure. Not that I think I would really have been able to forgive him. But maybe I would have been able to at least tell him how angry and hurt I was, and maybe that would have helped."

"I bet it would have."

"Who knows, right? Anyway, yeah, I'm sure that's a big part of why I'm not very good with people."

"That's *not true*," I say, before I can stop myself, and I'm pretty outraged, too. I've seen her with people. With *my* people, winning them over, making them laugh, stretching out of her comfort zone just to be part of their world.

"No, it kinda is. You don't know why I left New York."

And then she tells me the story. How she slept with a guy she met, how it turned out he was her boss's on-again, off-again boyfriend. And how the thing that made her boss so mad was that Lucy was a shitty friend and didn't make the effort to know her co-workers.

I know how hard it is for Lucy to open up. I know how much she doesn't like to talk about herself. And yet, she's just told me about her deepest fears, and how what happened with her boss tapped into them.

The only word I can think of is *honored*. I feel honored that she's telling me her stories. So even though I want to fix what's hurting her, I don't try this time. Because I know there's nothing I can say to make it better.

Instead, I pull her closer and hold her tighter, and we stay like that a long time.

One more trip, Easton's rafting trip, and then I'm done. My flight back to New York is three days from now. I know Gabe and I need to have a conversation, but I'm not sure how to start it, or what I would say.

So instead I put on my bathing suit and my base layer, because according to Gabe, we're in the in-between seasonal zone between bathing suits and wet suits, and I get in the Jeep with Gabe to head to a whitewater location that's good for beginners, on the Mionet River.

These words make no sense to me, "whitewater that's good for beginners," but then no words involving the term "whitewater" would really make sense to me.

When we reach the river, I'm relieved to see that it's a wide, lazy-looking river—with lush green vegetation rising to tall evergreen forest on either side. And the rafts are less intimidating than I feared, too. I know this makes me a dope, but I was totally picturing a big flat wooden raft with a pole. So when I see that "rafts" are actually inflatable yellow boats,

I'm relieved. Surely nothing bad can happen to you when you're in a big puffy yellow boat.

I mean, other than violent seasickness, which is pretty much a given.

Then Easton starts going over self-rescue techniques with us, and my heart is pounding so hard I have troubling listening to what he's saying.

"You okay?" Gabe asks me.

I don't want to tell him how much this trip freaks me out, so I nod and do my best to concentrate.

"...toes pointing up. Face out of the water, toes out of the water, if you can. The float position will reduce the risk of entanglement with rocks or other obstacles."

Rocks.

Obstacles.

Entanglement.

"Lucy?" Gabe's voice is soft and concerned at my ear.

"Promise you'll rescue me if we capsize," I instruct him.

He grins. "I promise."

My heart slows down. Because no one could look at Gabe freaking Wilder, six foot-plus and totally in control of the whole world, and still be scared.

"What did he say about float position?" I demand of Gabe, as we follow Easton's instructions for getting in the raft.

"Face up, arms outstretched, feet first, legs bent to absorb impact. Toes and face above water." He repeats Easton's life-saving guidance. "Then once you orient yourself, roll and swim aggressively to wherever Easton and I tell you."

"I'm not the most aggressive swimmer."

"You'll be okay," Gabe says. "I gotcha."

In the raft, Gabe is indeed right behind me, giving me

instructions as we go. And I'm pleasantly surprised to discover that in the cool breeze, without the gas-and-oil smells of an engine, I feel only slightly queasy. After a while, I start to relax and actually enjoy myself. The water is damn cold, but aside from the occasional spray in my face, I'm mostly pretty happy. The river is beautiful, the forest on either side rugged and green, mountains visible and snow capped in the dips between the trees, and everyone in the boat is in a great mood.

So far, we've only done Class I and Class II rapids, and mostly it's a rush. Like we're flying downstream, skimming over the surface of the world. I'm starting to think I freaked out for no reason when Easton eases us over to the bank and warns us that we have Class III rapids coming up. "The river's high today," he says. "There's more runoff than I was counting on, so these are probably closer to III-plus. But if you listen to what I say and do exactly what I tell you, we'll be fine."

"And if we don't?" one of the women on the trip asks.

"You'll still be okay, but you might be a helluva lot wetter," Easton says, managing to make it sound like sex. Do *all* Wilders have the ability to make effortless innuendo?

Her eyes track down the length of his body.

"He's going to do fine with the New Rush Creek," I tell Gabe.

"That's what I'm afraid of," Gabe says.

Easton finishes his instructions and lets us loose on the water again, and for a moment, I think he must have exaggerated the difference between Class II and Class III. But then it's like someone's turned the volume up on the lovely gentle shush of the river, and I stiffen.

The roar gets louder, like an animal coming for us.

"Well, shit," Gabe says quietly. "Easton wasn't kidding about the runoff."

The water ahead of us is a rough rush of brown and white, and looks nothing like the rapids we've seen so far. My heart's pounding again, and it feels like I can barely draw a breath. Nausea rises, hard and thick, and instinctively, I lean over the side. I'm going to throw up, and no way I'm going to do it all over my boatmates...

Easton's shouting instructions to us, telling us how to lean and shift, who should have a paddle in and who shouldn't. We're careening through the rapids and I can't do anything except hold on for dear life and scream.

"Lucy!" Easton is yelling. "Lean right. Right! Fucking right!" which I would if I could but gravity is doing something all wrong, and everything tilts off its axis and I know—we're flipping. I grab and grab, but I'm sliding and screaming, and then I'm tumbling under the icy surface, tossed and held. The cold knocks all the air out of my lungs; my head smacks against something, hard; my mouth flies open; and water rushes in.

Everything goes dark.

I n the tumult, I watch her go over the edge of the raft and into the rush of water.

I go in after her.

"Gabe," Easton yells, but I ignore him.

I see the flash of yellow that signals her life vest, and I'm on it in an instant, adrenaline driving me. There's nothing that matters except that yellow, which is Lucy, which is everything.

I see her head strike the rock, and a bitter rage flows through me. The world would not, it absolutely would not, do this.

I'm grabbing for her, for every bit of gear she's wearing that I can get my hands on. Tugging her by the loop on the back of her life vest, by her ponytail, getting her head above water.

She's unconscious.

I can't think about anything except getting her to safety. I'm on my back, trying to keep her afloat, trying to aim my feet downstream, praying that there are no strainers here. We

go under again, despite my best efforts, and the water is dark
and choking and I hate it fiercely.

And then we're out of the thick of it, back into calm, and
Easton's throwing out a line. I grab it and he tows us in, and a
moment later we're in the boat, among the stricken faces of
the other tour members. Easton gets a rescue blanket and
wraps it around her. She doesn't stir at all.

"Lucy," I beg.

If she's not okay—

She has to be okay. That is all there is to it. I will bargain
anything I need to. Wilder Adventures itself. Why did I think
saving this business mattered? We will find another way to
survive. But I will not survive without Lucy.

I will not survive without Lucy.

She opens her eyes and blinks at me, obviously confused
as shit, but definitely conscious.

I exhale for the first time in what feels like ten minutes,
even though I know she wasn't out anything like that long.

She sits up and coughs up a bunch of water, spluttering
and gasping until she clears her lungs. My relief is so fierce
that I almost laugh. I've never felt like this, like the feeling of
coming up for air from underneath a swirl of whitewater.

"I hate boats," Lucy says, her voice rough.

I clutch both her hands. "No more boats," I say. "I promise. You don't have to go in any more boats if you don't
want to."

"My head hurts," she says.

It's bleeding, and because it's a scalp wound, it looks ten
thousand times worse than it is, but even so it's scary. The
blood flow calms down when Easton presses a handful of
gauze to it. She might need stitches, but I'd bet not.

The other occupants of the boat are all spilling their relief in words and fussing and big sighs, telling her how glad they are that she's okay.

"No more boats for me, either," one of the men says, gray beneath his olive skin.

I don't care about any of them. I can't let go of Lucy's hands or stop staring at her beautiful, perfect face, or thinking, *I love you I love you I love you.*

I don't say it because she just almost drowned and she's bleeding and now she's shivering even in the rescue blanket.

But I think it, and then I think about how sometimes, there's no way out. I was always going to fall for Lucy, no matter what happened. I could make all the rules I wanted, tell myself all the lies I needed to, and in the end, it was going to come down to this.

I'm the guy who falls in love with women who leave.

"Mr. Wilder?"

I raise my head to see a nurse standing inside the doorway of the Five Rivers Regional hospital waiting area.

I've been sitting here, biting my nails—something I haven't done since I was fifteen—and practically jumping out of my skin, for what feels like hours but is much closer to forty minutes.

"Ms. Spiro is asking for you."

I leap up so fast I nearly trip over myself.

And then I stop, halfway across the waiting room, like I've run into a wall.

When we arrived at the hospital, Lucy was pale and

queasy but making jokes. About boats and how city girls should stick to dry land and 600-thread-count sheets.

She was hurt, and I hated it. It made my stomach clench.

And also she was tough as nails, and I loved it. It made me want to follow that goddamn gurney anywhere they took her. Hold her hand. But they asked me to wait in the waiting room, so I did.

If I go in there, I'm going to ask her to stay in Rush Creek.

I'm going to *beg* her to stay in Rush Creek.

And I've done that once, even though all the facts were stacked against me.

Ceci had told me, so patiently, why she couldn't stay in Rush Creek. She'd been away from her tenure-track job as long as her university's policy—and a whole lot of exceptions —could allow. She wasn't a small-town girl. She loved me, *but*.

But.

The thing about that *but*—which I understand now—is that it contains a whole world of information. If you love someone *but*, you love something more. Your freedom, your old life, a place.

Ceci loved me, but she didn't love me enough to stay.

I begged her anyway.

What I felt for Ceci wasn't half what I feel for Lucy.

And if it were only about that—my pride, the risk of getting hurt again—I would beg Lucy in a second.

I'd march myself right down to that exam room, and I'd fucking grovel.

One thing I learned from Ceci is that when a woman tells you she's not staying, you need to believe her. Not for your own sake, although it definitely would have saved me a lot of pain.

For hers.

Because after I begged, Ceci tried to stay. She stayed another six months.

She was fucking miserable, and we both knew it. Everything between us curdled and froze and dried up, even the sex, which had been pretty good. (Not Lucy good. But pretty good.)

When Ceci went back to Chicago, she started teaching again. Married a professor colleague five months later. They have a kid now. I see her on Facebook. She's beaming, happy.

I want Lucy to look like that.

Taking Lucy and pinning her down in Rush Creek would be like taking some fantastic, strong, exotic tiger and putting it behind bars in a zoo.

I want Lucy to be in her element. Powerful, dignified.

I want to think of her striding down the streets of New York, presiding over a glossy conference room, getting the primo coveted reservation in some chic new restaurant. Seeing an artsy flick the day it comes out, a once-in-a-lifetime art exhibit the moment it arrives. Her clothes cleaned and delivered. Her fashion up-to-the-moment.

"Sir?"

The nurse has both his eyebrows raised and is tapping a foot impatiently.

Even with all my doubts, I take another step forward, because I can't—won't—let Lucy be alone in there.

I hear a waterfall tumble of human voices behind me and instinctively turn, and there they are.

I texted them, and they came.

Lucy's mom and Gregg, my mom, Amanda, and Hanna, spilling through the main entrance with enough laughter and chatter and hubbub to be a dozen people instead of five, the best possible medicine for Lucy.

"That's who she *really* wants to see," I tell the nurse.

I head off the gaggle, and they start fussing immediately. Hugging, checking me over like I'm the wounded party. *Gabe, are you sure you're okay?*

Well, except for Hanna, who rolls her eyes in sympathy with me.

"I'm fine," I reassure them. "Lucy wants to see you. She's ready for company."

I follow the nurse and Lucy's friends and family down a fluorescent-lit hallway, past gurneys and carts and closets, to the room where she's waiting. They pile in, and I back into the corner closest to the door, letting them all have Lucy.

She's sitting on the edge of a padded exam table, wearing a hospital gown. There's a small patch on the side of her head where her hair was shaved. I imagine she must hate that. I can picture her fiddling with it in the mirror, trying to get the rest of her hair to cover it. Experimenting with the stash of cute, stylish hats she must own. I can't stand the ache in my chest.

Her family and friends surround her, fussing over her, hugging her, telling her she scared the shit out of them. They want the story, and Lucy tells it. The story is more dramatic in her retelling; she's animated, and with the color slowly coming back into her face, she has never looked more beautiful to me.

When she gets to the part where she goes overboard, her eyes flick to me. There's a question in her eyes.

I look away, because if I don't, I will shove them all out of the way and tell her she's never leaving Rush Creek. That she belongs here. Belongs to me.

She finishes the story, filling in the part where I dove into the water after her.

When all the storytelling and fussing is done, the nurse says that someone has to watch over Lucy tonight.

"Come stay with us," Gregg says.

Lucy's cheeks get pink. She casts her gaze my way again, the question in them.

Lucy's mom catches the movement and looks from Lucy to me.

"Unless—" she says.

"No," I say quickly. "You should be with your mom. She'll take care of you. I should—get going." I take one step closer to where Lucy sits. "I'm so glad you're okay."

Her eyes lock on mine, and I see the sadness in them.

Me, too, Luce, I think. *Me too.*

I turn to go.

"Wait," Amanda says. "Where are you going?"

"Easton and I have to file some incident paperwork." My hand is on the door, turning the knob. I'm out in the hallway. I draw my first full breath in what feels like hours.

"Gabe?"

Amanda has followed me down the hallway, her voice puzzled.

I almost don't turn around, but she calls my name again, and I do.

"You're leaving?"

"I have to go."

"Gabe, what the hell? Don't be a doofus."

She's worried. And mad. One thing I love about Amanda, you always know exactly where you stand.

I get it. I know Amanda loves Lucy, too. Hanna's become like a sister to Amanda, but Lucy—Lucy's a kindred spirit for her.

So I'm not the only one who's about to get their heart broken.

"I'm not," I say. "This time, I'm doing the smart thing. For me *and* Lucy. And if you took your own feelings out of it, you'd know I'm right."

And I turn and keep walking.

Two days after my rafting mishap, I give my final presentation to the Wilders. We're in the barn, where I stand in front of the pull-down screen and wait for the last of the brothers to plant their hot asses in their seats. In this case—of course—the stragglers are Brody and Easton. If I know my stuff, Brody will slink in and sink into his chair without making eye contact. And Easton will be all charm and sincere apology.

Meanwhile, Gabe sits stiffly in his seat, paging through my handouts, not looking at me.

Some people get super nervous before big presentations. I usually get pumped. I work hard, I know my stuff, and I polish every last word, so when I stand up there with my slides, I'm confident that I'll impress.

This time is no different, except that the only person I care about impressing has been avoiding me for two days, ever since he all but ran out of the ER.

I knew even before he bolted that things were over between us. I think I knew it in the Jeep on the way to the hospital, when he was so quiet, but for sure I knew it when he wouldn't jump in to tell the story of what had happened. When he wouldn't look at me.

I wasn't surprised, that's the thing.

This is Gabe's way of putting enough distance between us so that we both can walk away. It's what I need, too. If I saw him, I might tell him the truth, which is that I let myself fall in love with him even though he told me, a hundred different ways, not to.

I guess I'm never too surprised when it turns out I'm not what a man wants or needs.

And in this situation, it's definitely for the best, because I was getting too comfortable in Rush Creek. Too comfortable in Gabe's world, in his bed.

And I belong in New York City, the best place on earth for a woman who needs extra space between herself and other people.

Gabe did approach me this morning—wariness in every line of his face—to ask how I was feeling, and I told him I was fine, which was true. The headaches are mostly gone, and the dizziness only creeps up when I'm tired. I'm limiting screen time and resting as much as I can.

What I didn't tell him was that I'm definitely not myself yet. At night, I have weird jolts of terror every time I nod off, and even when I'm wide awake, I keep getting these flash visions of what it felt like to be disoriented under the water. Easton connected me with a wilderness therapist, which I didn't even know was a thing. She seems to know more about what my body and mind are going to do next than I do, which is super helpful. She says we'll work through it and I'll come out pretty much fine on the other side, with a nice, healthy fear of whitewater.

"You might never be gung ho about rafting again," the therapist said.

"I can live with that," I told her.

She and I will keep meeting by video call after I go back to New York, until I tell her I think I don't need her anymore. Being in a different location will help, too, she tells me.

A different location.

I'm looking forward to it. My streets, my territory, my city. Back where I belong.

Brody comes into the barn and drops—as predicted—into his chair without a word, his body language all *fuck you*. And right behind him is Easton, grinning at me.

"Thank you for joining us," I tease.

"I never miss a chance to see you in action," he says, with a smirk that on any other face would be over the top but on Easton's is hot fudge on vanilla ice cream, sexy but not smarmy.

I sneak a peek at Gabe, but he's still deep in the handouts. I search hopefully for a sign that he's upset by Easton's flirting, but nothing.

That's when my heart finally accepts it's really over, and clenches so hard in my chest that I wince.

I cover it with a smile and start my presentation, leading them through everything I've learned, all the data on who visits the new Rush Creek, how to reach them, and how that translates into new offerings and new branding.

"Not all of these will appeal to you. They're meant to be examples and suggestions. But I think it will give you a strong starting point. And let me stress: This is about adding new offerings, not getting rid of old ones. Clark will still offer survival trips, but he will also offer 'a night under the stars for beginners.'"

Clark tilts his head, what I've come to recognize as his, *I don't hate that idea* body language.

"For each segment of the business, I've proposed twenty new trip titles. You can think about what appeals to you and discard what doesn't."

I glance up to find Gabe watching me. His face is blank, but he's nodding. Warmth slithers through me. I hate that I still crave his approval, but this is his baby, his whole world, and I want to save it not only because it's my job, but for him.

Hanna crosses her arms. "So you make a plan, like, 'Star-Gazing for Book Clubs' or whatever, and then you... drop it in our laps and go back to New York?"

I will miss Hanna so much.

"Star Gazing for Book Clubs," I repeat slowly, and write it down, just to wind her up.

She knows it and gives me a look.

"Yes and no," I tell her. "I'll be available to consult via phone or video call if you have questions as you implement the plan."

"If we pay you more money," Hanna says.

"Hanna," Barb warns.

"No, it's a valid question," I say, smiling. "Yes. Once I fulfill the terms of this contract, additional work would be contracted separately."

Hanna doesn't push it any further. I could be insulted by her question, but instead, I'm pleased by it. Because Hanna has just admitted that my work has value to Wilder—and to her.

I finish presenting the new offerings and segue into messaging and branding. "You need very specific messaging to reach those women and couples. To appeal to their desire for unique experiences, luxury, and romance."

There's some grumbling around the table, mostly muttered *luxury*s and *romance*s, but nothing compared to the first day. Victory is sweet.

I talk them through the new language. Explain how they need to emphasize connection, learning, trust, comfort, friendship, and other non-tangibles. And they need to make a clear distinction between those trips and the ones that offer "challenge," "adventure," or "survival skills."

The Wilders (and Hanna) get it. They're nodding and making notes on their handouts, and the contrast between their frustration on that first day and their willingness to listen now could not be sharper.

I only had to weather seasickness, floundering in the mud, and a concussion to get them here.

Building trust is not for the faint of heart.

"You'll use a variety of warm marketing techniques—detailed in the next section—to entice people who go on the entry-level trips into more traditional wilderness experiences. You get them to fall in love with the outdoors, *then* convince them that if they're going to be camping regularly, they need a survival course. You get them comfortable on the water, *then* take them onto whitewater. You introduce them to the slow rhythm of a day on a boat, then teach them to fish. And not everyone will bite on the upsell—but a lot of people will, because they'll be comfortable with you as guides, and because you'll do a lot of talking about how passionate you are about your other trips. And no one can resist a hot guy who loves what he does."

I smile at Easton. Easton, of course, smirks right back. And not a single cell in my body is remotely moved by his perfect, beautiful, cocky face. Such a pity.

I smiled at him so I wouldn't have to look one more time at Gabe and discover that he wasn't looking back at me.

"I'M sorry my brother is an asshole," Amanda says, later that day, when we are celebrating with drinks at Oscar's.

I left the Wilder brothers—and Hanna—with strict marching orders. They all promised me they had it in hand, except they refused to go with the name I proposed: Wilder Romantic Adventures. It was a long shot; my feelings weren't hurt.

(Even though I already had the logo picked out.)

Gabe promised, too, still not looking at me.

I wave Amanda off. "It's *fine*," I say.

"How is it fine? He won't talk to you."

"I'm leaving anyway, right?" I say.

"But maybe you wouldn't *have* to leave. If he... I thought you two..."

Hanna interjects, "Ever the romantic. Didn't we go over this at the beginning? Wilder brothers don't fall."

And there it is. She's right. Even Hanna warned me.

"But I thought... I was sure..." Amanda starts, and then trails off again.

"You saw what you wanted to see," Hanna tells Amanda.

She could be saying those words to me, but I'm grateful

she's not. I'm grateful she doesn't seem to know how sad and hurt and lonely and deluded I feel right now.

Nan comes in the front door of Oscar's. She waves at us, then hurries over. Amanda grabs a chair from the next table and pulls it up. Nan sits and rests her chin in her elbows. "So. I heard you took a crack to the noggin."

I feel a tiny ping of the old anxiety—*someone is talking about me behind my back*—but it's way muted. I lean down and show her my stitches.

"They said twelve stitches," Nan says.

"How'd you know that?" I ask, although I'm long past the time when I'm surprised by the way news travels.

"Word gets around."

"Ahh."

"Gabe convince you to stay yet?" Nan demands.

Hanna looks at Amanda. Amanda looks at me. I give Amanda a tiny nod: I've got this.

"I don't think convincing me to stay was ever part of Gabe's plans."

"Then that boy's an idiot," Nan says.

"I appreciate the vote of confidence," I say, and I do. I want to hug Nan, and I'm not a hugger. Or I didn't used to be.

"Everyone knows he's sweet on you."

"Nan," Amanda says gently but firmly. "She has a head injury. Quit it."

Nan grumbles but drops the subject, switching instead to wanting to know if it's true that Brody got in a fight the other night, that Gabe had to haul him off Len Dix after Brody broke Len's nose, and that Brody spent the night in jail. Amanda straightens Nan out.

Nan frowns. "He has a kid. He needs to get his act

together. No one wants a daddy in prison. Lucy and I both know that from personal experience."

"Sorry," I say. "I missed that—what did you say?"

But I heard it. *Daddy in prison.*

For a split second, I think *Gabe told her.* But that doesn't make any sense.

Nan gives Amanda a look, then says, "My daddy went to prison for car theft when I was eight. Yours went for embezzlement, right? But it sucks no matter what. Sucks not to have your daddy around, sucks to have your daddy's crimes dictate what people think of you."

She puts a hand out, covers mine. It feels pretty good. I don't pull my hand away. I say, "It *does* suck."

And something in my chest thaws a little, and slides, the way ice slides over pavement when water gets in between.

"Where'd you hear my father went to prison?" I ask her.

"I play bunco with Barb and Adele. Adele told us."

My mom. My mom, the one who taught me to play my cards close to my chest, who said the more people who knew your secrets, the more people could hurt you. I try to imagine her chatting over bunco with Barb and Nan.

And the thing is, I can picture it.

I envy it, even.

Nan's hand is still on mine. Amanda is looking at me with sympathy that I can tell isn't pity. Even Hanna's face is scorn-free. Almost gentle, though I'd never tell her that.

I want to tell them I love them, but I hold back, because after all, I'm leaving.

It really is a good place, Rush Creek.

Just not my place.

40

The wilderness therapist warned me that with my concussion, even though it was mild, I'd have a tough time with the pressure changes and noise on the plane, and I'm sorry to report, she was right. She also said that the sights and sounds of New York would be hard to take —and she called that, too.

Everything from the moment I touch down at La Guardia to the moment I tuck myself into my own bed that night feels too loud, too bright, too rough around the edges.

Small town life can definitely lull you. I'd forgotten how much La Guardia looks like a work in progess. How hair-raising the traffic is leaving the airport. My Ryde driver is a charming woman with two kids in middle school, but she darts in and out of lanes on Grand Central Parkway with the speed of a Nascar driver and somewhat less skill. Gah.

The adrenaline makes my head start hurting again.

I long for the peace and quiet of my own apartment. The pale walls, the spare decor. They always soothe me.

But when I unlock the door and set my bags down, I don't

feel soothed.

It looks like someone sold everything off with plans to move out, then abandoned the plans and kept living here. There are only a couple of photos, one of me and Annie, one of me and my mom. There aren't a lot of things I'd call sentimental. Most of what's in here was picked out to reinforce the Lucy Spiro brand, so when I show myself on Instagram, you can see I know how to work with color and space and style.

I wonder if, like Gabe's house, this apartment tells a story about me.

If so, the story might be this:

When this woman was twelve years old, she discovered that at any moment, the people who say they love you will turn out to be lying to you. The people who say they're your friends will betray your secrets. The people who say they're your community will laugh behind your back.

Better not get too comfortable.

I want to text Amanda and say, *I just realized my apartment is exactly like Gabe's house!*

And then I want to text Gabe and tell him, *We're more alike than I would ever have guessed!*

But I don't. I shower off the smell of the airplane and put myself to bed, where I sleep as badly as you might expect, jerking awake periodically as if I've been plunged into cold water.

Each time, I lie awake a long time, trying to relish my 600-thread-count sheets while remembering the feel of being wrapped in Gabe's arms in a shelter in the woods.

In the morning, still headachy and out of sorts, I sit down at my desk and send an email to Gennie, officially giving my notice. After my Wilder (Romantic) Adventures presentation,

Barb wrote me the check she'd promised me plus a hazard pay bonus. It's enough to hire a virtual assistant, buy a work-horse design-friendly computer, load it up with the software and subscriptions I need, and get started.

I'm thinking about calling the new consultancy *Lucy's Look*. I play around for a while in my graphics software, trying out logo possibilities. I've just dropped eyeballs into the middle of the oo's and am laughing at myself for being a dork, when an email pings into my inbox. For a split, stom-ach-dropping moment, I think maybe it's from Gabe, and my pulse races out of control.

But it's not from Gabe. It's from Gennie.

I'm sorry to hear you're leaving Grand Plan. We'll miss your work. I meant what I said; you're excellent at this job. I wish you luck in whatever you pursue. Are you moving to Oregon? Insta-gram suggested the Wilder account, so I followed it. Cute pix of you (and those brothers are insanely hot). You look happy. Anyway, whatever (or whoever) you're doing, I wish you the best with it.

What the...?

When I last looked at that Instagram account, three weeks ago, it was crickets and tumbleweeds. I pull out my phone. Sure enough, there are all kinds of photos on the Wilder Insta, including several of me. On the boat with Brody—looks like Connor took it—working at the big conference table—I'm pinning that one on Amanda—out in the woods building a shelter—Clark? Really? Apparently, the Wilders actually listened to me when I said they needed to be way more active about taking and posting photos.

That makes me feel proud. And, suddenly, homesick.

Homesick?

You look happy, Gennie had written.

Do I not look happy most of the time?

I spin back through my own Instagram, and the answer is, *No*. I don't look happy. I look frozen. Even when I'm smiling— a just-right smile that I practiced for hours, because it's harder than it looks to take the perfect selfie—I can tell I don't mean it.

I look back at the Wilder photos, and there it is, a real smile. Even though I was puking twenty minutes later, in that picture my cheeks are pink and I'm grinning.

And then I scroll through Amanda's Instagram. There are so many great photos. Of Easton and me that first night at Oscar's, and of me (with a real smile) in the stupid cheese-bag dress, and of Gabe and me at the festival, dancing. You can't really see Gabe. You can only see my face over Gabe's shoulder, beaming, bright-eyed. I didn't even know Amanda was there; I was too wrapped up in enjoying myself.

The most recent photo is one Nan took of Hanna and Amanda and me that last night at Oscar's, the two of them flanking me. I half expect Hanna to look bored or scornful, but all three of us are smiling real smiles. And Amanda's arm is tight around me, a hug.

I sit there for a long time, staring at that photo, feeling that hug, and then I text Amanda. *Can I tell you a crazy story?*

Moments later, my phone rings.

"I'm sorry if I woke you up!" I say.

"It's three hours earlier here, remember?" Amanda says.

"Oh, right."

"Also, you can wake me up *any* time to tell me a crazy story. You wore a cheese-bag dress for me."

"Is that, like, a lifetime of favors?"

"Two lifetimes," Amanda says. "But the larger point is, I

love crazy stories, no matter what time of night. Bring it."

So I do. I tell her about sleeping with Liam, about how Liam showed up at my office and I thought he was there for me. About getting called into Gennie's office.

When I get to the part where Gennie threatened both Liam and me with strangulation, Amanda laughs, and then— surprising myself—so do I.

The story is pretty dang funny, actually, now that I have some distance.

Then I say, "I miss you and Han."

"Han and I miss you, too," Amanda says suddenly. "It's weird. You were only here three weeks, but it felt like you'd been here forever."

"It kind of did."

There's a long silence. I think maybe the conversation's over, and I'm sad, because if I stay in New York, Amanda and I won't have shared experiences anymore. We won't get bread and butter at Nan's or drinks at Oscar's. I won't get to play with her cute kids or hang out with her instead of going on her brothers' stupid trips. I won't get to help her build her business, and she won't get to help me build mine.

"And Gabe is a total fucking mess."

The mention of Gabe's name does terrible, wonderful things to my stomach. "A mess?" I ask, pretending I am only asking for clarification and not filled with hope that he is a mess over my leaving.

"Believe me, if there were anything left to tear to shreds and sell, he'd be doing it. Instead, he's tearing into his brothers and me."

I wince. "Ooh. I'm sorry."

"Nah. We're tough. And we all miss you, too. That said, he

better get his act together soon or we're going to disown him."
Amanda takes a deep breath. "But if New York is where you're
supposed to be, I get it. I would be the last person to tell
anyone else how to live her life. I mean, mine's kind of a
fucking mess right now."

Startled, I say, "Wait—what?"

"Yeah, things with Heath and me haven't been right for a
really long time. We married too young. I was pregnant. He
never got to choose me, he just got saddled with me—"

I try to cut her off, because I've seen Heath with her and I
don't think that guy looks saddled in the slightest. When he
thinks she's not paying attention, he looks at her like she
invented the alphabet. And maybe toilet paper. "He's crazy
about you, Amanda. It's all over his face."

"I want to believe you," she says. "But I don't."

If I were there, in Rush Creek, I'd take a stealth photo of
Heath silently admiring Amanda, and I'd make her study it
until she knew the truth.

"And none of this was what we pictured. He works like a
dog since he sold that app, and I think he thought I'd be at
home full time with the kids, but I'm doing the business and
the house is chaos."

"I didn't know things were that hard," I say quietly.

"I don't tell many people." Her voice breaks.

We're both silent for a moment.

I'm thinking about something I just learned. When you
let someone in, they might use what they know against you.

Or they might let you into their life. And, if you're lucky,
use what they know about you to have your back.

For the first time in my life, it feels like a chance worth
taking.

Easton finishes the presentation he's giving us about expanding the standup paddleboard tour offerings and diversifying into paddleboard yoga.

"You're going to teach *yoga*," Brody says, eyebrows practically touching in the middle.

"I'm going to hire someone to teach yoga."

"On paddleboards," Brody says.

"Standup yoga. It's a thing."

"It's fucking insane thing," Brody says. "Why not do goat yoga? Or goats-on-paddleboards yoga. Maybe you could do *seal* yoga. Seals like paddleboards."

"Look who's talking," Easton says. "I mean, sunset mani/pedi cruises, Bro? Seriously? Why don't you just do naked boat massage with happy endings?"

"Now there's an idea," Brody says. "I kind of like it. I've got good hands." He holds them up, then mimes a massage where he reaches around to cup someone's breasts. "Do you have Photoshop up? I'm making a flyer."

They've been doing this all week, messing around with

stupid shit instead of buckling down to make Lucy's vision a reality, and suddenly I've had enough. "Can you all stop messing around and just do the fucking work? I kill myself for this business, and all I'm asking of you is that you take it seriously for a fucking change."

They're all so used to my short temper by now that they barely turn around, but I see my mother's face go still.

My mother, even when we were kids, never yelled. She just wore the *disappointed face*.

Which was way worse than getting scolded.

I know I'm in for it.

After the meeting she calls me into her office.

"Gabriel Wilder," she says quietly. All disappointed face.

Oh, *shit*. Talk about pushing buttons formed in childhood.

"I know you're hurting—"

"I'm not."

"Oh, Gabe, don't lie to me. I gave birth to you. I could tell which of your cries meant you needed food versus sleep versus a diaper change. And I know you miss the shit out of Lucy."

She's right; there's no upside in lying to her. And I don't have the energy for it, anyway.

"Yeah," I say. "I do."

I miss her all the time. Every time Buck greets me at the door, every time I look at the washing machine. Every time I step inside the barn and she's not up in the loft. Every time I take a shower and there's no chance she'll slip in there with me.

Every time I lie in bed alone, missing what we had. The way she kissed, like she was all in, no turning back.

The no-condom games.

When she let me in.

"Gabe," my mother says, and I come back from Lucy La-La Land to find her looking at me, not with the disappointed face but with its close cousin, the deeply concerned face.

Just as bad.

She wrinkles her nose and keeps on looking concerned, like it's a full-time job for her. I know I'm not going to like what's coming next.

"Amanda told me you never asked Lucy to stay."

"It's none of Amanda's business. Or yours. Lucy needs to be in New York. She belongs there."

It's like I'm talking to the mountains; she doesn't even acknowledge what I've said. "I just want you to know, Gabe, if you ask for what you need, the world isn't going to end."

"I don't know what you're talking about."

I mean it. I was expecting her to give me a lecture about how Lucy wasn't Ceci and I should swallow my pride, but I'm lost right now.

My mom crosses her arms and fills me in.

"You should never have had to grow up so fast. If I could undo one thing, it would be my getting sick when I did."

I'm shaking my head, but she's shaking hers, too.

"You didn't get sick on purpose."

"I know," she says. "But you were too young to have to be someone's hero, and you really were my hero, Gabriel. I don't know if I could have gotten through that time without you being the kind of kid you were. But what I wish I'd seen sooner is that somehow you got it in your head that it was your job to take care of everyone. The one time you asked for what you wanted, it ended up with Ceci miserable, and that messed with your caretaker brain even worse. So after that, I think you decided it was always going to be about what everyone else needed. But you're allowed to need things, too. You're allowed to need Lucy."

The whole time she's talking, my chest is feeling like something is clamped around it, and the longer she talks, the tighter it gets, until the part about "you're allowed to need Lucy." And then it kind of cracks. Like an ice fissure opening up, dark and dangerous.

Because I think she's right. I think my mom nailed it perfectly. I've believed I don't get to need anyone or anything, that it's not my job to need. It's my job to make sure everyone else has what they need.

She looks at me like she can see straight through me. Moms, man. What a mindfuck.

"The thing about Lucy belonging in New York, Gabe? That's just bullshit you tell yourself so you don't have to do the right thing. Tell her, Gabe. Tell her you need her. Give her the chance to say she can't give you what you need, but don't take that chance away from her. Or from yourself."

And then she delivers the biggest mindfuck of all, because Moms don't hold themselves back when the shit gets real.

"I know all about what you feel like you owe your dad, Gabriel Wilder. I don't have to be psychic to guess. Maybe you promised him you'd take care of me. I don't know. I don't know what he said to you or what you said to him."

She takes a deep breath.

"But here's the thing, Gabe. Your dad would want you to be happy. And you know it."

I HAVE to go on three different airline sites to find something available in the next 72 hours. Who knew people wanted to go to New York City so badly? I think it's a major error in judgment, but then, I'm not the target audience for a big city.

I'm not sure if I should be flying into La Guardia or Kennedy but I decide it doesn't matter. Go big or go home, right? The least of my worries is how much I spend on a ride service to get from the airport to Lucy's apartment.

Finally I get desperate and type, "I want to fly to New York City as soon as possible," and then I find something. It's three hours from now, Bend to Seattle to La Guardia.

I buy and print the ticket, and then run next door and basically ransack my house packing an overnight bag. It looks like someone tossed it, but I don't have time to care. Buck's going to stay with Amanda and Heath and the kids. I probably won't be able to convince him to leave afterwards, because he'll be in doggie heaven. I load his stuff into the car and shuttle him to Amanda's.

"You have her apartment address?" Amanda asks.

I shake my head.

"I don't know it. But her mom would."

So, my last stop in Rush Creek is Adele and Gregg's Airstream.

Adele comes out, looking like Lucy plus twenty years and filling me with fresh longing for Lucy.

"Hey, Gabe, what's up?" she asks, and I explain that I need Lucy's address.

"Huh. You do? Why?"

Valid question, so I explain. "I'm going to New York to try to talk her into being with me."

Lucy's mom tilts her head to the side and gets a funny look on her face. "Huh," she says again. "Not sure…"

Okay, I wasn't expecting this. I figured Lucy's mom would be gung-ho about the idea of me going to get Lucy, of bringing her back here, and the fact that she's hesitating so much sets me back on my heels. Does she know Lucy's going to say no to me?

I can't let myself think that. I can't picture failure. I am going to go to New York and I am going to show Lucy Spiro why saying yes to me will be the best decision she ever made.

"Lucy loves New York," Adele tells me.

"I know."

I want that address, so I'm going to have to fight for it, and I can do that. I've had plenty of time to think about this, and I know myself now. I know myself and I know I should have fought for Lucy to begin with, and I know this is my last chance to get this right.

And I'm willing to beg. Whoever I have to beg, including Lucy's mom. This is a version of the old, busted asking-the-dad-for-permission ritual.

"If she belongs there, then I'll make it work for me."

Adele's eyes get bigger.

"I asked Clark if he would be willing to take over the business if I need to move to New York."

"What will you do there?"

"I don't know," I admit. "But I will figure it out. Maybe I'll do the East coast marketing for Wilder Adventures. Maybe I'll parlay my outdoor experience into working for one of the big gear companies. But I *will* figure it out—if she'll have me."

I definitely have Adele's attention now. I take a deep breath. "Because Lucy is *fearless*. You should have seen her in the woods. On the water. If something freaks her out, she does it anyway. I thought I was so brave before I met her, but I'm realizing that's bullshit because I'm your basic coward about the things that matter. I let her leave because I wasn't strong enough to tell her I need her. When she was in the hospital, I just walked away—and I'm so, so sorry about that."

I can't read Adele's expression. I can only keep going and hope I'll convince her. It's good practice for what I'm going to need to do in New York... only in that case I'm planning to do it on my knees if I have to.

"The only thing in the world Lucy's scared of is that people won't love her. And she doesn't need to be scared of that anymore. Because there are so many people here who love her. If she comes here, we will love her every day, in every way. And if she stays there, I love her, and I'm never going to stop, unless she tells me it's hopeless. And possibly even not then, because I don't seem to have any control where she's concerned. And I will make sure she's surrounded by other people who love her. So that's what I'm going to New York to say."

Adele seems to be crying.

"Well," she says. "You can tell her yourself, because she's right here."

And then I look up and sure enough, Lucy is standing in the doorway of the Airstream. She comes running down the steps and catapults herself into my arms, and I catch her and lift her up. She wraps her legs around my waist and we both hang on for dear life.

"Did you hear all that?" I demand.

"Every word," Lucy says. "But if you feel like saying any of it again, I won't stop you."

"And?" I prompt.

Her eyes are teary, too. "And I love you, Gabriel Romantic Wilder."

I scowl at her, but I kiss her anyway.

42

LUCY

"**I** have something for you," I tell Gabe.

I run back into the Airstream—my mom follows me in, giving me a big smile and a shoulder squeeze. I find what I'm looking for and bring it out. Hold it up for him. It's the woven wall hanging from Five Rivers Arts & Crafts that he admired at the Spring Festival.

He takes it from me. Touches it like he can't believe his luck.

"I saw you looking at it that night at the festival. I even thought I saw you go for your wallet. I know you like the just-moved-in look—"

He wrinkles his face at me.

"—but I thought maybe you could try hanging this and see how you feel about it."

"I fucking love it." He ducks his head and kisses me. Hard. "Let's go home."

"About *home*," I say. "Hanna says her roommate is moving out next month."

"*Hanna?*"

"Yeah."

"Hanna wants you to move in with her?"

I shrug. "Unless someone makes me a better offer."

"Oh, City Girl. I am going to make you an offer you can't resist."

I don't doubt this.

However, his offer-making is delayed slightly because we have to pick up Buck on the way back to Gabe's.

Amanda comes running full tilt out of the house and hugs me so hard the wind gets knocked out of me. Then she punches Gabe in the arm. Hard.

"Asshole!" she says.

"I got her back, didn't I?"

"You *cheated!* You should have had to go all the way to New York."

Gabe has apparently just realized something. "Wait a second," he says, slowly. "You *knew* she was here? And you were going to let me fly to New York...?"

"You walked out on her at the hospital," Amanda says. "You owed her a really, really good grovel. And having to fly all the way to New York only to realize she was here would have been a pretty great grovel, you have to admit." She frowns. "I feel like you're going to have to do something else epic to make up for it now. I was trying to save you that brainstorming session. It was in your best interest, I swear."

"I'm so sorry about the hospital," Gabe says to me. "I mean, like, really, really, really sorry. I was being a straight up idiot—"

Normally I'd say, "It's fine," because the part that matters is that he was coming for me, but this time I say, "Yup!" and Amanda laughs her ass off.

Then someone lets Buck loose and he barrels out of the house over to us. He completely ignores Gabe and throws himself at me, almost knocking me over and then almost knocking me over again by trying to lift me off my feet with a nose in my crotch.

"Buck!" Gabe chides, but he's laughing.

"You secretly want to do the same thing," I murmur to him.

"Not so secretly," Gabe murmurs back.

"TMI!" Amanda howls. "Get out of here. Go do all the things! And don't tell me anything about it! That's the one limit on my friendship with you, Lucy. I cannot know anything about my brother and underpants games. Otherwise, you can tell me anything."

"Understood," I say.

She gives me a big hug. I hug her back.

Gabe and I load Buck and all his stuff in the Jeep and drive back to Gabe's house.

"You gave a really good speech back at the Airstream," I tell him in the car on the way back. "But you actually had me at *I need Lucy's address in New York*. Maybe I'm too easy."

"I like you exactly the way you are," he says, giving me a brief but heated look.

"Gabe," I say. Because he got to say his piece, but I have a few things to say, too. "It's not all on you. I should have told you how I felt. I'm going to get a lot better at that."

"You can start now," he says hopefully.

"I love you."

"Damn, that sounds good," he says. "It is going to sound even better when you say it when I'm inside you."

"Oh," I say. "Oh, yes, it will."

I get distracted for a moment thinking about that, but then I snap back to the present and explain my plan to Gabe. I am still going to open my marketing consultancy. I'm just going to do it here, out of the new space I leased over Nan's bakery for a very special friend-of-the-owner rate. I'll still help Rush Creek and other Pacific Northwest businesses market to women. And in addition? I'll specialize in helping East coast-based clients reach Pacific-Northwest-based audiences.

"So basically, I'm a translator," I say. "I translate Fifth Avenue and Dior and Louboutin into rain jackets, undyed hair, and..."

"Geoducks," Gabe suggests. "We can still grab a little bit of the clam season. We'll go on a field trip to the Seattle area—"

"No boats."

"You'll like the ferries, I promise. No engine smell, no rocking, and no whitewater."

"I'll take it under advisement. Anyway, yes, you'll have to finish my Pacific Northwest education."

"Happily," he says.

He parks in front of the house, and Buck sprints for the front porch and then hangs there, patiently waiting for us to let him in. Gabe does, and then scoops me up and carries me over the threshold. And up the stairs. And straight into his bedroom.

He deposits me on the bed and begins stripping off my clothes.

Then he makes me an offer I can't refuse.

EPILOGUE

My house is stuffed with people. The walls vibrate from all their energy. My brothers; Amanda and her family; Lucy's mom and stepdad-to-be; the Perezes; Hanna and her brothers; a bunch of other local friends... it's a bash.

Clark and Easton are manning the grills in the backyard, and the smell of charbroiled burgers, dogs, chicken breasts, and grilled vegetables wafts through the open back door, along with conversation and shouts of laughter. Kane and Amanda keep the salads replenished and make sure the drinks are flowing.

It's the first party I've thrown... basically ever. And I'm having a blast, watching my mom gossip with Lucy's mom and Nan, my brothers—well, Easton—hitting on the single women, and Lucy chatting with everyone like she was born to make new friends. Which really? I think she was.

The party was Lucy's idea. She decided we should have a house re-warming party, since we finally finished decorating. The beautiful weaving she bought me from Five Rivers launched us on a campaign to fill the house with lots of things we love—new furniture, rugs, framed posters, throw pillows (Lucy), and objet d'art (also, obviously, Lucy, because I didn't even know what that meant before she told me).

Lucy made the rules. She said both of us have to love whatever new thing we buy. It can't just be there to look good on an Instagram post. Which means that some of our rooms are Frankenstein's monsters. They don't match perfectly, but we love being in our house. Together.

I've also slowly won Lucy over to the pleasures of being *out* of our house. She doesn't exactly beg me to take her hiking and camping, but she's a willing participant—and she's slowly accumulating the gear. Boating is still off limits, and I get that. But I might see if I can convince her to try fly fishing. The scenery's beautiful... and her being there would make the scenery that much more beautiful. Plus it takes a long hot shower to rinse all that river mud off.

I'm standing in the living room, and from my vantage point, I can see the front porch, where Rachel chats with Amanda. Rachel reappeared in town recently, and no one really seems to know why—although I suspect Amanda does and isn't telling. Amanda and Rachel worked on the yearbook together in high school, and they're obviously enjoying seeing each other again.

Brody appears—he must have come around the house from the backyard, where a lot of people are gathered—and says a few words to the women. Things between me and Brody aren't great. It's the only sore spot in my life. He's been cooler than usual toward me since the night I rescued him from the fight at Oscar's. Brody and I, we've always butted heads. He has issues with authority, and it's tough taking orders from your big brother who's not even two years older than you—I get it. I've always hated that there's friction between us, but I've never known how to fix it. I want to—but I'm not sure he does.

Heath calls Amanda's name from around the house, and she leaves Brody and Rachel alone together. Rachel's head is tipped to one side, and Brody seems to be explaining something to her, looking as animated as Brody ever gets. Rachel's eyebrows are scrunched together. But eventually, she nods a few times, and they shake hands.

Huh. It looks almost like some kind of business deal. Not exactly what I was expecting when Amanda left them alone together.

Now that I have Lucy in my life, I've turned into That Guy, the one who has to shut the fuck up or be an evangelist for love and monogamy. I want Brody—all my brothers, actually —to feel about someone the way I feel about Lucy. A year ago, I thought Zoë, Justin's mom, might be that person, but it doesn't seem like it. Zoë and Justin are with Len Dix now, which is what I assume the fight in Oscar's was about that night. The confusing part to me is why Brody cares, since he walked away from his engagement to Zoë.

Anyway, I guess part of me now hopes Brody's *person* could be Rachel.

I just want Brody to be happy, and not only so he'll stop giving me the cold shoulder.

I can't help it. I'm a fixer.

Lucy comes into the living room holding a big plate of barbecue. "You should get some before it's all gone."

"Not a chance of that. We bought enough for ten times this many people. We're going to be eating leftovers for days."

She smiles at me, then sets her plate on the coffee table—

yes, we bought a coffee table—and steps into my arms for a hug. She has her hair in those big loose curls, but she doesn't seem to mind that it's getting flattened and mussed up. She is so soft and warm, and she smells unbelievably good, like the floral shampoo that has taken up permanent residence in my —*our*—shower. She did something super naughty with that shampoo the other day, and—

"Gabe," she chides. But she doesn't sound upset in the slightest. She wiggles a little, her hip bumping my erection.

"I can't help it," I whisper. "I was thinking about what you did in the shower with the…"

"Oh. Yeah. That was…"

I take her face in my hands and kiss her. It quickly escalates to not-safe-for-a-family-party, and I pull back. "Send all the people home."

She laughs. "I love you, Gabriel Wilder."

"I love you, Lucy Spiro."

Amanda bounds into the living room and hisses, "Luuuucy! Holy shit! You have to hear this! Brody asked Rachel to do one of her mom's parties on his boat!"

Needless to say, because Brody's been so prickly lately, getting his part of Wilder Adventures squared away has been… tricky. He doesn't want to take suggestions from me or Lucy, and some of his early efforts to win over the New Rush Creek clientele have… bombed. So this is good news.

Except Lucy and Amanda are giggling. A lot.

"Does he *know* what she's selling?" Lucy demands.

Amanda shakes her head. "I don't think so."

"Ohhhh." A smile creeps across Lucy's face. I recognize it. It's a mischief smile.

My body doesn't know whether to turn on fight-or-flight or rev up for fun. "I'm not going to like this, am I?" I growl.

Both women turn to look at me. Lucy tips her head to one side. She studies me.

"If it concerns the business, you need to tell me what's going on," I remind her.

She bites her lower lip, and her cheeks turn pink. Then she gets up on tiptoes and whispers in my ear, her breath teasing my body toward the fun side of the equation.

"Oh," I say. "That should be very interesting."

I can't help the grin that spreads over my face at the thought of the surprise Brody is in for.

The next few weeks at Wilder (Romantic) Adventures should be very interesting indeed.

ACKNOWLEDGMENTS

First of all, a shout-out to my amazing readers. This is all for you, and I couldn't do it without you. I've felt so grateful this year to get to know many of you better through my newsletter and readers group. And special thanks to Laura Luallen and Meredith B, who won my contest to name Lucy's (unimaginative, unsympathetic) ex-boyfriend. They both suggested Darren, and Darren it is!

Every book is different. This one has been a sheer joy for me from beginning to end, and I'm deeply grateful to all the people who helped make it so. Thank you first and foremost to my early readers Dylann Crush, Christina Hovland, Christine D'Abo, Brenda St. John Brown, and Claire Marti. This book (and my sanity!) was in the best possible hands when I turned it over to you.

Huge thanks also to the women of the Romance Market Mastermind—Dylann Crush, Megan Ryder, and Dawn Luedecke—for talking me through the tricky, raw, and uncomfortable bits of figuring out how to tell the story readers want to read, and for all your support and enthusiasm. This is your book!

Thank you, Dylann, Christy, and Brenda for being there and listening even on those tearful days, and for bearing with me through my crisis of confidence right around the time I finished writing and started editing!

Christine, I can't begin to tell you what your sane, steadfast, and *balancing* presence has meant to me. Also there is no one I'd rather have in my corner during a plotting crisis. All the hugs!!

Gwen Hernandez, I am so grateful for the events that brought us together and for our regular chats, on all the topics. I look forward to them every time.

Thank you Rachel Grant and Kate Davies for being there for me through so much, including this pandemic. Whether it's tapas or Zoom, I know I can count on you, and that means so much. I can't wait until we can retreat together again—it will be such a perfect bookend.

Thank you to my agent, Emily Sylvan Kim. It is the loveliest feeling to know you have someone in your corner.

Thank you, Sarah Sarai. Sarah is an eagle-eyed copy editor with a wicked sense of humor, and copyedits are always a blast (and a vast improvement).

Thank you to my other beloved author friends, including but not limited to the authors of the Corner of Smart and Sexy, Small Town World Domination, Wide for the Win, Tinsel and Tatas, and my two ongoing newsletter swaps.

Thank you, XPresso Book Tours, especially Giselle, for the cover reveal and release support.

This year I've benefited from the wisdom of some amazing authors and author resources, and I wanted to name just a few: Skye Warren, both the Romance Author Mastermind conference and the Ads for Authors Intensive; Zoë York's *Romance Your Brand* book; Sarra Cannon's HB90 planners and other online resources; and Alex Newton's K-lytics. Of all the things I did this year, finally listening to the experts was one of the best.

I cannot imagine doing any of my jobs without the love and support of my amazing friends, Aimee, Chelsea, Cheryl, Darya, Ellen, Gail, Jess, Julia, Kathy, Lauren, Molly, Soomie, and Tracey. An extra shout-out to Aimee, who got me pointed in the right direction on Cuban-American culture and food. Any and all errors or flights of fancy in that department are mine and mine alone.

And last, but absolutely, positively, never or ever least, abundant hugs (and cookies) for my in-home cheering squad, Bell Boy, Bell Girl, and Mr. Bell. If it weren't for your affection, devotion, and patience, these bare bears wouldn't exist at all. And dinner is never boring. I love you all so much.

ALSO BY SERENA BELL

Wilder Adventures

Make Me Wilder

Walk on the Wilder Side

More titles coming soon!

Returning Home

Hold On Tight

Can't Hold Back

To Have and to Hold

Holding Out

Tierney Bay

So Close

So True

So Good (2021)

So Right (2022)

Sexy Single Dads

Do Over

Head Over Heels

Sleepover

New York Glitz

Still So Hot!

Hot & Bothered

Standalone

Turn Up the Heat

ABOUT THE AUTHOR

USA Today bestselling author Serena Bell writes contemporary romance with heat, heart, and humor. A former journalist, Serena has always believed that everyone has an amazing story to tell if you listen carefully, and you can often find her scribbling in her tiny garret office, mainlining chocolate and bringing to life the tales in her head.

Serena's books have earned many honors, including a RITA finalist spot, an RT Reviewers' Choice Award, Apple Books Best Book of the Month, and Amazon Best Book of the Year for Romance.

When not writing, Serena loves to spend time with her college-sweetheart husband and two hilarious kiddos—all of whom are incredibly tolerant not just of Serena's imaginary friends but also of how often she changes her hobbies and how passionately she embraces the new ones. These days, it's stand-up paddle boarding, board-gaming, meditation, and long walks with good friends.